Beyond the Fame

A Hate to Lovers Romance
Settle Myer

Contents

Author's Note

Content Warning

This book includes adult themes and deals with tough topics which you will find listed below. Some may include spoilers.

This book has adult themes and deals with difficult topics including fatphobia, bullying, terminal illness (cancer), loss of a sibling, loss of partner, loss of a parent (off page/mentioned), grief, attempted suicide (off page) & suicidal thoughts, addiction & alcoholism, depression, parental abuse (mental), grief, graphic sex

Help is available

Suicide & Crisis Lifeline — Call or Text: 988

https://988lifeline.org/

https://afsp.org/

https://nami.org/Home

Please consider donating to St. Jude:

https://www.stjude.org/

To the big boys: you deserve to be the main character of your own spicy romance book

Chapter 1 – Jensen

4 ½ Years Ago

I've never hated anyone more in my life.

Rebecca Taylor is a menace.

It's nearing the end of negotiations on script changes for *Tyler's Team* with Rebecca and the movie's producers, and Rebecca is refusing to budge.

We've been going through the script, page by page, and we're still discussing changes to two key scenes that Rebecca is fighting wholeheartedly against. This is why we haven't signed off on the final manuscript, which should have happened hours ago.

I'm pissed, tired, and ready to walk out the door like the three other directors before me. Whoever gave her final say on the screenplay was an idiot. She may have written the book, but she clearly has no idea what goes in to making a movie.

Every time Rebecca scoffs or whines about a change, I grit my teeth and ball my fists. The way she's latching on to the control she has, waving it around in my face... it's fucking infuriating.

I take it back. I don't hate Rebecca; I hate how much control she has over this screenplay. I hate that she's stolen that from me. Having control over the artistic vision of a project is what I love about directing. It's how I cope with the fucked-up world. I lose myself in the jobs that I sign on to and it's freeing.

"Miss Taylor," the movie's executive producer, Shyon Maronne, says with a sigh. "I understand this is your brother's story—"

"*Do* you understand?" Rebecca bites out. She grinds her jaw, narrowing those vicious blue eyes at Shyon, who is sitting next to me.

I shift in my seat, ignoring the way my cock reacts to her authoritative tone. I may despise Rebecca Taylor right now, but that doesn't mean I don't want to fuck her.

I accepted this job knowing how difficult she's been. I came into negotiations ready for battle. I was ready to fight for my revisions. What I wasn't ready for? A beautiful woman who makes me squirm.

Rebecca is nine years older than me and a force to be reckoned with. The skin-tight dress she's wearing magnifies all her curves. I've caught myself staring at her voluptuous breasts far too many times, wanting to hold them in my hands. I've imagined wrapping her long light brown hair around my fist so I can tug her head back and stare into those *vicious blue eyes.*

She's making my job harder; however, I'm weirdly turned on with how stubborn she's being with her refusal to cave. I can't help but admire her tenacity. She knows what she wants, and she has all the power. Except, power needs a source and if she doesn't give in soon, the producers, and their money, will bail. I'm surprised it hasn't happened yet. It's clear the production company keeps pushing for this project to get made because the book was such a success. Fans will show up in droves to see this movie, and I know that's the main reason this project is still alive. But if it doesn't work out this time, the production company might have no choice but to table it.

"My brother died, and this is all I have left of him," Rebecca continues. "This is his legacy. You're trying to change the good things that he did, and I—"

The threat of tears cuts off her words, and I avert my eyes. She's nearly broken down three times now. The first time it happened, I had a knee-jerk reaction to reach for her—to hold her hand. The second time, my stomach flipped, and my hand twitched with that overwhelming need to console her again. This time... this time I force myself to look away because if I have to see her heartbreak one more time...

What the hell is wrong with me?

I don't do emotions, especially the type that could crush my heart.

Emotions are messy. All of them.

I've only let myself truly care about one person and he's currently destroying his life. My best friend's addiction is killing him, and he won't let me help. He won't stop going out. He won't stop drinking.

We hardly see each other anymore. We're both busy with our careers. Mylan Andrews is the type of person who needs companionship. He needs someone by his side to help guide him. I haven't been able to be that person for him lately.

When we are both free for a night, he drags me with him to a club. I shouldn't go. It enables him, but I also want to protect him. When I'm there, I can make sure he doesn't get out of control. His bodyguard and assistant also help keep him out of trouble, but we're tired. We're running out of hope.

And this time, it's all my fault.

Six months ago, I introduced him to Olivia Hadford, an up-and-coming plus-size model. I had no choice. She was determined to insert herself into our conversation at the premiere party for Mylan's last movie. The same movie he kept showing up late to set to, kept flubbing his lines, and almost didn't make it through filming before his manager sent him to rehab again.

It's been over a year since his second stint. He was doing fine in his recovery until Olivia showed up.

She ruined him. She made him fall in love, then destroyed his heart. She knew he was an addict—an alcoholic—and used it to her advantage. She recorded videos of him in vulnerable states and sold them to the tabloids. When a reporter from *Entertainment Now* tipped Mylan off two weeks ago, he was devastated, and they broke up. He's been coping with booze and pills.

A brutal cycle he can't seem to escape.

I'm trying to be there for him. *I'm trying.* But I have a feeling I'm going to lose him, and *he won't let me fucking help.*

I swallow the lump in my throat and sit up straight in my seat. Now isn't the time to drown in my regrets.

"Rebecca," I say, a little rougher than I meant to. She immediately interprets my tone the wrong way and sharpens her distasteful glare. I adjust my black-rimmed glasses and clear my throat. "We've explained this several times. Book adaptations are tricky. With books, you have pages upon pages of details. Yours was... what? 90,000 words? About 400 pages? We only get a fraction of that for the movie.

We have two hours to tell Tyler's story. These changes are necessary for certain parts of the book and important scenes to translate better from paper to screen."

She huffs, likely because she knows this. She knows this because every other director before me must have given her the same speech. Then why is she being so goddamn difficult?

"Look, you're a new author. This is your debut novel. To have a movie deal with as much control as you have is unheard of."

"And what about you, *Jensen*?" The way she says my name is so condescending, it should piss me off. Instead, it only makes me want to fall to my knees before her. Submit to her and take care of her and—

What the hell? I'm losing my mind. *She's* making me lose my mind.

"Aren't you just a baby director yourself?"

Baby director? Was that a quip about my age?

I may have just turned twenty-six, but I've already directed two Oscar nominated films. And before that, I acted. I've been on TV and film sets since I was five years old. I know what I'm doing.

I bite my tongue before saying something I'll regret. She waits as I form a response, refusing to release me from her fiery stare.

Be nice, Jensen.

"What I'm trying to say, *Rebecca*, is all this control you have: filming locations, casting, final script approval... it won't work if you won't let us do our job. Logistics-wise, we have to make sure the camera shots work. Many of these changes are based on the filming locations we all agreed upon. You know, the ones in your hometown in Arkansas and at Tyler's alma mater that you were so adamant about keeping true to the book?"

Her unrelenting gaze falters, and she casts her eyes down to her clasped hands resting on the table.

"Look, I read your book—"

Her head jerks back up. "You did?"

"Of course." Her defensive posture loosens slightly, so I feed off that. "It was a beautiful book, Rebecca. I understand how much this means to you, and I promise not to tarnish Tyler's story with these changes. I promise they're only so we can make production as smooth as possible within the budget and time-limit we're given. Okay?"

Her eyes glaze with the tears that have been teasing her all day.

"I think this has gone on long enough," Shyon says, standing.

Rebecca tenses at Shyon's words and she erects those defensive walls once again. Damn it. I was finally getting through to her.

"Accept these changes or we're withdrawing our funding." Shyon buttons her fitted blazer and turns to the two other producers in the room. "Let's break for ten minutes and upon returning, we either part ways or celebrate the start of this project. Your decision, Miss Taylor."

Shyon leaves in silence, followed by the other two producers, and Rebecca's lawyer, who has been sitting in the corner. He's only there to go over any paperwork we sign.

The moment the door closes, Rebecca's bottom lip trembles and that uncontrollable need to want to comfort her returns.

"Rebecca," I whisper.

She stands and I lean back at the abrupt move. Without a word, without even a glance my way, she runs out the door.

I find her a few minutes later in the bathroom at the end of the hallway, her hands planted on the ceramic sink and her head down. She sniffles, not hearing me walk in until the door bangs loudly as it shuts. She straightens and turns away from me, but I can see her wiping her cheeks in the mirror.

"What do you want?" she asks.

"I wanted to make sure you're okay."

"Why do you care?"

I can't answer that.

"Just go away and leave me alone."

"I will when you tell me you're okay."

She scoffs. Something she's been doing to me, and my words, all day long.

"I'm fucking fine."

She moves to leave, keeping her head turned away from me as she walks by. She's trying to hide her face. Her tears.

But I saw.

"Wait." I place a hand on her shoulder to stop her.

She immediately jerks away from my touch.

"Don't. I don't want to hear anything you have to say."

She stares me down, challenging me to make another move. She's putting on a strong front, but I can see she's worn down, ready to give up.

She's hurting, and she's about to break.

I can make it better.

"Then I won't say anything," I whisper and lift my hand. She flinches and I pause, waiting for her to curse me out again, to slap my hand away. To do anything. Instead, she does nothing—says nothing—but her eyes tell me all I need to know. They plead with me. Beg me.

Make it better.

My calloused fingertips move forward until I'm wiping away the tears falling down her cheeks.

She closes her eyes at my touch. Her reaction to me is intoxicating, and I need more. I pull her against me, burying my fingers in her hair with one hand, and rubbing her back with the other.

For the next five minutes, I let her cry into my chest.

I leave Rebecca in the bathroom after she told me she had to fix her makeup and return to the conference room before Shyon and the other two producers.

What am I doing?

I hugged her.

I can't remember the last time I hugged someone. It's not something I like to do because of how I grew up. My parents never hugged me. They never showed me affection. Hell, Mylan might have been the first person to ever give me a true 'I care about you and love you, my friend' hug. But Mylan Andrews's love language is also touch and now he forces me into hugs all the time, especially when he's drinking, high, or in need of attention.

I don't even hug the women I fuck. They always want to cuddle after sex. I'm a big guy, and I'm sure I'd be great at cuddling, but cuddling, hugs... they're all too intimate.

Just like emotions, intimacy is messy.

I don't do it.

Then why did I like hugging her?

I need to shut this down now. Especially since we're going to be working together.

Rebecca enters the room and sits across from me. She doesn't say a word, but I can feel her eyes on me, waiting for me to glance up. I don't. I can't. If I do, I'll give in to her. This woman makes me want to do things—feel things—I refuse to let myself experience. Not because I can't, but because I fear what will happen.

Because the first person I let myself care about is losing himself to his demons.

Rebecca leans forward, about to speak, but her lawyer walks in, followed by Shyon and her underlings. Knowing Rebecca won't say anything with them in the room, I finally look at her. She's still staring at me, confused and hurt.

The producers resume the negotiations, reiterating their ultimatum: either Rebecca accepts the changes, or they're done. If that happens, the movie will never get made. After three directors left over quote, "creative differences," they struggled to find someone who wanted to take on this project.

I was the first director in over a year to show interest.

I read the screenplay, more curious about what was so important about this story for the author to be so resolute about not compromising.

Then I read the book and understood why this screenplay was so important to her. She wrote it true to the book, but unfortunately, book to movie adaptations have to be altered. I don't know what happened with the other directors—maybe their changes were too extreme. Maybe they just didn't want to fight, feeling it was a waste of their time.

For me, it's not a matter of getting my way. As I told Rebecca, my revisions are solely for a smooth production. But I can't direct a movie that's not funded. The production company is determined to get this movie made, but if these producers pull their money, Rebecca and her script will be placed on the blacklist, and no one else will want to make this film.

She must have realized this and finally agreed to changes in the final two scenes. We end the meeting signing the lawyer-approved paperwork.

"Ms. Taylor," Shyon begins, standing. "I hope we don't run into any more issues as we continue pre-production. We've already wasted too much time on these revisions. We begin casting this month and six months from now in May, we start filming. Think you can manage that?"

Rebecca offers a solemn nod, which Shyon accepts and leaves with her two shadows, and Rebecca's lawyer following. I need to get out of here before Rebecca says something about that moment in the bathroom.

I'm not fast enough.

"Jensen," she says as I reach the door.

She stands to walk to me, and I freeze, refusing to look at her. When her floral scent hits me, I close my eyes, and my body instantly relaxes. Her nearness soothes me in a way I can't understand.

"What did I do?"

Her voice is small and full of hurt. I hate myself for causing that uncertainty. I should say something... tell her she did absolutely nothing wrong.

All I want to do is hold her in my arms again.

I shake my head. No. I can't. I won't. Not while my best friend is crushing my heart. It won't be able to handle one more hand wrapped around it, and I have a feeling if I let this woman claim my heart, she'll never let go.

"Can I offer some advice?" I ask, my voice cold and my eyes focused on the door. I continue before she can answer. "Just... stay out of my way. If you're going to be on set, let me do my job, okay? You've already made this much more difficult than it needed to be."

"What?" she whispers, in shock.

"Goodbye, Rebecca."

"Jensen?" she says my name in a sob.

"What happened in the bathroom... that wasn't me. I just felt bad for you is all."

I force myself to look at her. The hurt I caused, the confusion wrecking her face, it all transforms into a wrath that should send me running in fear. It's impressive.

"You're a fucking asshole, you know that?"

I wince and almost apologize. I almost tell her I don't mean it, but I say nothing and walk out the door because I really am an asshole.

Chapter 2 – Rebecca

Present Day

I've never been to a wedding. How sad is that? I'm thirty-nine years old and not once have I received a wedding invite.

Over the years, the friends I had in high school and college got married. I saw the beautiful photos of the ceremonies on social media. Maybe their invitations got lost in the mail. Maybe only close friends and family were invited. Or maybe they were never really my friends to begin with.

Like many young girls, I always dreamed about the day I'd say 'I do.' I'd dress up in the extravagant wedding gown my mother bought me. It wasn't a real wedding dress, of course. It was bright pink with a sparkly light pink tulle skirt. I spotted it in the toy section at Walmart. My mother told me it was a princess dress. I don't remember this part, but apparently, I threw a tantrum and demanded my mom call it a wedding dress from that day forward.

I wore that pink dress all the time, every day, until it got too covered in food stains and dirt, and Mom made me take it off so she could wash it. I'd wear it to bed, so when I woke up in the morning, I was ready to begin preparations for the ceremony. My wedding guests—all the stuffed animals I owned—were meticulously placed in rows upon rows in my bedroom.

My first husband was my blue rabbit, Leon. Who names a stuffed animal Leon? I remember hearing the name once. I was outside playing and came in to get a glass of lemonade. I stopped to eavesdrop on my mother's phone conversation about her annoying boss, Leon, and his new secretary and something about rabbits. Now that I'm older and look back on a conversation I wasn't meant to hear, she'd clearly said they were 'doing it like rabbits,' but I was six and I didn't know what 'doing it' meant. So, all I gained from that conversation was my mom's boss Leon was a rabbit, and for a while I thought all rabbits and bunnies were called Leon.

I know. It makes no sense. How could her boss be an animal?

Mother used to tell me I had an overactive imagination. One that gave human names to stuffed animals. One that took me to fantasy lands where I had magical powers and ruled the equally magical creatures who lived there. One that took me on endless adventures and gave me the happiest memories of my childhood. One that I tucked away when it started giving me attention at school. Bad attention. The kind that left you with unwanted wedgies. The kind that ended with you locked inside lockers, or with food "accidentally" dropped on you during lunch.

Middle school was brutal. The teasing got worse the weirder I got. The day I became the laughingstock for wearing my bright unicorn T-shirt with mismatched cat-print pants to class, I went straight home and threw that outfit away. I didn't stop there. I tore my pretty pink wedding dress—which no longer fit me—to shreds. I divorced all my stuffed animal husbands, including Wyatt the giraffe, Henry the elephant, Sheila the kangaroo, Gregory the tiger, Perry the platypus, and even Leon the rabbit.

I ripped all my fantasy posters down from my bedroom walls and dug into my allowance stashed in a shoebox under my bed. I rode my bicycle down to the Dollar General and bought all the teeny bop magazines in stock and replaced the silly posters with ones of boys the pretty popular girls fawned over during lunch: the boys with swooshing blond or black hair, dark blue eyes, and flirty expressions.

I also bought a stack of fashion magazines. I circled outfits similar to what the popular girls wore and showed my mom, begging her to take me shopping.

She was more than thrilled because I'd never shown an interest in spending 'girl time'—as she liked to call it—with my mother. We didn't have much money, so I was surprised she bought me fifteen new outfits that day. She made me promise not to tell Dad we racked up hundreds of dollars on a credit card at the mall in Little Rock.

I wore my new outfits to school, and by the end of eighth grade, I had worked my way into the 'it' crowd. My popularity only grew when I got to high school, mostly because of my brother's reputation.

Tyler Taylor was the star quarterback of the Silo Springs High School football team. He was royalty, ruling the school alongside his cheerleader girlfriend, Lana Young.

Word got around that I was Tyler's sister, and suddenly, every girl wanted to be my friend. It was obviously because of him. Still, I didn't mind. I was no longer the strange girl with the strange imagination and strange clothes. I was getting invited to parties, shopping trips at the mall, movie nights, and weekend sleepovers. Of course, all the sleepovers were at my house on the off chance they'd run into my brother when he'd make the drive home from college to visit.

The fascination with my brother lasted throughout my high school years as his success on the Arkansas State University football team grew. He'd always get featured on the news during their sports reports. My brother was a local celebrity, and while I always knew he was special, I was ecstatic everyone else was finally seeing his brilliance.

Senior year of high school, my girlfriends and I would make the three-hour drive to Jonesboro for Friday night home games to watch Tyler play. After the game, we'd sneak into frat parties and get drunk, make-out with college boys, and crash at Lana and Tyler's apartment.

Then the unthinkable happened.

Tyler collapsed on the football field.

My brother was diagnosed with cancer.

And six months later, he died.

All my life I was known as Tyler's sister—always a second thought, always cast aside and forgotten. Then I became the sister of the college football star who died.

He was my best friend. He was the one who'd officiate all my fake weddings. He'd let me chase him around the woods behind our home, pretending to be the bad guy, and I was a spy assigned to arrest him. He'd dress up with me in colorful costumes when I wanted to play an alien queen coming to conquer the human lands.

He's the reason I never wanted to be a pretty princess.

Why be a princess when you can be a queen?

He was confused when I stopped playing pretend and traded the costumes for the fashionable outfits. Yet, he supported me in whatever adventure I chose for my life. He was always supportive—always observant. He saw everything. Even when he came home from college to visit, and my so-called friends ignored me to chat with him. He told me I shouldn't let them treat me like that. I should never be someone's second choice. I told him I didn't care. I didn't. At least, that's what I convinced myself. Did it hurt to be pushed into the shadows while my perfect brother shined brightly? Yes, but that small boost I got when people paid me attention hoping Tyler would pay *them* attention was all I needed.

No, that's not true.

All I needed was Tyler. He made everything better. He was the only one to light up my dark days.

Before he left for college, Tyler would write me notes and hide them in my backpack. It was the first thing I'd look for in first period.

Sometimes there'd be jokes.

How do you make a tissue dance? Put a little boogie in it.

That was the first ever note he wrote me. I laughed so hard; I almost peed my pants.

Most of the time, the quotes were encouraging.

You are worth it. Kick ass today.

You're a badass, don't forget it. Make today your bitch.

You're my favorite sister in the entire world. Oh, shit. You're my only sister. Statement still stands.

Yeah, he cursed a lot.

Tyler was the only one who saw me. When he died, a part of me disappeared with him. Who would see me now? Definitely not my parents. It's almost as if they forgot they had two children. As if they forgot one was still alive. As if the child who died was the wrong one.

I desperately needed their love. I needed them to see how broken I was without my best friend. Any time I'd try to talk to them about my grief, they'd wave me off, tell me it's too hard to talk about it. Yet, they could talk about Tyler's death with Lana, with my grandparents, and their friends. Why not me?

I didn't understand it.

I had no one, and that's probably why I started writing the book my senior year of college.

Despite my parents' protests, I delayed going to college so I could grieve. I also took on a light class load my freshman year. Instead of the typical four-year college stint, mine took nearly six years.

I was studying journalism. I always had a knack for telling stories. So, I poured my grief and emotions into *Tyler's Team*, telling the story of my brother's inspiring life and how he raised money for cancer research until his last breath. I shared all his selfless acts of kindness throughout high school and college.

I also wrote about his romance with Lana.

Their love was one I'd always dreamed about—a love I hoped to one day have with someone. They were childhood friends before becoming a couple, and not one moment did I feel like Lana was taking him away from me. She treated me as her own sister, including me in conversations, taking me bowling or out for ice cream.

When they left for college, I missed their friendship. Until I found my own friends, real or not.

I never thought anyone would read the book I wrote, and I hadn't planned to do anything with it. Then I was telling my roommate, Ashley, about it. She was an English major, and she offered her expertise. It also helped that she read a lot of books. Something I used to do before I forced my true self to hide behind the manufactured woman I am today.

Ashley told me it was the best book she'd ever read. She cried, she laughed, and she encouraged me to send it out to literary agents. I did, and on top of the dozens of rejection letters, I also got dozens of responses offering representation.

Years later, when the book was released, it skyrocketed to success after an A-list celebrity chose it for their monthly book club. Then Hollywood came calling. I never realized how tedious the process was to turn a book into a movie. I was constantly told that my situation was special. It differed from other authors. I had an overwhelming amount of offers from movie producers to buy the rights for *Tyler's Team*. Enough that I was able to make counteroffers. My only stipulation was that I got to help write the screenplay and approve any changes made. My agent even got me final approval on casting and filming locations.

Eighteen years after my brother Tyler died, the screenplay was written, and the book was finally being made into a movie. Eighteen years and I was still grieving my brother's death. Lana, his fiancée, was still grieving his death, but she moved on. She met Mylan Andrews, who was cast to play my brother in the movie. The two hit it off. They both healed each other.

I needed that. I needed someone just as fucked up as me to understand. To see me like Tyler saw me. To see the woman I used to be.

There was a brief moment I thought Jensen Boliver could be that for me.

He's nine years younger than me, bossy as fuck, and an asshole. We fought nonstop over changes to the script, and I hated him so much for it. Jensen was my last chance to get the movie made, and near the end of negotiations, I knew I was going to have to relent. All the other directors who signed on dropped out after I refused to compromise to their demands.

Jensen was going to be the same; the producers were going to walk away, and the moment I realized I was fucking it all up, I rushed out of the conference room where negotiations were being held in Downtown Los Angeles.

I wasn't gone long—five minutes at most—when Jensen found me.

I think about that day a lot—how he just held me, neither of us speaking. He was so big compared to me and in that moment, I felt safe. I felt cared for. No one had cared for me like that since Tyler had. Not even the men I dated.

After that final meeting, I stopped Jensen before he walked out the door. I wanted to thank him for comforting me in the bathroom. I thought maybe my first impression of him had been wrong. Maybe he wasn't an asshole. I wanted to get to know him, but whatever compassion Jensen had offered me in that bathroom just minutes before was gone. He closed himself off. He almost seemed angry that he'd let himself be nice to me.

Whatever.

I didn't need his pity.

I didn't need him at all.

"Welcome. How can I help you?"

The hotel clerk's accented voice draws me from my thoughts about *him*.

"Hi, Rebecca Taylor. I have a reservation."

The woman, who looks to be in her early twenties, types away at the computer with her purple painted fingernails.

Her rows of braids are pulled back into a wonderfully full ponytail. Her dark brown skin glows with a sheen of sweat from the tropical climate pouring into the open-air hotel lobby.

I've been to Hawaii before—Maui and Oahu—but only for book signings. Both times, I only had one day, barely getting a chance to explore. I want nothing more than to go chasing waterfalls, to walk through lava caves, to soak my feet in the ocean, or lie on the sandy beach and enjoy the sunset.

This time, I'm in Kauai for a wedding; my first one.

Ginger Ann Cartwright and Bruno Stein are getting married.

The two met during the filming of *Tyler's Team* four years ago and they fell in love. Bruno was Mylan Andrews's bodyguard before quitting a few years ago to start his own personal security business that he runs with Ginger, Lana's best friend.

Going to set and watching Ginger and Bruno fall in love then seeing Lana and Mylan's romance unravel... made me sick to my stomach with jealousy.

How horrible is that?

I'm happy for them, all of them. Really, I am.

I brush the toxic thoughts away. This weekend isn't about me. It's about Ginger and her dream wedding. She chose Hawaii because her mother always wanted to visit. She never got the chance before she passed away over three years ago, so holding the ceremony here is a tribute to Gracey Cartwright.

I glance around the bustling lobby. People are sitting on white cloth furniture, chatting and drinking or snacking on bowls of cut fruit. Others are watching the sun setting over the ocean. The resort is on the beach and the lobby offers the perfect view of crashing waves. Beautiful bodies of all shapes and sizes relax on towels spread out across the sand, or underneath umbrellas, hiding from the harsh rays of the sun.

"You're with the Stein-Cartwright Wedding?"

"Yes ma'am."

The clerk smiles. "Do I hear an accent?"

I snort because *she* has an accent to *me*. "I lived in the south a long time ago. Can't seem to shake the twang."

"I understand that. You shouldn't try to shake it, though. It's cute."

The woman's flattering—and somewhat flirtatious—words help soothe my rattled nerves. I've been stressed while writing my new book, but also because Ginger asked me to be a bridesmaid.

My first ever wedding and I'm *in* the wedding.

I was surprised Ginger asked me. We've had our issues in the past. She's Lana's best friend, and she wasn't too happy about the things I said when Lana stepped away from the process of the book being turned into a movie. That was a rough time in my life. I apologized for what I said. Words I never meant. Words I thought would protect me and my feelings.

Over the past four years, my relationship with Ginger has gotten better. Now me, her, and Lana text non-stop and we take week-long girl trips together once a year.

"Oh no," the clerk whispers.

She glances up at me, then back down at the computer screen. She types frantically and winces.

"Mrs. Taylor."

"Oh... I'm not married."

"Right. Um. Sorry, but it appears your reservation was canceled."

"What? How?"

"I'm not sure. It must have been a glitch. We had a similar issue last week with another reservation."

"Okay. Can you, um, uncancel it?"

She winces again, and my heart drops.

"We are fully booked for weddings. We have three this weekend alone. Unfortunately, I have no available rooms to offer you."

"Well, that's a problem since I'm in one of those weddings."

"Right... um... shit."

The woman slaps her palms over her mouth. "I'm sorry. I did not mean to curse." She wrings her hands. "I don't know what to do. I am still new. This is only my second week."

I feel bad for her. This isn't her fault. At the same time, I want to scream at the top of my lungs. I don't need this right now. I love Ginger to death, but I will head back to the airport and go home to finish writing my book if they can't figure this out.

Ugh. No, I won't, because I'm already here. It'd be a waste of money, and how could I leave Kauai without exploring or appreciating its beauty?

But where the fuck am I going to sleep?

I can't stay in Mylan and Lana's room because her grand-parents are flying in tomorrow and staying with them in their two-bedroom suite. Maybe I could crash on their couch?

What about Eloise? No, I mean, we're cool, but I really don't know her that well. I met her when she was Mylan's personal assistant. Now she's a successful photographer. She shows up to the gatherings Lana forces us to attend, but mostly, Eloise keeps to herself and doesn't really share her life with any of us.

There are other resorts on the island, but I don't have a car to drive back and forth between hotels.

"Fuck!"

The clerk jumps at my outburst, and I immediately apologize.

"Would you like me to get the manager?"

I rub my temples. "What will the manager do? You said there are no rooms to put me in."

"You can stay in my room."

My heart leaps into my throat.

I recognize that voice. The last time I heard it was a year ago when Bruno and Ginger got engaged. It belongs to the man who drives me crazy. Who I constantly find myself thinking about.

Jensen.

I turn around and find his light green eyes, surprisingly, not hidden behind black-rimmed glasses. He also liked to hide his brown hair underneath beanies, but he's ditched that too. His hair is cut short at the sides, longer on top, allowing for those loose curls to fall perfectly across his forehead.

And now he has a beard.

Fuck me, it's a sexy beard.

He's not even wearing a long-sleeved flannel top. Instead, going casual with a black graphic t-shirt with some science fiction design on the front. The fabric stretches across his meaty chest and broad shoulders.

During the filming of *Tyler's Team*, the tension between us grew. We avoided each other as much as possible, only speaking if it involved discussing the script or the camera shots. Even when I saw him at the movie's premiere, and then again at the Oscars, we both refused to speak to each other.

It wasn't until last year that... something happened between us.

Something that has my thighs clenching, remembering. My heart beats faster with need. I hate how much I want it to happen again.

"You," I growl out.

Chapter 3 - Jensen

Last Year

L AX is literally hell.

Between thirty minutes of taxiing to the gate, to dodging the crowds walking through the airport just to get stopped by people who recognize me either from my acting roles or my directing jobs, I finally make it to baggage claim. It's nearly an hour after my flight landed from New York City where I was doing press for my new movie: *Galaxies of Enzine*. I'd always wanted to direct a science fiction movie, ever since watching *Star Wars* as a kid and aspiring to be George Lucas one day. I started prep work on *GoE* shortly after wrapping *Tyler's Team*. It took a year to film and another two years to edit and add special effects. I've been doing press junkets for the past couple weeks ahead of the film's release this month.

Interviews I should still be doing, but Mylan's girlfriend basically threatened violence if I didn't show up to their little get-together.

I find my luggage on the carousel and make my way to the line of drivers holding signs with names written on them.

"He got a flat tire?"

Wait the fuck up. I recognize that voice.

"Can you send someone else?"

My feet move against my will and follow Rebecca freaking Taylor's soft Southern accent. I hadn't seen her since the Oscars last year. I had every intention of avoiding her, but of course the *Tyler's Team* cast sat at the same table and Rebecca was directly across from me. Both of us had dates too. Dates neither of us paid attention to because my eyes kept wandering to her, and I'd catch her eyes on *me* every time.

The only time we spoke all night was when she congratulated me on winning the Best Director statue. She even sounded genuine about it, despite her not getting nominated in the original screenplay category.

I was surprised she had talked to me at all. Especially after I snapped at her the night of the wrap party in Silo Springs.

"There's no one for an hour? Okay. No worries. I can call an Uber. Thank you."

Rebecca's back is to me, and I can't help checking out her perfectly round ass in her skin-tight jeans. Jeans? I'm surprised she's in casual attire. I've only seen her in form-fitting dresses.

Not that I'm complaining. She's gorgeous no matter what she wears. My dick agrees, pressing hard against my zipper.

My eyes continue to explore Rebecca's body. She's wearing purple heels and a light purple dress shirt that's more of a crop top, showing a belt of tanned skin above the band of her pants.

"I'll give you a ride," I say the moment I reach her.

She jumps at my voice and spins around. Her startled face morphs into one of hatred.

"You," is all she says.

"Me."

"Go away."

"You need a ride, don't you?"

"Not from you."

"Nonsense." I snatch the suitcase on the ground next to her legs. "You'll ride with me."

I walk away, carrying both of our bags before she can stop me. Though her protests made it very clear she does not want to ride with me.

"Jensen Matthew Boliver, you get back here right now with my luggage."

I smile at her using my middle name. I never told her my middle name. That meant she Googled me.

She was thinking about me.

We approach the area where drivers line up to wait for their clients. I find a man holding my name and follow him out to the parking lot. Rebecca trails behind with loud steps and feisty words the entire time.

"I can carry my own bag, you know."

"At least slow down. I have heels on, asshole."

"Pleeeeeease stop."

"I swear to God I will kick your ass. I don't care if I get arrested."

We arrive at a black SUV, and I hand the driver our luggage. He puts them in the back and by the time Rebecca catches up, I have the door open and ready for her to get in.

She stops a few feet away and crosses her arms, tapping her foot.

"I'm not riding with you."

"You are. Get in, princess."

"Do. Not. Call. Me. That," she seethes and narrows her eyes at the nickname.

I don't respond to her overreaction. Instead, I stand there, door wide open, staring. Waiting. A game of chicken for who will make the next move first.

"This is kidnapping," she says, dropping her arms in defeat.

She's flustered. Blush pinks her cheeks, neck, and chest. It's beautiful, and I wonder how else I can make her blush.

"Get. In." I nod my head to the inside of the SUV. "We're going to the same place."

She huffs and rolls her eyes, but finally relents, mumbling something about me being bossy the entire time. I close the door, relishing my victory before getting in on the other side.

The driver takes off and I activate the privacy screen as a habit. I always request one when hiring a driver. Most of the time, I'm on calls or going over scripts, and I don't want to distract them or them to distract me.

We drive for thirty minutes before Rebecca unleashes all hell on me.

"You are insufferable. You could have at least asked me if I wanted to ride with you. Don't you remember we hate each other? Why would I want to ride with you forty-five minutes to Lana and Mylan's house in Malibu when we can barely stand each other? I swear, Jenny."

My eye twitches at the nickname. I'm going to get my revenge on Mylan for letting it slip that one day on set.

She's still talking about God knows what, and I've had enough. I unbuckle my seatbelt so I can reach her, and grab hold of her chin.

"Shut. Up."

"Make me, asshole," she snarls.

So, I do. My lips crash against hers. They're soft, plump, and eager. She parts them and I slide my tongue in.

Did she just moan?

My palm moves to the back of her head, and I grip her hair to have full control. My other hand skates down her front, stopping at her breast to squeeze and knead and tweak her hardened nipple through the fabric of her shirt.

She definitely moaned that time.

I need more.

My hand moves further down while I continue to drown her cries of pleasure with my kisses. I pause at the buttons of her jeans.

"Tell me to stop," I say against her lips.

"Don't fucking stop," she demands and claims my mouth again.

That's all I needed to hear. I unbutton her jeans and push her panties aside, allowing my fingertips to tease her pussy up and down the slit.

So fucking wet.

"Is this for me?"

"Yes," she whines. "Please."

I plunge my fingers inside her, and she arches away from the seat. She fists the cloth of my flannel at my sides.

"More, Jensen," she moans. God, my name on her lips sounds fucking amazing.

I add another finger and pump, in and out, in and out.

"Faster." Her breaths are short and quick. "Harder."

My thrusts become brutal. I'm not holding back, and she eats it up, tightening her hold on my shirt enough I swear I hear it rip.

She whimpers when I stop kissing her, which I only do so I can trail my lips along her jaw and down her neck. I lash my tongue against her skin and suck as the urge to leave my mark on her overwhelms me.

I want to consume this woman.

"Don't you dare give me a hickey, Jensen," she says, her words husky.

I tease her with a nip of my teeth followed by a lick, and her pussy clenches around my fingers.

She groans. "Fuck you."

I chuckle against her neck before finding her mouth again. Her kisses are so demanding. I never want them to end.

The heel of my palm presses against her clit, and she bucks in the seat. I keep the pressure there as my fingers drive into her fast and furious.

She's close, so I remove my hold on her hair and end my kisses to cover her mouth with my hand just in time to quiet her orgasm.

I wait for her walls to stop pulsing before taking my fingers out and she watches as I bring them up to my mouth to lick them clean.

That breaks the spell. She shoves me away and buttons up her jeans.

I scoot back to my side of the vehicle.

She narrows her eyes at me. "You're disgusting."

"Was I disgusting a few seconds ago when I made you come?"

She scoffs and jerks her chin at the privacy screen.

"Do you always fuck women in the backseat of cars?"

"No."

"That's not why you put up the screen?"

"No."

"Whatever."

"Becky," I muse. She absolutely loses it.

"Fuck you, Jensen."

"Well, if you want..."

She growls. It's adorable and makes me laugh, which she does *not* appreciate.

"That will not be happening again. Ever."

I would respond, but we're pulling into Mylan and Lana's driveway. When the car stops, I wait for her to get out first.

"Go ahead," Rebecca says, digging in her over-sized purse. "I have to fix my makeup."

I grin, spotting her smeared lipstick.

Her head snaps up. "Wait!"

I pause before opening the door. The driver is already at the back and taking our luggage out.

Rebecca extracts a makeup wipe from her massive purse and holds it out to me. She waves her finger at my mouth. Curious, I take out my phone and open the camera.

Her lipstick is all over me too.

I laugh, pleased with myself for our disheveled appearances.

"Asshole," she mumbles.

I wipe away her red lipstick and smack my lips before exiting the vehicle, surely annoying Rebecca.

Lana and Mylan's butler opens the door as I'm approaching, and I give her a nod before walking in. When I round the corner to the living room, I'm met with Mylan and Lana being disgustingly cute and handsy with each other.

That unnerving yearning for companionship hits me head-on so I kill it with humor.

"Get a room."

My best friend whips around and smiles at me. My stomach drops. He looks so healthy. We haven't seen a lot of each other these past few years, but every time we do, I'm always surprised by his appearance.

During the height of his addiction, he'd hide the physical signs well. He'd cover the dulled, gray skin and dark circles under his eyes with makeup. Mylan had always been built, but he'd lost a lot of weight before going into treatment because he wouldn't eat when he was drinking or getting high.

But now? He seems so happy. He's gained back the weight and muscle he lost because of his disease. His skin is clear and smooth, no longer suffering from dehydration.

Mylan greets me with our secret handshake—three palm slaps, two fist bumps, a fist to the chest over the heart. We made it up as teens with our other friend Rey, the three of us bored as fuck on set in between scenes.

The heels of Rebecca's pumps click loudly on the marble floor. I step back from Mylan and adjust my black-rimmed glasses, folding my arms over my flannel-covered chest.

"Wow. Did you two come together?" Lana asks, glancing behind me.

"Ugh, no," Rebecca blanches. I turn to look at her as she tosses her long, light brown hair over her shoulder and crosses her arms like me. She's still flushed from what we did, and I realize I did, in fact, make her blush for reasons other than pissing her off.

"Wrong. She *came* with me, but we're not *here* together," I say, giving Rebecca a teasing smile, which makes her blush deeper.

Rebecca explains the situation with her driver getting a flat tire. Her voice fades away as I replay the memory of her coming on my fingers.

Oh, this is going to be fun. There's no denying Rebecca enjoyed my touch and my kisses. Now I'm going to use that to make her squirm every chance I get.

Chapter 4 – Jensen
Present Day

S he's as beautiful as ever.

Rebecca's flawless but pissed off face scrunches up—likely planning my murder at this moment. I scan her body, from her tapping sandal-covered foot then up her tanned, smooth legs pouring out of white shorts. The body-hugging crop top she wears dips to showcase her plump tits that I desperately want to put my mouth on.

I salivate, remembering her taste—a taste I never expected to have. That moment in the car when she let my fingers inside her was a product of built-up sexual tension between us. A year later, and my hands itch to touch her again. I barely got a chance to memorize the feel of those wonderful curves.

Rebecca isn't a plus-size woman like Lana and Ginger, but she's not thin like Eloise. She's in between. I believe the term is mid-size, though I fucking hate all the labels that are assigned to our bodies.

"It makes sense, Becky. My suite has an extra bedroom that no one is using."

She balks at me using the nickname she despises and anxiously plays with the strands of her perfectly styled hair that falls in waves over her shoulders.

"Because, *Jenny,*" she begins. I walked right into that. I use the nickname *she* hates; she uses mine. I don't let her see the effect it has on me and smirk, which just pisses her off more. "I would rather have nails hammered into my eyeballs than stay anywhere near you."

"No reason to lie. Just say you don't want to stay with me because you find me irresistible, and you'll have a hard time controlling yourself around me." I glance at the clerk, giving her a wink, which makes her blush.

Rebecca groans. "You are so wrong, it's sad."

"And where will you be sleeping tonight?"

"I'll figure it out. I'm sure Lana and Mylan will let me crash on their couch. Believe it or not, I don't need you to keep saving me."

She's being such a fucking brat.

I step to the counter next to where Rebecca is standing, and she backs away. That's the difference between her and Lana. I've seen the way Lana doesn't back down around Mylan. She's fierce and defiant. I know Rebecca is all that, yet she doesn't trust herself to let it show.

I lean in to the clerk, who is flustered and maybe it's because she recognizes me. Or maybe it's because of that wink. I could never understand why women found me attractive. I've struggled with my body image my entire life. It's something I've been working to fix for the past four years, but learning to love myself, when my whole life people told me I shouldn't, has been difficult.

Sometimes I'm my own worst enemy because when women see me and want me, it should make me feel good. Instead, I wonder if it's all a ruse. Do they ignore how my body looks because of my career? My money? My fame? I never let them stick around long enough to find out.

"I'd like to check in. Jensen Boliver."

The clerk composes herself and taps away at the keyboard. I turn to Rebecca, who saw the whole flirty interaction with the clerk. She radiates disgust, and I swear there's a hint of jealousy there too.

Jealous? Good.

"Oh yes, here you are, Mister Boliver."

Rebecca sneers.

"Great. Can you give me two key cards, please?"

The clerk flicks her eyes at Rebecca, then back to me. She doesn't hide the scowl, clearly wanting all my attention.

"Of course," she says through a forced smile.

She takes a few seconds to scan the cards before setting them down on the counter and telling me it's room 909 on the top floor.

"Do you... do you mind taking a picture with me?" the clerk asks shyly. I glimpse at Rebecca, and she rolls her eyes. "I recognize you from that show. The 80s one you were in—*Metal & Mayhem*. And now you direct movies? That's so cool. I really loved that sad one from a few years ago."

"Why thank you..." I glance down to her chest at her name tag. "...Vilonia. Beautiful name. I'd love to take a picture with you."

She nearly runs around the counter. "Thank you so much. I already got a photo with Mylan Andrews. He checked in a couple of hours ago with his girlfriend. They were so nice, like you." She holds her phone up in selfie-mode.

"Actually." I pass Vilonia's phone to Rebecca. "Becky, do you mind?"

Fire as hot as a thousand suns shoots back at me behind her sharp blue eyes.

"Sure," she grits out.

I wrap my arm around Vilonia's waist, which she takes it upon herself to move my hand lower, so it rests near her ass. Rebecca, of course, notices it, and that blaze behind her glower intensifies.

I relish her jealousy.

Rebecca snaps a few pics before handing Vilonia her phone. Then she swipes one of the key cards off the counter and stomps off, dragging her oversized suitcase behind her.

"Thank you, Vilonia." I smile, grabbing my card and luggage.

I walk off and try to catch up with Rebecca. Once I do, she's already inside one of the resort's three elevators, standing in front of the button panel.

"Becky," I warn, still a few feet away.

The elevator she's in is nearly packed, and everyone watches in confusion as she frantically stabs at the panel, clearly pushing the 'door close' button, as she makes no attempt to keep them open for me.

She raises a brow, sneers, then flips me off before the doors shut.

Really mature.

It's check-in time at the resort, which means a crowd has formed, all waiting for an elevator to take up to their rooms. After several minutes of waiting, I'm finally on my way up to the top floor.

It takes about five minutes to drop other guests off before the elevator stops on the ninth floor. I make my way down the hallway towards the suite at the end. The entire hotel is an open concept. To my right, the wall is gone, allowing for spectacular views of the setting sun. I pause and close my eyes, letting the salty air rush over me. This is the first vacation I've had in years. The last one was with Mylan, before he went on a downward spiral with his addiction and alcoholism. We spent a week in Switzerland. It was by far the best week of my life. That country is beyond beautiful; as if a painting came to life and exploded to form the landscape, resembling worlds from some of my favorite science fiction movies.

Mylan was my vacation buddy until he decided he no longer cared about his life. I can't even think about those years or the depression that I fell into. How defeated I felt when my best friend refused my help and was determined to die.

I immersed myself in my work to escape the stress and even though Mylan finally got help, thanks to finding Lana, I still haven't slowed down. I still haven't let myself process the hurt. The apology letter he wrote during his year-long recovery helped me understand. It allowed us to reconnect. It did not, however, heal the darkest parts I can't seem to shake.

I open my eyes and my breath catches in my throat. This sunset is unreal. The vibrant colors—dark blue fading into purple, pink, orange, and yellow. Not a cloud in the sky obstructs this view and I consider staying here until the day melts into night.

But I have a bratty woman to deal with.

My bodyguard, one I hired through Bruno's company, was originally going to share the suite with me but he had a last-minute family emergency. Instead of replacing him, Mylan told me not to worry because he'd hired enough security to protect us all while we're here. I don't need a bodyguard as often as Mylan does, only when I'm traveling or going to crowded events.

The suite is fantastic. Modern yet true to the tropical island motif. To my right, a kitchen with sleek stainless-steel appliances and a bar overlooking the living area. To my left, a glass dining table with four white cloth-covered chairs.

The living room is massive, with stark white furniture and a thin smart TV hanging on the wall. In the far-left corner is an office set-up with a wooden desk to match the wooden coffee table and side tables.

Rebecca must have opened the room to the outside. Sliding glass doors reveal a balcony overlooking the sea. A slight breeze rakes over me and I inhale salt, fresh air, and a hint of flowers, though I couldn't say what kind. The sounds of the waking night filter in—waves crashing against the beach, the pulse of a whistling insect or maybe it's a frog singing songs, the faint notes of music, and people outside laughing and talking.

"Isn't it wonderful?"

I turn around to find Rebecca leaning against the doorframe to what I assume is the bedroom she chose.

"You're willingly talking to me?" I ask smugly. She flinches, almost as if remembering she hates me and shouldn't be having a conversation with me.

She scans my face, her brows pinching together. "Where are your glasses?"

"Ever heard of contacts?"

"Yes, dumbass, but I've never not seen you wear those stupid glasses."

"One, they're not stupid. They're sexy and you know it." I shrug. "And two, we're on a hot tropical island. Contacts seemed like the smart option."

She waves a finger around her mouth and chin. "And what's with that? Did you lose your razor?"

I rake my palm over my nicely trimmed beard, enjoying the way Rebecca's kissable lips part ever so slightly as she follows the movement.

"If you stare any harder, your eyes will fall out."

She straightens her back and clamps her mouth shut.

"I chose the smaller bedroom. They both have their own bathrooms, so as far as I'm concerned, we won't have to cross paths while we're here."

"Except we're both in the wedding and we're going to cross paths the entire time we're here."

Bruno asked me to be a groomsman, and I almost thought he was joking. I've known Bruno since he became Mylan's bodyguard a decade ago, but we were never really friends. He's older than us, closer to Lana and Ginger's age. We always thought of him as the tough big brother. Over the years, he loosened up. He'd still be intimidating in public while working, but in private, he'd joke around with us, talk about women, or his family. Having someone in your life that long, it's inevitable to form a connection with them.

While I never had that deep of a connection with Bruno, we've become friends these past few years. He's no longer Mylan's bodyguard. Now he's just one of the guys.

Rebecca purses her lips and turns on her heel, back into the bedroom. Before she closes the door, she pauses. "I appreciate you offering me the room. Thank you."

Then she slams the door so hard, so childish, I can't help but laugh out loud.

I bring my belongings into the other bedroom. Rebecca said her room was the smallest, but damn, my room is almost twice as big as the living area. There's a king-size bed with a light gray comforter. A matching gray couch and armchair next to it. A wood desk in the corner, and another thin smart TV hanging above a wooden dresser. The balcony extends to this bedroom, accessed by a sliding glass door built into a wall of windows.

I unpack my clothes since I'll be here for four full days. Tonight is dinner with the friends group. Tomorrow is the rehearsal dinner followed by Bruno's bachelor party—though it's basically just going to be me, Mylan, and Bruno hanging out—the wedding is the next day, and I decided to stay two extra days for some much-needed relaxation before heading back to Los Angeles to take care of things ahead of my next project. My assistant already has a long list that I'm dreading tackling.

I desperately need a shower.

The bathroom holds a massive glass cubed shower and an equally massive jacuzzi next to it. Thoughts of fucking Rebecca in that jacuzzi cross my mind.

She said she'd never let me touch her again. I won't if that's what she wants. The moment I sucked her release off my fingers in the back of that car a year ago, regret replaced her lust. She accused me of being disgusting, all because the SUV had a privacy screen, which I activated the moment we pulled away from the airport. She thought nothing of it at first, but her expansive imagination must have thought I regularly fucked women in the backseat of my chauffeured car, all because of a stupid privacy screen.

Rebecca is the only woman I've ever *wanted* to touch or fuck in the back of a car.

Thoughts of that infuriating woman have me jacking off and blowing my load all over the shower tile before turning off the water. I dry off and return to the bedroom, staring down at the outfit I laid out.

I frown, remembering the email Ginger sent.

No flannel or beanie hats allowed. I'm talking to you, Jensen.

Rude.

Not only did Ginger forbid me to wear anything in my comfort zone, but both Mylan and Bruno warned me to show up dressed to impress.

I mean, seriously. I don't always wear flannel and jeans. Sometimes I'll wear a t-shirt with a lightweight hoodie over it... and jeans. Plus, they've seen me at award shows. I wore a fucking tux to the Oscars. I wear suits to attend movie premieres. Still, those are formal events. Tonight... it's casual. It's dinner with friends. A dinner that Ginger threatened immediate ass kicking if I showed up looking like I was ready to chop wood.

A month ago, when I told my therapist about Ginger's threat, first, she laughed, then she challenged me to use this as the next step in my body acceptance journey by wearing something I usually wouldn't. Something that doesn't hide my body. I've been testing it out this past month and if I'm honest, coming up with a new outfit every day has been fun. I've been getting a lot of compliments too.

I hate when she's right.

The dinner is being held in the outdoor area of a restaurant on the property. It's the end of August and hot as hell, so, swallowing my anxiety, I dress in an approved short-sleeved blue button up with colorful palm tree designs paired with tan cargo shorts. Both show off parts of my body I rarely let the public see.

I stick my feet in a pair of white Vans and check my hair in the full-sized mirror across from me.

Ready as I'll ever be.

I open the bedroom door and step out at the same time Rebecca does.

We both freeze, staring at each other, mouths gaping.

I'm the first to break. My eyes travel down her body. She changed into a tropical-themed romper with yet another plunging neckline that hugs her tits to perfection. The romper's shorts showcase her long, tanned legs and wonderfully thick thighs. Thighs that I want, no *need,* wrapped around my head.

She's put her light brown hair up in a messy bun with flyaways framing her face. Her makeup... I've never seen her so natural in my life. She's beautiful, heavy makeup or not, but with the light mascara, gold eyeshadow, and light pink lip gloss on those plump lips... she's a goddess.

The longer I stare, the harder my dick gets. When my eyes find hers again, she's blushing. Her breaths are shallow, and I glance at her now-hard nipples poking against the thin fabric of her outfit.

Fuck yes. She's reacting to me too.

"I see you're ditching the flannel and hipster jeans."

I cock an eyebrow. She's baiting me. She *wants* to fight with me.

I shrug. "Bride's orders."

"Didn't realize you had tattoos."

My shorts and shirt offer perfect views of the ink covering my arms and legs.

"I have more you can't see."

"Oh? Where?"

"Do you want me to take off my clothes and show you, Becky?"

"That's not..." She snaps her mouth shut.

I've won this battle.

"We're late," she mutters and walks towards the door.

I follow her and a barrage of fruit and flowers hits my nose... cherry blossoms and peaches. It takes everything in me not to grab her so I can bury my nose in her neck.

I move past her and reach the door first. I open it and wave my hand at the hallway.

"After you, princess."

She crosses her arms, which amplifies her cleavage, and I steal a look before focusing on her pouty pink lips.

"I'm *not* a princess."

"Then what are you?"

"A queen and if you call me princess one more time, I'll cut off your balls and toss them into the ocean."

I put up my hands, feigning fright. "I'm so scared."

Rebecca moves at lightning speed, and I yelp the moment her hand cups my balls.

What the actual fuck?

This position places her mouth inches from mine. "Good. You should be scared," she whispers, her breath fanning across my lips. I can taste a hint of wine. She clearly sampled the bottle left on the kitchen counter; a gift from the hotel for high-profile wedding guests.

Why is my cock getting harder?

Why do I *like* this?

Rebecca must have felt my growing boner because she immediately releases me.

The way she sizes up my crotch has me fidgeting on my feet.

"Hmm."

It's all she says before walking out the door.

Chapter 5 – Rebecca

Holy shit.

Holy shit.

Holy shit.

I can't believe I did that. I can't believe I just sexually assaulted Jensen Boliver. My hand was on his balls.

And his cock.

Jesus, that thing is huge.

I cringe at my actions because if it were a man cupping a woman's cunt...

Unacceptable.

Embarrassment has me speed walking down the hallway to the elevator. I'm trying to run away from Jensen but after I stranded him in the lobby earlier, he doesn't let me make it to the elevator by myself this time.

He pushes his way inside just before the doors shut. He pauses to make sure we're alone, then he plants his hands on either side of my head, caging me against the wall.

His cologne and musk overpower me—amber, honey, and oranges.

I want to bottle up that scent and inhale it like a drug.

Ugh. No, I don't. I hate this man. Not to mention he's way too young for me.

Only nine years younger.

My thoughts are ganging up on me, teaming up with my body.

"Oh, Becky," he purrs. His hot breath against my neck sends a shudder through me. "You're going to pay for that."

I swallow hard, struggling to look away from his green eyes. An instrumental ukulele version of Somewhere Over the Rainbow plays faintly over the elevator speakers. A soothing song that does nothing to slow the fast beats of my heart. It beats frantically because... that's how turned on I am.

"What... what are you going to do?" My voice wavers. Not with fear, but with lust. My cheeks burn with it. I squeeze my legs shut, attempting to ease the ache he's causing, but Jensen tsks, shoving his knee between my thighs to spread them back apart.

"You're not even a little sorry, are you?"

No. I should be. I don't answer, but I don't have to. He sees it all over my face.

"Bad Becky." He moves his hand to my throat and grips it, squeezing gently, but dear lord I want him to squeeze harder. I close my eyes, leaning my head against the wall.

The elevator jolting to a stop on the fourth floor to let someone else on ends this... sexually charged moment.

I pop open my eyes and he's stepped to my right. An older couple with silver hair gets on and pays no attention to our corner. Instead, they're watching a TV built into the wall, playing the resort's commercial on the screen, talking about all the fun activities and excursions to participate in.

Out of the corner of my eye, because I refuse to look at him, I notice Jensen adjusting his dick, trying to hide his erection.

I want to help him with that.

No.

Bad Becky.

The elevator makes it to the lobby without picking up more passengers. Jensen places his hand on my lower back, leading me out and guiding me through the crowd. Tourists pack the lobby, some holding drinks and chatting, others roll their luggage, trying to dodge people who are standing in their path to the elevator.

When a drunk man carrying a cocktail bumps into me, Jensen snakes his hand around my waist and yanks me against his side.

The protective move nearly has me wanting to finish what we started in the elevator, no—something I started in the room when I touched Jensen without his permission.

I'm an asshole.

We finally squeeze past all the bodies and follow the signs to the restaurant. A hostess guides us to a private area near the back of the patio setup where our friends crowd around a table fit for eight.

We're the last ones to arrive.

Mylan sits next to Lana, dressed in a short-sleeved button up decorated with colorful lilies. His dark curly locks frizz slightly because of the humidity. His tanned arm is slung over Lana's bare shoulders—tinted pink from likely being in the sun today—and he's holding on to the tail of her red braided hair. Ginger and Bruno are across from them. Ginger is wearing a form-fitting white sundress, her natural coiled hair longer than last time I saw her. Her skin glows as Bruno whispers sweet nothings (I assume) into her ear. He's wearing a Hawaiian shirt, his blond hair in a low ponytail, and his face is a shade of red—also likely sunburned—compared to the rest of his lightly tanned skin. Eloise is next to Ginger, choosing a long sundress to wear. For once she has her blonde hair styled down.

Mylan is the first to see us walk in. Jensen's hand is still resting on my lower back, so I peel myself away before anyone notices and walk to the two remaining seats across from Eloise and next to Lana.

"Rebecca, finally!" She stands and gives me a crushing hug that I desperately wanted to linger. She releases me and frowns. "Why are you all flustered?" Her hazel gaze moves to Jensen trailing behind me. "Oh. That makes sense. Hi, Jensen. Love the beard."

"Thank you, Lana," Jensen responds, then throws a smirk my way. Jerk.

Mylan and Jensen do their silly best friend handshake, then he sits down next to Lana, whose eyes dance between the two of us.

"Are you and Jensen here together?" she asks, and I want to murder her.

"Yeah, why are you two arriving together?" Mylan adds, and I contemplate double homicide.

I take the chair beside Lana. Jensen sits next to me and wags his brows, feeding their speculation.

"Well," I begin, "the hotel messed up my reservation. My room was canceled because of some glitch, and they didn't have another room to give me. Jensen offered to let me stay in the second bedroom in his suite."

Mylan chokes on the sip of water he just took.

Lana's mouth drops open. "That was very kind of you, Jensen."

I scoff.

"Rebecca," Lana scolds, "when are you going to realize that Jensen is a nice guy?"

"He's really not."

"I'm literally sitting next to you, Becky, and you're not using your inside voice."

"We're outside." I turn back to Lana. "See what I mean?"

That mischievous grin of hers grows bigger. "Mhm."

"Whatever you're thinking, you better stop right now."

Mylan peers at me around Lana. "What would Lana be thinking?"

"None of your business, Mylan Andrews."

He shrugs. "No worries. Lana will tell me later."

A server interrupts the vulgar gesture I was about to give Mylan to take our drink order. I choose a glass of red wine and Jensen orders a Tom Collins.

"How you doing?" Jensen asks Mylan, while bent over me far enough he's basically in my lap. "You're okay with us all drinking tonight?"

I press at Jensen's chest, attempting to move him out of my personal bubble, but he's too big and doesn't budge.

"Jenny, I told you to stop asking that every time I'm in the same room as alcohol."

I expect Jensen to get mad at his best friend for using the nickname he can't stand. Instead, he relaxes his face. But not before I caught the worry pinching his brows.

Mylan must have seen the worry too because he softens his voice. "I'm four years sober and going strong. You know, one of the pillars of recovery is to find a purpose in life. I'm doing just that through service to others with my foundation."

Oh yeah, Mylan created Beyond the Bright Lights to help people like him get treatment and offer resources in the days, weeks, months, and years following rehab.

Mylan plants a kiss on Lana's cheek before continuing. "And I have my sweet donut offering me support and unconditional love."

Lana flips me off when I fake a gag, not only at the cheesy words, but at Mylan's ridiculous nickname for her.

She nudges my shoulder with hers. "How's the book coming along?"

"You're writing another book?" Jensen butts in before I can answer.

"Yes," I say to him without a glance, and to Lana. "It's... coming along. I'm at a block, but I'll get through it. I'm staying a couple of extra days and plan to take my laptop out to the beach and write."

Which reminds me, I need to ask Jensen if that's okay. It is *his* suite I'm staying in. I wonder how long he booked it for.

"That sounds like a wonderful idea," Lana beams at the same time Jensen asks, "what's it about?"

I huff out my frustration and whip around.

"It's about a magical land split in two, ruled by the queen of the west and the king of the east. A knight, whose loyalty is to the old king, kidnaps the young queen. This knight is ordered to deliver the queen back to his king for death, allowing him to take claim over the entire realm. But on the journey back, the more time this knight spends with her, the more he realizes he can't let the king kill her—"

"Why can't he?" Jensen shockingly sounds interested.

"Because they're soulmates."

"So, it's enemies to lovers."

"Who says they fall in love?"

"Oh, I just assumed... since they're soulmates."

"Just because they're soulmates doesn't mean this is a love story. My book is about a powerful queen who's been doubted her entire life. She's lost everything. Her family was all killed by the old mad king from the western kingdom. She has to prove that she's worthy to rule and the only way to do that is to kill the mad king herself and avenge her family. The twist is that she actually orchestrated the kidnapping, unbeknownst to the knight, so she can execute her plan."

Jensen clamps his mouth shut, his lips in a fine line while he thinks about his response. "I'm just saying if the main characters are soulmates, readers are going to expect a love story."

"That's exactly what I told her," Lana says.

I sigh. "Yeah, yeah. I'm already working on the love part. Here's the problem, though. The mad king finds out about her assassination plan. He has spies everywhere. He also knows the queen and the knight are soulmates, so he goes to the village witch and has her put a curse on himself and his knight. If the queen kills the king, the knight dies too. The witch is the only one who can remove the curse. Not even her death can remove it. So, the king has the witch killed to prevent the curse from breaking."

"Holy shit," Jensen says with awe.

"Right?" Lana adds, equally impressed.

Jensen sits back in his chair and crosses his husky arms over his expansive chest. The sleeves of his shirt bunch up, allowing me a peek at the rest of the ink on his right arm. The entire thing is a galaxy with stars and planets and some sort of spaceship that looks to be firing lasers. There's a weird furry creature—a Sasquatch, maybe?—and a couple of robots, one tall and gold, the other resembling a trash can. Wait... I know where this is from. Star Trek, I think? Or is it the other Star one? Both are movies I stayed far away from fearing I'd get made fun of for liking them. Whichever movie it comes from, I want to trace my fingertips over the art, appreciating its beauty. Or is it the beauty beyond the ink I want to appreciate?

"That sounds like a great story. Why are you having a hard time with it?"

"Because she wants the mad king to die so badly, she doesn't believe her love for the knight is strong enough to save him."

He doesn't respond for the longest time, and I can feel his eyes on the side of my face.

"Have you never been in love before, Becky?"

"Why would you ask me that?"

He shrugs. "Just curious. If you've never been in love, then that might be why you're struggling to write about it."

"Have *you* ever been in love?" I snap.

Silence. Again. When I finally turn to look at him, his eyes are down, inspecting the contents of his glass. He lifts it to his lips and pours it all down his throat. Before the bottom of the glass hits the table, a server is at his side asking if he wants another. Jensen nods and gives the man his empty glass.

I've seen this side of Jensen a few times before. It's the same man who disappeared that day in the conference room during script negotiations after showing me his vulnerability in the bathroom. The man who broke down the night of the wrap party for *Tyler's Team* and refused to let me in.

Before I can say a word and ask him what the hell his problem is, Ginger stands and clinks her glass with a fork.

"Thank you all for being here tonight." She waves her hand to all of us around the table. "After my father passed away when I was in my twenties, and I lost my mother a few years ago, I had no one left because I was an only child. You are the family I chose, and I am so grateful you chose me too. Thank you for traveling to spend this special moment with me and my future husband, my Ehemann, Bruno. I know a destination wedding isn't the most convenient and definitely not cheap, but you're all rich, so I don't feel that bad."

Lana snorts and I smile before glancing at Jensen. He's still inspecting his new drink as if it has all the answers to life.

"Tonight is special, just us, our chosen family. Because tomorrow Bruno's parents, Lana's grandparents, and all the other guests will arrive as we celebrate the beginning of our forever." Ginger raises her glass. "Cheers!"

She places a gentle smooch on Bruno's lips that he decides isn't enough and goes in for a deeper kiss.

I'm so caught up in their love story that I startle when the server appears by my side to ask if I want more wine. I hadn't realized I'd already drank it all. The man moves on to Jensen, who just finished his second glass of hard liquor.

Jesus, this is going to be a long night.

The dinner was divine. I had two pork manapua with a side of veggies. The sandwich is like Chinese bao with a fluffy white bun and sweet pork inside. Jensen got an ahi tuna poke bowl and I grimace because I am not a fan of fish—any fish, even tuna. For dessert, I ordered a chocolate Haupia Cream pie. The sweetness burst inside my mouth, and I swear I nearly orgasmed.

I noticed Jensen staring at me after each bite of food I took, not just dessert, but the manapua too. When I questioned him about it, he glanced away and kept his head down, eating his poke.

By the end of the night, Jensen had had at least five Tom Collins. I can't believe he's still sitting upright.

Jensen lets out a gurgle of a laugh, and I sigh before looking at him.

"What's so funny?"

Lana and Mylan have already called it a night. Eloise stayed and is chatting enthusiastically with Bruno and Ginger about the ceremony. She even brought her camera and has been showing them test shots. I noticed Ginger hadn't been drinking tonight.

I already hate myself for drinking too much. Enough that I'm pretty dang tipsy. Still, I don't stop the server from bringing me another glass of wine.

Jensen leans into me, his arm brushing against mine. "I was just thinking," he begins, his words slurred, "about how we've never kissed, yet I've had my fingers inside you, and you've now fondled my cock and balls."

My eyes widen, and I turn to see if our friends overheard. They don't stop their conversation to gawk our way in shock, so I assume they didn't.

"Shut the fuck up," I hiss at him. "And we have kissed, you idiot."

"Oh, yeah, the car." He smiles as if remembering every hot detail. "Let me kiss you again, Becky."

"In your dreams."

"We do kiss in my dreams," he says, then to himself he not-so-quietly adds, "we do a lot more than kissing."

My heart flutters at his words, but I ignore the traitorous bitch. She has no idea what she wants. Besides, he's clearly drunk, and the booze is making him talk nonsense.

I chug down my drink and stand.

"I'm leaving." I wave at Bruno, Ginger, and Eloise, not wanting to interrupt their conversation. They wave back and I'm high tailing it out of there before Jensen can keep confessing things my body wants to hear but my brain can't comprehend.

Once inside the elevator with four other resort guests, I lean back against the wall and let out a long breath, relieved to be away from that man. As the doors close, I see Jensen's face appear between the cracks.

Was he chasing after me?

I exit on the ninth floor and try not to trip over my feet as I walk to the room. I probably shouldn't have had that last glass of wine. Right before I tap the card to let myself in, I hear a loud thud on my right. I turn my head to find a wasted Jensen face down on the cemented floor of the open-air hallway, steps away from our door.

He rolls over, breathing hard. He must have been running to catch up with me. His face is red and there is a line of sweat beaded along his forehead.

I cannot with him.

I walk to where he's lying and hold out my hand. "Come on."

He accepts my offered help and nearly topples me over.

"You gotta help me out, big guy."

"Don't call me big guy," he slurs.

Yeah, I wasn't talking about his body, but I can't tell him I said that because of his massive dick.

Finally, after a few false starts, Jensen is standing on both feet. I peel my hand away and notice blood on my palm.

"What the hell?" I grab Jensen's right hand and turn it over. "You're bleeding."

"I fell." He pouts and points at his left knee, which is also scraped and bloody. "It hurt."

He shoves his palm in my face.

"Will you kiss it and make it better?"

I smack it away and take hold of his wrist, dragging him behind me to our room.

Our room.

I hate how much I love the sound of that.

I take him into his bathroom—holy shit, this is nice—and sit him on the toilet. "Be a good boy and stay."

He scoffs at my words but doesn't complain as I walk away and search for a first aid kit. I've never seen one in a hotel room, likely only available if I go downstairs and ask the front desk clerk. Good thing I have a little kit in my purse. My clumsy ass has needed a Band-Aid after slicing my finger on God knows what far too many times.

I bring the kit—which holds a few Band-Aids, antiseptic wipes, and healing ointment—back into the bathroom, where I find Jensen hunched over with his eyes closed.

The moment I place his right hand in mine to clean it, his head jolts up.

"What are you doing?" He tries to jerk his hand away.

"You hurt yourself when you fell, remember? I'm going to clean it, so I need you to stay still."

I hear him hiss in a breath when I wipe the wound with the antiseptic towelette.

"Come on. It's not that bad," I say with a smile.

He relaxes at my playful tone. Silence stretches between us as I work, and when I look up, he's staring at me.

"You're so beautiful, Rebecca," he says in a whispery voice.

Rebecca.

He didn't call me Becky.

Heat pools between my legs at how intimately he said my name. I ignore it and keep cleaning his injuries. Once finished bandaging his right palm, checking his left and finding no scrapes, I kneel and get to work on his knee.

He watches me in this highly sexual position and if we weren't in the bathroom—him perched on a freaking toilet drunk—maybe I'd help him with that erection forming.

After placing the last Band-Aid over his cut, I stand and he crushes me to him, wrapping his long, tattooed arms around me. He buries his head into my soft stomach and inhales deeply.

"You smell amazing." His hands flatten on my back, moving up and down. "Like peaches and flowers."

My fingers find their way to the mess of soft, loose curls on his head, and I scratch my nails over his scalp.

He moans and pulls back to rest his chin on my stomach just above my belly button.

"Let me kiss you, Becky."

Oh, so we're back to Becky now?

That breaks whatever spell this man was putting on me. I free myself from his arms and step back.

"I'll help you get into bed."

His shoulders slump, and he pouts again as we leave the massive bathroom. I stop him at the side of the bed and fold back the blanket and sheets.

"Take off your clothes," I say and turn around to find him something to sleep in.

"*You* take off my clothes." I don't see the smirk, but I sure heard it.

I ignore the cocky asshole and rifle through the dresser drawers—impressed that he unpacked—until finding a pair of plaid pajamas. Of course, he'd have flannel pajamas.

He's so ridiculous.

Yet, why do I find it adorable?

Shaking my head, I turn around to hand Jensen his sleep clothes. He's all but naked except for his boxer briefs and the full erection he's sporting.

I've been with men of all sizes—short, tall, big, small.

Jensen is a big guy. Plus-size, I suppose. Over three hundred pounds if I had to guess and maybe six-two compared to my five-five. His body matches the lumberjack outfits he favors. Hairy chest, beefy arms and thighs—all of which are covered in tattoos. Designs that I can't focus on because I want to get a good look at the rest of his body.

He doesn't have abs. His stomach jiggles like mine, and I let myself imagine kissing along his chest, down his torso until reaching that thick and long—

I look away, blushing, my mouth definitely not watering at the thought of taking his dick down my throat.

"Here." I hold out the clothes to him.

"Were you checking me out?" he asks, taking his pajamas.

"No, you're just drunk," I lie and quickly add, "I'll get you some water."

I leave before he can call my bluff. By the time I return, Jensen is in bed, pajamas on, his back against the headboard, and sheets covering his waist.

I hand him a hotel-provided bottled water, and he gulps it all down within seconds before placing the empty bottle on the table next to the bed.

"Sleep with me," he demands, grasping my hand.

"Hell no."

He rolls his eyes. "No, not sex. Just sleep."

I pause, narrowing my eyes at him.

"I'll be a good boy, I promise."

"You're crazy." I turn to walk away, but his grip on my hand tightens.

"Please, Rebecca," he asks in a whisper.

Ugh. Why did he have to say my name again? Does he realize the power he possesses by using my actual name instead of Becky? Except, right now, he's not making a power play. He's... vulnerable. Or maybe it's the booze. Either way, the desperation in his eyes squeezes my heart.

I give him a curt nod.

He lets out a shaky breath, then smiles wide and scoots over. He holds open the sheets for me to get in.

Jensen snuggles up to my side, laying his arm across my waist and tangling his legs with mine. His beard scratches my arm and I barely stop myself from petting it. I breathe him in—his boozy breath, his sweat mixed with that alluring amber, honey, and citrus scent that I can't get enough of.

He's knocked out cold within seconds. The heat radiating off his body wraps around me, and I relax. A few minutes pass and I fall asleep too.

Chapter 6 - Jensen

I wake on a gasp and pain rips through my skull. I groan as I flop over onto my stomach. Am I dying?

What the hell happened last night?

What did I do?

Did I really cuddle with Rebecca until we both fell asleep?

I hate cuddling.

But I loved cuddling with her.

My arm slides out to the other side of the bed.

Cold.

She left me. Of course she did.

I lift my head and spot a glass of water and two pain pills sitting on the table next to the bed.

She left me, but she *thought* of me.

The ache of abandonment fades, replaced with a feeling I'm not used to—something I was denied growing up.

I roll myself out of the bed, groaning some more when I sit up. After popping the pills and washing them down with the entire glass of water, I rest my elbows on my knees and rake my hands over my face and through my hair.

I'm an idiot.

I never drink this much.

Why did I drink this much?

Maybe it was Rebecca talking about her book and how excited she sounded, how that excitement dissolved to anger when I asked her about love, how she erected that mask of loneliness I know all too well—I drank to numb it all.

I could never understand why Mylan lost himself to his addiction all those years. But last night, this morning, I get it. I understand now how easy it was for him to escape.

My phone beeps with a text notification.

Mylan

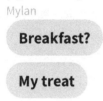

I roll my eyes at his dumb joke. The resort is all-inclusive. Breakfast is free. Still, I huff a laugh and smile.

Mylan

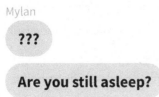

> **Damn, how late did you stay last night?**
>
> **Okay, fine. No breakfast**
>
> **Lunch?**
>
> **Dude, it's almost 2**
>
> **Are you alive? I'm about to come check on you**

My stomach dips while reading the text he just sent. Two in the afternoon? I slept for sixteen hours?

Me

> **I'm awake. Guess I needed to catch up on sleep**

It's not entirely wrong. It seems I've been needing to catch up on sleep for the past five years.

Mylan doesn't answer immediately, so I head into the bathroom to shower the previous night away. I change out my contacts for a new pair of dailies, then strip my pajamas. My cock jerks remembering Rebecca checking me out. At least, I think she did. Unless my drunk self imagined it.

Next, I remove the bandages on my palm and knee. Thankfully, the scrapes weren't deep and they're barely visible today.

Rebecca was so focused as she took care of me last night. Fuck, it felt good. Then I had to ruin it. I vaguely remember the conversation, but I'm pretty sure I asked her to kiss me. No, not ask... demanded.

It's strange how I'm not embarrassed. How I'm not shutting down my emotions to protect them from inevitable harm. I think it's because she didn't hesitate to care for me. She *wanted* to help me.

Because Rebecca is a good person. Too good for me. She's seen me at my worst far too many times, and yet, she never runs away.

After my thirty-minute-long shower, I dress in a white shirt with green and yellow palm leaves on it and forest green swim trunks. I still have a few hours to kill before wedding activities, so I have every intention of walking down to the beach, jumping into the ocean, and floating on my back until my skin prunes and sunburns. It's something I used to do when my nanny took me to Santa Monica when I was a kid. She was always the one taking me to the pier because my parents were too busy to be a part of my life.

I check my phone again and see a whole new round of texts.

Mylan

> You haven't been sleeping? Every-
> thing okay? Want to talk about it?

> ???

> You didn't fall back asleep, did you?

> I guess you're showering or some-
> thing. Don't forget, wedding re-
> hearsal is at 7, followed by dinner,
> then the bachelor party. Ginger said
> don't be late or you're out of the
> wedding

> Also, loving the new look. The beard
> is badass. And I always told you
> to show off those tats. Women
> love them. It's sexy #showmeyour-
> tats #justsaynotoflannel #lumber-
> jacknomore #dresstoimpress

I fire off all my responses.

Me

> Just got out of the shower. I'm fine,
> nothing to talk about. I won't forget
> and I won't be late

Then I reply to the text about my 'new look' with a whole paragraph of middle finger emojis. He sends five hysterical laughing emojis back. A wave of warmth spreads through my chest. We've been repairing our friendship for the past few years, and I'm so glad to have my best friend back.

My feet trudge leaving the suite and I swallow the nausea as I walk down the hallway to head to the beach. I decide to take the stairs—all nine flights—because the elevator will only remind me of last night and how I caged Rebecca against the wall. I don't need my dick getting hard before going out in public.

The hotel lobby is just as busy as last night when I exit the staircase. I hiss at the bright light filtering in and put my sunglasses on—I don't even remember hooking them onto my shirt.

My stomach is killing me, so I stop by the hotel's café and grab a coffee, a sandwich, a cup of fruit, and a bottled water. I sit to eat and inhale everything within five minutes.

Despite the sunny and warm day, the beach isn't too crowded. Lounge chairs are placed throughout the sand facing the ocean.

As I'm walking to an empty one, a flash of red stops me in my tracks. The moment my eyes find *her*, time slows down. Okay, maybe not, but I've surely died, and this is heaven. Rebecca walks out of the water soaking wet. Her red two-piece suit clings to her body, leaving little to the imagination. Her top barely covers her tits, her nipples hard as rocks and poking out.

God, I want to put them in my mouth.

Water drips down her soft stomach and my tongue goes dry, desperate to lick it up. Her bottoms are high-waisted, sitting above her wide hips and showcasing those godforsaken thick legs.

I stand there, staring like a creep and move my towel in front of my hardening cock.

She sees my... excitement and smiles, knowing exactly what she's doing to me.

"Jenny," she purrs and despite me hating the nickname, the way she just said it speaks right to my dick. "You're alive."

I compose myself enough to plaster on a smirk. "Were you worried about me, Rebecca?"

She narrows her eyes at me saying her real name. Becky gets a reaction out of her, but *Rebecca* makes her feral.

"Not at all. If you died, I'd get the suite all to myself."

She tosses her wet hair over her shoulder and walks past me, close enough that I inhale the salt and ocean scent mixed with her sweet perfume.

My anticipation of seeing her after last night is keeping me on edge. While I'm not embarrassed about what happened, I at least expected her to question me about the things I said or the cuddling.

She's acting like none of it never happened. Fine. I can play that game too.

She settles into a lounge chair, picking up her sunscreen bottle. I will absolutely lose it if I watch her spread that lotion across her skin. I throw my towel into the empty lounger on her right and start unbuttoning my shirt.

"What do you think you're doing?" Rebecca pauses her sunscreen application to gawk at me.

I tilt my head. "Going for a swim."

My shirt is now off, and I relish the way Rebecca checks me out before quickly averting her eyes.

"I mean, why are you putting your stuff next to me? Go sit somewhere else."

I lean over her, as close as possible, to set my shirt next to where I threw the towel. With my lips mere inches from her mouth, I say, "No."

She inhales sharply, her eyes flickering to my mouth as if anticipating a kiss.

Boy, do I want to kiss her.

I even lean in a little more and she holds her breath before I suddenly stand up straight.

She throws her sandal at me as I walk off, chuckling all the way to the water.

I've been floating for at least thirty minutes by the time she joins me. I didn't expect her to, but here she is.

"What's wrong with you?"

"Right now? Nothing."

"You're being creepy with your sunglasses on, floating like a dead body. People are staring."

"I don't care."

"What are you even doing, anyway?"

"Haven't you ever just floated in the water before? It's relaxing."

She says nothing at first, so I lift my head to look at her. She wants to try it, but she's glancing around the water, at the beach, worried people will judge her or something.

"Stop thinking about it and just do it, Becky."

She sighs dramatically and I laugh out loud. I find myself laughing around her a lot lately. I close my eyes again and hear her splash around before finally settling on her back.

"I feel silly," she says after about a minute of silence.

"Who cares?"

She scoffs.

"Seriously, though. Why do you care? Everyone here is a stranger. We'll never see them again."

"Unless they take our picture and sell it to the tabloids."

"You're famous enough to get recognized?" I tease.

"For your information, yes. I do get recognized. In fact, my publicist texted me this morning saying there were already pictures posted online from dinner last night."

Clearly, she didn't look at those pictures or read the articles or she would have commented about the speculation of bad blood between us. She was giving me a murder glare the moment someone snapped the shot.

I wave my arms in the water like I'm making a snow angel. "Yeah, well, that's expected. Especially since Mylan is here. The paparazzi always find him."

"What about you? Don't the paparazzi scramble to get shots of you too?"

"I'm like the Robin to his Batman. He will always be the one they want. I'm just a bonus. It's always been like that, though."

"Jealous?" Rebecca teases.

A laugh bursts from my throat. "Not at all. Most of the time when I'm in the press, it's about my weight. It used to bother me. I mean, it still does. But... I don't know... I've been working on this part of my life with my therapist for a while now, and I'm over it. I just want to live my life without worrying about the world's warped opinion of what the perfect body should be."

It took me far too long to reach this level of body acceptance. It's a work in progress, but I'm trying.

"What I'm saying is... life is too short to let other people's opinion dictate the way we live."

"You sound like my therapist."

My eyes shoot open, and I turn my head to her.

"What? Surprised I'm in therapy too?"

I don't answer. How can I answer that? Her seeking help for her mental health is none of my business. I have no room to judge. Not that I would. No one should.

"I started going after the first director dropped out," she says quietly.

"You don't have to—"

"I know."

We laid there in silence, only the sounds of the waves fill the air. A slight breeze skims across our bodies to cool the scorching sun beating down on us.

"It took me a long time to get over my brother's death. He was my best friend. It's why I fought so hard against changes to the script."

My arm floats close enough to Rebecca that my fingers graze hers. She doesn't move it away.

"So, I went to therapy to talk about it. About why I refused to give in to the directors. She helped me realize I never properly grieved. Because my parents didn't let me grieve with them. I convinced myself they hated me. At least, I think they wished I had died and not Tyler."

"You really believe that?"

The water splashes as she shrugs. "They never outright said it, but I can tell. They can barely look at me when I visit them. When I call, they try to find any excuse to get off the phone. After Tyler died, I needed their love, yet all they ever did was push me away."

This time, when my fingers graze hers, I latch on. She lets me, and I weave them with hers.

"Have you talked to them about this?"

"Yes. They deny it. Then they act so hurt, like I was the one who emotionally abused them."

I squeeze her hand.

"Anyway, that's just part of why I'm fucked up."

"I don't think you're fucked up."

She doesn't respond to that. I wait, wondering if she has more to reveal to me. I also wonder when she's going to realize we're still holding hands.

"What about you?"

"What about me?"

"You said you're in therapy."

"Oh."

"Sorry, that was so invasive."

"No, it's fine. Um, I've been going since I was a teenager."

"Really?"

I laugh nervously. "Yeah, I'd get depressed about auditions. The way Hollywood perceived me as a fat person, always casting me as the fat friend, the comedic relief, or the butt of the joke. I'd also talk about my parents. They weren't terrible parents, they were just... vacant."

"That's horrible. I'm so sorry, Jensen."

I wave off her sympathy, not wanting to go into detail about any of this. "I've accepted it by this point."

"Parents should have unconditional love for their children. We should never have to accept anything less."

"Yeah, I agree."

We float in silence for a few minutes before she speaks again.

"What about Mylan?"

"What about him?"

"Do you talk about him in therapy too? Because I see the way you look at him. The fear in your eyes that he's going to slip up again."

Fuck. She can see all that?

When I don't immediately answer, she keeps talking. "Dang it. Here I am being an asshole again, asking you questions I have no business asking."

I've noticed how strong her country twang gets when she's flustered. And when she's excited. Like last night, talking about her book. It's so freaking sexy.

"You're not an asshole, Rebecca. Well, not all the time, anyway." I laugh when she gasps. "But yeah, I talk about Mylan with my therapist, but I'm not worried about him anymore. He's four years sober. It's the longest he's ever been sober."

"I think you're lying. I think you're still worried about him."

"I'm not."

She snorts.

"I'm not, seriously. I mean, yes, I will always be concerned that he could lose control again. This time, though, I think he's got it. He has Lana, and he's in a good place."

"But?"

"Jesus, are *you* my therapist?"

She laughs and that might be the first time I've ever made her laugh. I like it.

"Tell me," she urges, in such a supportive way, it has me *wanting* to tell her. She waits while I compile my words.

Words that my therapist wants to hear, but I always skate around.

"I had no one growing up. Sure, my parents gave me everything I ever wanted. I was never told no. They cared with their money, but I never had their love or their time. I met Mylan when I was seventeen. He was just as in need of filling that hole of parental abandonment as I was. So, we became friends. We stuck together, had each other's backs, supported and loved one another like we were family. We are a family."

I never told Mylan about what I went through at home with my parents. He had his own family issues to deal with.

"He was the one who told me to pursue directing. I'd always have my camera out filming on set. Don't get me wrong, I loved acting, but no matter how great I was on the screen, all anyone ever saw was my weight. I couldn't change the way people saw me, but with directing, I could create art the way I wanted. To be behind the lens meant I had the control. It was liberating.

"Mylan was always there for me, no matter what. He saw me and not my fatness. Then when he lost control... I left him and..."

My throat stings with an emotion I keep caged. I release my hold on Rebecca's hand and rub my palm over my face.

"I need to get out of the water." I stand up, surprising Rebecca enough that she stands too. Talking about this has me flustered and my brain hurts. I want to run away and hide, ignoring everything I'm feeling right now.

"Jensen," Rebecca says.

"I don't want to sunburn."

"I'm here to listen if—"

"It's getting late. We should probably get ready for the rehearsal dinner."

I leave Rebecca in the water, grab my clothes from the lounger, and practically run back to the room.

Chapter 7 – Jensen
4 Years Ago

I'm sitting on the couch at my Silver Lake home, re-watching Jurassic Park for the millionth time—Spielberg is one of my favorite directors—when my phone vibrates with a text.

Mylan

I'm sorry, Jenny. I love you

I frown at the nickname. Mylan overheard my mom calling me Jenny once. The next day on set, he blurted it out to get my attention. I got so pissed. He asked why I hated the name so much and I couldn't tell him how it brings up all my horrible childhood memories. Mylan has been through too much in his life to worry about mine too.

I re-read his message and my heart skips. I hadn't heard from him in several weeks after I left him at a club in New York City. He'd just been fired from a Ron Howard science fiction flick. He dragged me out with him to cope with booze. Our friend Rey met us there, but he couldn't stay long. Eloise was back at the hotel, helping the publicists deal with the aftermath of the firing, so it was just me and Bruno taking care of him. We didn't know he had coke and was snorting it all night. He was so out of his mind; he started singing and dancing on furniture.

His break-up with Olivia months earlier was a catalyst to this downfall. He was fired because he kept going out, kept getting drunk, and was too out of control for me to handle. It's not like I could physically stop him.

He refused to listen, refused to get help, and not just for thirty days, but longer this time.

Me

What do you mean? What did you do?

He doesn't answer immediately and the pit of my stomach twists.

Something's wrong.

I stand up and run to my kitchen where I grab my keys off the table next to the garage. I barely close the door to my Audi before I'm backing out of my driveway and speeding towards Mylan's place in Beverly Hills.

Thirty minutes later I arrive at a freaking crime scene—red and blue flashing lights, police, EMTs.

What the fuck happened?

I fly out of the car and run up the driveway to find the EMTs rolling Mylan out on a stretcher. He's pale and unconscious and hauntingly still.

"What happened? What the fuck happened?"

Tears well in my eyes, and I swallow the tightening in my throat.

A police officer holds up his hands, stopping me from trying to get to the ambulance to my friend. "Sir, please get out of the way."

"Jensen!" Eloise runs towards me with wet streaks down her face.

"What the fuck happened? Is he okay?"

"He... he..." She breaks down and I immediately wrap my arms around her petite body, which shakes violently.

"Is he alive? Please tell me he's alive."

"He's alive," Bruno answers solemnly and walks up to where we stand, his eyes lowered to the ground. "He overdosed. It... It was intentional."

"He tried to—" I can't even get the word out. This isn't like him. What the hell?

"I had to give him... I had to..." Eloise hiccups into my chest, so upset she's unable to speak.

"She gave him CPR. The EMTs said she saved his life. If she hadn't found him..." Bruno answers for her, his accented words trailing off.

"He'd sent me a text," Eloise says, her voice muffled because she'd yet to pull away from me. "I got it right as I was parking to drop off a pile of scripts for him to read... I found him and..."

She bursts into more tears.

"I got a text too," Bruno says quietly. I'd never seen him so sad. He's typically a happy man. "I was in the gym. I didn't hear my phone go off."

"Hey," I whisper into the top of Eloise's head. "He's going to be okay. If he really wanted to... if he really wanted to end things... he wouldn't have texted all of us."

It's the only comforting words I can offer, and I'm not even sure I believe them. I should have been there for him more. We've been best friends for nine years now, yet these past few years, we've grown further and further apart. The more I'd beg him to get help, the more he kept pushing me away.

After the ambulance leaves with Mylan, we pile into my car, and I drive us to the hospital. It's hours before the doctor comes to the waiting room. He tells us Mylan is stable and resting. Despite visiting hours being over, he still lets us go back.

Seeing my best friend, the one person who has been by my side, who's had my back, and loved me like a brother, restrained to a bed because he's a danger to his own life, is unsettling. My throat burns, my eyes ache with tears. I never cry unless it's on cue for a scene. I never cry because no one's ever been worth the tears.

Why? Why did he do this? I don't understand.

I tell Eloise and Bruno I can't stay. It's too hard. I ask them not to tell Mylan I was here then leave, making it just outside the door before I finally break down. I bend over, hands on my knees, and cry and cry and cry.

After a few minutes, I hear talking from inside Mylan's room.

"It was an accident," Mylan says, his voice scratchy and raw.

"Bullshit," Bruno growls. "We all got a text."

He doesn't defend himself.

"Is Jensen here?"

Bruno and Eloise say nothing.

"Right. Of course. Why would he be?" He doesn't say it angrily. Just sad. Defeated. "Look... I'm going back to Forest Ridge after they release me from here. Okay?"

"Stay longer this time," Eloise sobs.

I hate him so much right now for doing this to her. For doing this to me and Bruno. We're his friends. We care about him. Does he not realize that?

"Please, Mylan," Eloise pleads. Her voice is so small and broken.

"I'm sorry, Eloise. I really am. I... I don't know what I was thinking. I... I'm sorry. It won't happen again. I promise."

I t'd been a month since the worst night of my life. Reports about Mylan's overdose went viral the next day. Except, the media reported it was accidental. Mylan's publicity team is that good and kept the truth hidden.

Mylan stayed in the hospital's psych ward until they were confident he was no longer a danger to himself. They sent him to Washington for rehab. Eloise says Mylan's progress impressed the psychiatrists at L.A. Med enough that they didn't recommend a longer treatment. That doesn't surprise me. He's a fucking actor and can convince anyone he's fine. He's convinced me too many times to avoid going to rehab. They ultimately left the decision of an extensive treatment program up to Mylan.

What about the counselors at the rehabilitation center? He'd been there twice already. Would they try to talk him into staying longer like I did? I called his phone and left a million voicemails, sent him dozens of texts pleading with him to do the year-long treatment, but either he ignored every single one, or he shut off his phone and never got my messages.

I can't make him do something he's not ready for.

"What do you mean you have to drop out of the project?" Shyon, the executive producer, says.

I'm at the production company's head office with her, and the two other producers who seem to be attached to her hips. Sitting across the table from them is my friend Rey Michaelson, who's been cast as Tyler Taylor in *Tyler's Team*. He's the lead and now he's telling us he can't film the movie... with a month and a half before production begins.

Rey combs his fingers through his light brown hair, his blue eyes encased in shadows as he fidgets in his seat.

"I'm sorry, but it's out of my control," Rey says in his British accent. He grinds his jaw and shakes his leg.

"You signed a contract," Shyon points out, not a caring bone in her body. All that matters to her is money.

"Then I'll pay to break it," Rey yells. "I don't fucking care how much. Bill me, sue me, do whatever you need to do." His hands ball into fists on the table. "I have to go back to the East Coast indefinitely. It's a family emergency." His words die out. The pain taking claim of his voice. "I have no choice."

"This is—" Shyon begins, but I cut her off.

"This is fine. We'll find another lead. No problem."

Rey finally looks up, his eyes filled with concern and fear. "Thank you, J.B. I owe you."

I've known Rey as long as Mylan. He's a year younger than me and was cast to play mine and Mylan's bandmate in *Metal & Mayhem*. The three of us became close. We were inseparable while filming that show. Then it was canceled, and all our careers took off. Suddenly, we were too busy to hang out, especially Rey. He strayed from our friend group as he built his successful career.

I've missed the three of us. That's why Rey got the role in *Tyler's Team*. I advocated for him because I wanted to work with my friend again.

Rey stands. He's slightly shorter than me, six feet I'd say, and slim like Mylan. He's your typical Hollywood heart-throb with washboard abs and swoon-worthy hair, who already has a long list of movies. Rey claimed his spot as the next big action star.

But this is a setback for him.

"Call me if you need anything, okay?" I hold out a hand and he gives it three slaps. Not quite the secret handshake Mylan, Rey, and I created but that's understandable. He'd called me last night to tell me what happened. He's mourning and his life is about to change drastically.

Shyon sighs dramatically the moment Rey leaves.

"What the hell are we going to do? We start filming in less than two months."

"It'll be fine."

If only Mylan wasn't in rehab right now, he'd be perfect for this role.

I t's been three weeks since Rey dropped out of the project and we have to make an offer to someone today or we'll be forced to delay production, which starts in three weeks. We've reached out to dozens of actors on our list and, as expected, they had other projects secured.

"We've got our Tyler Taylor," Shyon says, barging into my office without knocking.

"What do you mean? No one consulted me about a new lead."

"This is above your head, Boliver."

"Who is it?"

"Mylan Andrews."

"No. No fucking way. He's still in rehab."

"He's getting out next week."

"Are you kidding me? Do you think it's a good idea to put someone on set who just went through a recovery program?"

"It doesn't matter what I think. This is coming from the head of the production company."

"How?" I grumble.

"Mylan's manager called in a favor. We're told he's doing well in recovery. We've been assured that Mylan will be ready, in character, and lines memorized by the time filming starts. That means we won't need to push back production and cost us a fortune."

"He's an addict."

"Who's been rehabilitated."

"This is a mistake."

I'm angry they're letting this happen. Surprised? Not so much. I've heard stories of celebrities going through treatment *while* filming. How they'd get escorted to set, film their scenes, then get carted right back off to the facility.

Eloise has been texting me updates and said the counselors at Forest Ridge want to keep him longer. But money talks, and I'm sure Mylan's manager and lawyers got involved to convince the rehabilitation center that he didn't need the longer treatment.

I don't doubt Mylan would do a great job with this role. When he's clean, he's brilliant. But I worry it's too soon. He's going to relapse and this time, what if it actually kills him?

Chapter 8 – Rebecca
Present Day

R ehearsal for the ceremony takes place on the beach along the shore as the sun sets over dark blue water. The sky is painted in an array of purple, pink, red, orange, and yellow accented with brush strokes of puffy clouds.

Ginger glows in her flowing maxi dress of bright tropical flower designs. Bruno beams as he stares across at his soon-to-be wife, his long blond hair floating around his face like he's some book cover model, ready to devour the woman in front of him.

They're so sickly in love it makes my stomach hurt with envy.

Eloise glides around, snapping photos, likely plotting out the best angles to get the perfect shots for the ceremony tomorrow.

I'm Ginger's only bridesmaid with Lana, her maid of honor. Mylan is Bruno's best man and Jensen is his only groomsman. Which means I'm paired with the moody man to walk down the aisle together. I tried talking to him, but he remained distant and vacant, only offering grunted responses. I even gripped his arm harder than normal, hoping to get some sort of reaction out of him, but no.

Now he's across from me and I stare at him, tuning out the wedding planner as she blurts out instructions. He's refused to make eye contact with me ever since he stormed out of the water earlier today following our conversation about Mylan.

Why does he do that? Why does he show an ounce of humanity only to retreat the moment he realizes he's revealed too much?

I'm sure it has something to do with what he told me about his parents. Or how he cared for Mylan and nearly lost him.

He needs someone to treat him like he matters. He needs someone to care about him, to care for him.

That could be me.

Before the thought settles and grows, the rehearsal for the ceremony ends and we're all heading back into the resort for dinner.

"Well, would you look who it is!" a scratchy voice, as thick as molasses, says when I approach the front of the restaurant where everyone gathers waiting for our table. "I didn't get the chance to say hello before the rehearsal. How are you, honey?"

"Gram," I smile, hugging Lana's frail grandmother. She's wearing a lovely purple dress with sewn in beads in a swirling silver design. Her thinning white hair is braided at the nape of her neck. "I'm doing well. So wonderful to see you. Are you and Pa excited to walk Ginger down the aisle?"

"I'm just tickled pink," Gram says the same time Pa says, "You're losing your accent, girly."

Lana's grandfather, Pa, stands next to Gram wearing high-waisted blue slacks and a white dress shirt underneath a matching blue suit jacket. He's missing all his teeth and reminds me of Popeye when he grins.

"Nothing worse than a Southerner sounding like a Northerner," he adds.

I gasp. "I do not! I still have my twang."

Pa bursts out into a fit of giggles, slapping his leg with one hand and waving the other around my face.

"You always were so easily riled up."

Gram gives Pa an eye roll before turning back to me.

"How are your parents, honey? I haven't seen them in a while. They've sure been traveling a lot."

They're traveling because I paid off all their bills. I bought them an RV so they could take that cross-country road trip they've been talking about since Tyler and I were kids. One that we were supposed to go on to celebrate Tyler's college graduation, but he got sick instead.

"They're good. They're spending a week at the Grand Canyon."

Mom sends me pictures. That is the basis of our communication lately. I'll call them, but as I told Jensen, they aren't very chatty on the phone. I just want to hear about their life and if they're having fun on the trip.

They didn't even ask if I wanted to come. I would have if they had.

"That's just wonderful. I wish Pa and I were healthier to travel more. Unfortunately, this will probably be our last big trip."

"Everything okay?"

"Oh, yes, honey. We're just old. Time to slow down is all."

"Table's ready!" Ginger sings, and Gram squeezes my arm before walking away.

Dinner was uneventful. We mostly talked about the excitement of the wedding tomorrow. Jensen sat far away from me, and I hate how much that hurt. Following dessert, Gram and Pa call it a night after flying all day. Mylan had sent his jet to pick them up in Arkansas, then they boarded a commercial plane in L.A., sitting first class (paid by Lana and Mylan) for the rest of the trek.

I briefly met Bruno's parents before they also retreated to their rooms with jet lag since they came all the way from Germany. His dad, Karl, could be his twin—tall, bulky, blond. His mother, Sofia, is the opposite: petite with brown hair.

We leave the restaurant. The guys hit up the resort's casino and poker room for Bruno's bachelor party and we head to the hotel's outside bar/pool area for Ginger's celebration.

The massive patio allows people to spread out, either taking a dip in the pool, soaking in one of the four hot tubs, hanging out at the bar, or dancing on the designated dance floor. The calming music playing over speakers hung around the area soothe my pounding head after drinking too much last night. I'm going easy tonight, only having one glass of wine. Besides, Lana doesn't drink, and if I remember correctly, Ginger wasn't much of a drinker either, and she's definitely not indulging the night before her wedding.

I recognize some of the other people who are here for the wedding but can't quite remember their names. People Ginger and Lana went to high school and college with and people who they worked with at Lilies Bar & Grill in Silo Springs. Apparently, Lana bought all their plane tickets and paid for their rooms.

I scoff. Everyone else got a room but me. Now I'm stuck in the same suite as an emotionally closed off man who keeps opening the door and letting me peek inside.

"Oh no, why are you pissed?" Lana muses. She looks radiant tonight, wearing a red body-con dress. Her dark red hair, that she's been dying for almost a decade now, hangs over her shoulder in a perfect French braid.

"Why are men?"

Lana and Ginger burst into laughter, not even needing me to fill in the blank.

"Is Jensen getting on your nerves?" Lana asks, snickering.

"I'm so proud of him," Ginger adds. "He hasn't worn a thread of flannel yet. I'm really digging his new look. The beard is so freakin' hot. It suits him."

"Yes!" Lana says. "I never knew he had all those tattoos. They're super cool and sexy. And I can see his eyes better without the glasses. They're so pretty."

Ginger goes on. "He's sweet too. I saw him helping Gram and Pa walk up the sandy beach after the rehearsal. Swoon."

She literally said swoon out loud.

I know exactly what they're doing. They're trying to butter him up, so I'll take a bite. They even look at me expectantly.

I hold up my hand.

"Did she?" Ginger gasps.

"I think she did," Lana counters.

"Objection!" Ginger squeals and heads turn our way.

"Stop," I hiss.

"Ma'am." Ginger's voice turns serious. "Impersonation of law enforcement is a crime."

Here we go.

These two are obsessed with *Law & Order* and for as long as I can remember, they've been quoting that damn show. Their favorite is holding up their hand to plead the fifth to avoid talking about something.

Apparently, I'm not allowed to participate.

Lana joins in on the fun. "Rebecca Marie Taylor, you're under arrest. What do you plead?"

"Not guilty," I say, smiling despite how ridiculous this is.

"Confess. It's the only way to prevent you from going to jail." Ginger crosses her arms to amplify her seriousness.

I purse my lips, not wanting to talk to them about this, but at the same time, I really need to talk to them about this.

"Jensen," I begin.

"I knew it!" Lana yells.

"Never mind."

"Sorry," she quickly adds. "Sorry, I'll shut up."

I give Lana a warning scowl, then proceed to tell them everything that's happened between us—that day in the bathroom during script negotiations, the car last year, me groping him yesterday before dinner, and the heated exchange in the elevator that followed.

"I knew something was up with you two when you came to Ginger's engagement party last year," Lana says.

Ginger nods her head, agreeing. "Yeah, you did have a bit of a post-orgasm glow going on."

"That's not a real thing."

"Oh, it is." Lana blushes. She's probably thinking about Mylan giving her an orgasm glow.

"You should fuck him," Ginger blurts out and more heads turn our way.

My face flushes with heat, both embarrassed by having this personal conversation in such a public place but also because the image of Jensen on top of me, fucking me, flashes across my thoughts.

I squeeze my thighs together.

"It's obvious you both want to," Lana says.

"It's not that obvious."

"Becca," Lana says as if I'm an idiot. "The tension between you two is suffocating. Please, put us all out of our misery and just... do it."

I glance around the bar area. While Lana, Ginger, and I sit on a wicker couch in a corner, the rest of her small bachelorette party guests stand nearby. Everyone's drinking, laughing, enjoying life. I should be doing that too. I'm not getting any younger. I remember what Jensen said about not caring what people think about me. It's hard not to when I was bullied in school for being myself.

"Where's Eloise?" I ask, attempting to change the subject so I don't have to talk about Jensen anymore.

"Oh, probably flirting with someone, somewhere." Lana offers.

"And my flirting game is weak," Eloise giggles, magically appearing, and plopping down on the couch next to Ginger. "I should have brought a date."

"Why didn't you?" Lana muses.

Eloise shrugs, and I don't expect her to go into detail. She never talks about her personal life with us.

"I'm a romantic. I thought I would meet someone here and have a whirlwind romance. We'd fall in love and live happily ever after together."

"Aww," Ginger and Lana coo at the same time.

Eloise rolls her eyes but smiles. She starts snapping photos of us all.

"Well," I begin, "you still have time to meet someone."

Eloise scans through the pics she just took and grins before turning her camera around and extending her arm to show me one of myself. I look... amazing. My skin is tanned from spending hours at the beach today. My hair, despite being slightly frizzy, gives me an island vibe to match my tropical sundress.

Eloise pulls the camera back to her lap and sighs. "The dating scene is so exhausting. I think I'm just ready for a relationship." Ginger and Lana perk up, desperate to learn something, anything, about this private woman. "I grew up in a super religious home, so when I came out to my parents, it was rough. They disowned me at first. I was devastated, and I just needed to forget about them, so I dated a lot. Fucked a lot. I was trying to fill the hole they created. I was trying to find my place again. Now that I'm mending my relationship with them, I think I'm finally ready to find a partner."

"And what *do* you want in a partner?" Lana wags her eyebrows. Eloise's head jolts up, almost as if she forgot we were here, and realizes she's sharing part of her life with others.

Instead of retreating as I expected, she blushes and answers. "I want a woman who will give me multiple orgasms."

"Amen," I say, and we all giggle.

"I want a partner who can make me laugh because I don't laugh enough. I want someone who will support me no matter how crazy my dreams may be. I want a woman who will spend the day doing nothing because I let myself get overwhelmed with life too often."

She frowns. It's brief before she replaces it with a sad smile.

"Anyway, I should go. I need to charge my camera and unload the pictures I took today." She stands and offers a small wave before quickly leaving.

"That was unexpected," Ginger says. "Seems like she's finally comfortable enough around us to open up."

"I adore her," Lana beams. "I'm so happy you hired her."

"Are you kidding me? She shot for freakin' Vogue. She offered to charge us half her rate, but I refused. She deserves it all."

"Cheers to that." I lift my wine glass. Lana and Ginger raise their non-alcoholic drinks and we finish the night talking about men, laughing at inside jokes, and gushing over Ginger's big day.

Chapter 9 - Jensen

"**F**ull house!" Bruno slams his cards down on the table's green felt so hard, my stack of chips bounce and tip over.

"Fuck off, man," Mylan grumbles, tossing his cards to the dealer and crossing his arms over his wide chest.

Well, a full house definitely beats my straight.

"This is Texas Hold'em. You want to win?" Bruno chuckles. "Play better. Jetzt geht's um die Wurst."

"What does that mean?" I ask.

"Now it's about the sausage, boys," Bruno answers.

"Try again, buddy." Mylan shakes his head.

I've missed hearing these Brunoisms. Words or phrases that Bruno doesn't quite get right after translating them to English. Bruno moved to the U.S. from Germany a decade ago. I'm pretty sure he knows exactly the right words to say by now, but he likes to mess with everyone just to be funny.

"It's all or nothing. You will not win if you half dick it with these bets."

"I think you mean half ass it," I offer.

"I said what I said."

"It's not about the bets," Mylan says, exasperated. "I'm just not getting good cards."

"Excuses do not pay the rent."

Mylan groans. "The Brunoisms are killing me tonight."

"Sorry, boss. I'm just really nervous about tomorrow."

I laugh at Bruno, not only being self-aware of his confusing phrases but also calling Mylan boss, despite not being his bodyguard for four years now.

"I'm pretty sure I don't deserve Ginger."

My stomach tightens at his words. How could he say that? Bruno is literally the nicest guy. Even Mylan, despite his dark days of addiction, is the most caring man I've ever met. Me, however, I'm a cold-hearted asshole who can't seem to drop this indestructible wall I've built around my emotions.

Though Rebecca sure has been chipping away at that wall lately.

"Who you thinking about?" Mylan asks, next to my ear.

I must have missed Bruno's entire conversation about being nervous about his wedding because the next hand has been dealt. I tilt back the corners of my two cards just enough to see what I got, hiding them from Mylan's prying eyes.

Pocket Rockets. Nice.

"Who says I'm thinking about someone?"

"Is it Rebecca?"

"Absolutely not," I lie and shove my sad stack of chips into the center of the table. "All in."

"She'd be perfect for you, you know?"

I watch as everyone around the table folds, except Bruno and Mylan.

"She's insufferable."

"So are you."

I give him the side eye and sip on my vodka tonic. It's my first and only drink of the night.

The dealer lays out the flop: ace of diamonds, king and jack of spades. Nice. I have triple aces now. Bruno adds a stack of chips to the pot and Mylan calls.

"We're not compatible," I finally say to stop Mylan's searing stare on the side of my face.

"How do you know? Have you two actually sat down to have a civilized conversation?"

Yes.

Talking to Rebecca on the water earlier today was... nice. Aside from Mylan and my therapist, I've never revealed that much about myself or my feelings to anyone. Even in the press, I keep my words limited to work, only offering small glimpses into my private life. She didn't even judge me when

I talked about therapy, my parents, or me abandoning My-lan.

"Just... try it. Try not to be an asshole to her."

"She's the asshole."

"Fine, you're both assholes. Maybe you can bond over it."

I scoff. "She hates me. What's the point?"

"Are you sure?"

"What?"

"That she hates you? I mean, I've seen the way she looks at you. And the way you look at her."

I cringe internally, remembering saying those exact words to Mylan that one day on set years ago when I realized how important Lana was to him and the hope it gave me that she could be the one to save him from his disease.

I was right.

Doesn't mean *he's* right, though.

The dealer lays down the turn, another ace. Four of a kind? I got four of a kind? Hell yeah.

Bruno's face is set in stone as he makes another bet against Mylan. Mylan curses under his breath and folds.

"Show your cards," the dealer says, and I toss mine over towards the pile of chips in the center.

Bruno whistles. He has three kings. Even if the river reveals another king, my four of a kind would trump his.

I won. Holy shit. I won. I never win. I'm typically a horrible poker player.

The dealer turns the final card, and it's a seven of clubs.

"Congrats, Jenny." Mylan claps his palm on my shoulder. I don't even care that he called me the nickname and scoop the pile of chips towards my chest. I'm smiling. Big, hurting-my-cheeks smiling.

Mylan leans into me and says, quietly, "Why don't you go find someone and celebrate?"

He shows me a text on his screen from Lana saying Ginger's bachelorette party is over. She's back in their room in their suite and is ordering him back to—okay, the rest of that text was not meant for my eyes.

If Ginger's party is over, that means Rebecca is probably back in our suite too.

Without saying a word, I stand and turn away from the table.

"What about your chips?" Bruno yells after me.

"Keep them."

"It's like $10,000," he adds.

"Wedding gift," I say and exit the poker room.

My steps pick up as I move through the casino. I can't think about what I'm about to do because then I'll second guess myself. I'll let my fear consume me and shut down these intense feelings for Rebecca; feelings I keep pushing down and now they're ready to burst free.

I concentrate on putting one foot in front of the other. The casino's not that big, and it's right next to the lobby, so it's less than a minute before I'm at the row of elevators. There's a crowd waiting, and I consider taking the stairs up nine floors, but the elevator closest to me opens, and I slip in before the crowd converges.

Of course, everyone is getting out on a different floor.

I tap my fingers on my thigh.

Don't think about it.

Don't think about it.

Don't think about it.

You want to do this. You want her. *Will she want this too?*

I nearly lose my mind before arriving on my floor. I sprint down the hallway, sweating as I scan my card and enter the room. The door shuts behind me and I pause with my hands on my hips to catch my breath.

Rebecca stands at the door to her room, holding a bottle of water halfway to her mouth, frozen by my odd behavior. She's wearing the hotel-provided slippers and robe. I wonder if she's naked underneath. Her hair is down, not wet, so she doesn't appear freshly showered.

Good, because I'm about to get her dirty.

I stalk towards her, and she steps back. The door frame stops her from getting away from me.

"I'm going to kiss you, Rebecca. Right now. Right fucking now. If you don't want me to kiss you, say it."

I snatch the water from her and toss it across the room, not even caring that it spills out and soaks the floor. My hands reach out to cup her face in my palms. My mouth hovers over hers.

"Say it," I whisper.

"I don't want to say it."

"You want me to kiss you?"

"God yes."

My lips capture hers—hungry, messy, desperate. I swoop my tongue inside, exploring every inch of her mouth. She tastes like sweet wine. She lets out a quiet little hum and fists the fabric of my shirt to bring me closer to her until our bodies fuse.

I thread my fingers into her hair and tighten my hold on the strands to tilt her head back so I can move my kisses away from her mouth, down her chin to her neck. Her skin radiates sweetness—cherry blossoms and peaches.

My other hand snakes around her waist and finds her ass. I squeeze firmly before sucking hard on the skin of her neck, desperate to leave a mark.

She groans.

"You like that?"

"Yes."

"What else do you like?" I ask as I perfect this hickey.

She removes my hand from her ass and guides it behind the fabric of the robe to her breast.

"Touch me, Jensen."

I've never wanted anything more in my life, but first, the robe has to go.

I curl my fingers over the thick belt. "May I?"

She bites her bottom lip and nods, her breathing labored and pupils blown out.

I untie it slowly, never glancing away from Rebecca's ocean blue eyes. Once the robe is loose, I let it fall off her body. Her nipples pebble and goosebumps rise over her skin.

Rebecca Taylor is naked before me.

I step back to admire her. Her body is a piece of art. She tries to cover her stomach and I don't think she realizes she's doing it. I move her arms out of the way.

"Rebecca, your body is better than anything I've tried to imagine these past four years. Let me memorize it so I'll never forget," I say.

She holds her breath as my fingertips trace the stretch marks on her stomach and sides. Her skin is so soft and tanned except for the white patches her bathing suit covers. My fingers move to her breasts, grazing her rose-pink nipples, which makes her whimper again. My thumb grazes a scar underneath her breast, and I find a matching one on the other side. I make a mental note to ask her about those later.

She groans. "Please, Jensen, you're driving me crazy."

I cup her heavy breasts in my hands and latch my mouth over one of the hardened tips. My tongue lashes out while the pads of my fingers twist and tug her other nipple.

Rebecca arches away from the door frame. "Fuck yes."

I relish the way her body reacts to my touch.

My knee settles between her legs, and she starts grinding her bare cunt on it. She's so fucking wet I can feel it through my shorts.

She rides my knee while I work her breasts, pinching and pulling, sucking and nibbling.

It didn't take her long to get worked up and the moment she buries her fingers in my hair, clutching the locks hard, I know she's close.

"Jensen," she moans my name again and starts shaking with an orgasm, soaking my shorts just above my knee.

We stand there for at least a minute, holding each other, both of us breathing roughly. My dick aches with how hard it is for her. When she finally composes herself after that release, I lift my head. Our eyes meet, and she's scowling at me.

I don't know why that makes me laugh, but I do, which only makes her scowl harder.

"That's never happened to me," she says.

Before I can ask exactly what she means by that, she's spewing out words.

"You made me come... just by..." she points at her breasts.

"And I..." she points at my knee. "I mean, it has been a while since I... fuck, Jensen, I dry humped your knee."

My smirk turns into a full-blown cocky-ass smile. "There was nothing dry about what you just did."

She winces after seeing the wet spot on my shorts, so I distract her by brushing my mouth against hers, teasing her with near-kisses.

"Do you regret it? What we just did?"

She's confused by my question but shakes her head.

"You don't regret me making you come this time?"

Now she understands. This wasn't like last year in the back of the car. This time, she's not in denial about how she feels about me.

She shakes her head again, a lazy smile spreading across her face.

"Good, because we're not done."

I clutch her hand and lead her away from her room to go into mine. I swing her around and gently drop her onto the bed. She scoots to the middle.

"Tell me what you want," I demand.

"I need you inside me."

"Not yet."

She frowns. "Why?"

I crawl to her and hover over her, making sure not to put my weight on her. I do, however, grind my cock into her pussy. She gasps and digs her nails into my arms.

"Because I won't want to fuck you once." I kiss the exposed skin between her breasts. "I will want to take you just like this." Next, I kiss just above her belly button. "I will want to take you from behind so I can see that pretty ass bounce on my dick."

At the mention of my cock, she tries to reach down for it, but I'm faster and pin her hand to the bed. I hold down her other hand as well.

"I will want you on top so I can bury my face between your tits while you ride me. I want to fuck you on the balcony; I want to bend you over that chair; I want to fuck you in the jacuzzi after pounding you in the shower."

I cover her nipple with my mouth, lapping my tongue over it roughly. She sucks in a breath.

"Fucking you the way I want will take all night, and Ginger will murder us both if we show up to her wedding tired and sex ruined."

I stand up before she can protest and capture her by the waist, sliding her down until her legs hang off the edge of the bed. She yelps at the fast movement.

"Beautiful," I say, admiring her spread out before me.

My hands worship every inch of her, over her soft stomach, up her sides, until I cup those plush tits. My fingertips graze over the scars I felt earlier, then I tease her hard nipples again. She whimpers. They must still be sensitive from a few minutes ago.

My lips trace the exact route my hands took, up her stomach, past her belly button until I'm placing gentle kisses along her collarbone. I can only hope my beard tickles her skin in a pleasantly torturous way.

"Jensen, please," she begs.

"Have you decided what you want?"

She groans.

"Tell me and I'll do it. I'm yours tonight, Rebecca."

"Keep calling me that."

"Rebecca," I say seductively and huff a breath on the tender spot on her neck that now has a dark pink mark forming.

She grabs my hair again and pushes my head toward her cunt.

I tsk.

"Use your words, Rebecca."

"I want your mouth on me."

"Where?"

"Everywhere."

"Be specific."

"Jensen," she whines.

"You're in charge here. Haven't you been wanting to boss me around?"

She tries to squeeze her legs on me, but I pry them back open. I lean into her pussy and inhale deeply.

"I'm waiting for my order, my queen."

She sucks in a breath, her grip on my hair tightening. "I want you to taste me."

"Yes, my queen."

"Shut up," she growls, and I laugh, my hot breath fanning over her wetness, making her shiver.

I get on my knees and toss her legs over my shoulders, wearing her thighs like fucking earmuffs. Then I dive in, consuming her like a hungry man getting his first meal in days. My tongue lunges inside her, licking up her pleasure before teasing her clit. I suck it with fervor, and she arches her back off the mattress. Her nails dig into my scalp, and she clamps her thighs on my head.

"Fuck, yes, Jensen," she yells before I spread her legs back apart.

"Tell me I'm yours," I say and plunge a finger inside her.

"You're mine." She pants as I pump slowly.

My mouth returns to her clit. By the time I'm adding a second finger, she's close to coming again. Her walls pulse and suck around my digits as I thrust them in and out, over and over.

She needs more, so I curl the tip of my middle finger to find that spot. The moment I graze it, I drag my teeth over her clit. She screams and explodes with another orgasm. Her thighs squeeze my head again, burying my face deeper as she rides her release. When her body finally lowers down to the bed, she lets out a shaky breath before spreading her legs to free me.

I crawl up her body, placing soft kisses along her stomach, then between her breasts, and up her throat. I pause, not sure if she wants me to kiss her while my beard is covered in her release.

To my surprise, she crashes her lips to mine, letting out a quiet hum as she tastes herself on them. She nips my bottom lip, and I grind my hard dick against her still swollen pussy.

She reaches down for it again.

"No," I laugh and jump up from the bed.

"Why not?"

"Because tonight isn't about me."

I've spent four years fighting my attraction to Rebecca. She's the first woman I've wanted to take my time with and prioritize her pleasure over my own. I plan to spend these next few days losing ourselves to each other and catching up on what we've been missing.

Plus, as much as I want my dick in her mouth, she can barely keep her eyes open. I can see she's had a long day and we both have an even longer one tomorrow. I'm going to need her energized for what I have planned tomorrow night.

I hold out my hand, and she scowls at it.

"Come on. I'm going to clean you up."

Her eyes widen, it was fast, but I caught it. Despite her confusion, and her wariness of me not letting her go down on me, she places her hand in mine. I walk us to the oversized bathroom and start the water in the jacuzzi.

Rebecca stands there watching it fill but turns her focus on me once I start stripping.

I unbutton my short-sleeve shirt and shed it off my body, tossing it to the marbled floor. My shorts follow. Rebecca's blue eyes widen at the sight of my dick straining against my black boxer briefs.

When I wrench them down, my erection springs free, pointing directly at her. She steps forward and I hold my breath, expecting her to wrap her fingers around it.

She doesn't. Instead, she places her palms on my chest and runs them up and down my pecks, over my arms, then around to my back before resting on my love handles.

She presses light kisses along my chest—gentle, tiny kisses that make my heart thunder behind my rib cage. I let out a shuddering breath.

"Are you okay?" she asks, tilting back. Her brows pinch with concern.

"Yes," I nearly whisper.

I don't tell her I never let women touch me so intimately. How I never let them explore my body the same way I give such detailed attention to theirs. I don't tell her that the last time I had sex was over a year ago.

I'm nervous.

Rebecca's fingertips skim along the ink on my chest (dark storm clouds with lightning strikes placed throughout, which I got at the beginning of Mylan's downfall when I was deep in my own depression). On my left arm, I have a nature half-sleeve: trees, a mountain, a river, birds.

It's the full sleeve on my right arm that piques her interest. "What is this from?" Her touch hovers over a scene from my favorite movie.

"Seriously?"

She laughs. "Yes, seriously."

"Star Wars."

"Oh, it's cool."

"Cool?" I scorn.

"I've never seen Star Wars before."

"What? Why? How?"

She smiles, sadly. "Long story."

My eyes flicker back to the jacuzzi and there's enough water now, so I turn off the faucet. I get in first, then Rebecca steps in, sinking down in front of me. I adjust my cock so it's not poking her in the back.

"Can I wash you?"

"Yes, please," she says and relaxes her entire body.

I pick up my body wash and pour some into my palm, foregoing the loofah just so I have a reason to touch her. Lathering up the soap the best I can, I spread it up and down her arms, over her breasts and down her stomach. I cup water into my hands after each pass and rinse the soap off.

The moment I'm done, she twists around in the tub and grabs the body wash I just used on her and squirts some in her palm.

The control I have while Rebecca cleans me, her hands exploring every inch of my skin, is impressive. My anxiety about people touching me fades the more I'm with this woman. There's something about her that brings out the parts of me I've always kept buried.

I wait for her to talk, to tell me what made her sad just a few minutes ago. I don't pressure her, though. I want her to be comfortable talking to me. My body hums with excitement because I have never wanted something like this before with a woman; something as simple as talking, sharing, confiding.

"I used to be a strange kid. Well, not strange to me, but other people thought I was weird," she finally says once she's finished washing me. She gives me a sad smile and turns back around. I draw her against my chest. "I'd dress up in costumes and pretend I ruled magical worlds. I'd wear mismatched clothes with unicorn designs or clothes with a bunch of cats on them. I used to love escaping in my imagination."

I smooth my palms up and down her arms, letting her know I'm listening. She melts some more against my chest.

"In middle school, kids started making fun of me. I was bullied a lot, so I stopped dressing like that. I stopped my imagination from taking me to those magical worlds."

"Where you were queen?"

"Yes." She laughs, the vibration spreading throughout my body. "Tyler was the one who told me I should never settle for being a princess. He told me I should strive for greatness and become a queen."

"Ah," I say. "That's why you told me to shut up when I called you my queen."

She laughs again. "Yeah."

"And that's why you kept getting mad when I called you princess."

"Yes." She doesn't laugh this time, but I heard the smile in her voice.

"Well, only a queen would fondle a man and put him in his place like you did to me."

"Ugh," she says and covers her face with her palms. "Don't remind me."

I kiss the top of her head.

"Don't be embarrassed. I liked it."

"You did?"

"Did you not feel how hard I got?"

She giggles, and it's so freakin' adorable.

"I'm used to being in control: with directing, with my press interviews. I'm not a fan of surprises. I like when things are planned and organized. But that can get exhausting. I rarely give myself a break. So, when you grabbed me and took control of the situation, being demanding as fuck, I don't know. It was sexy. I didn't think. I just wanted. I wanted you, I wanted to please you, I wanted you to order me around."

"You *do* take direction well," she giggles again, her fingertips drifting across the top of the water.

I have a feeling she said that to distract me, so we'd stop talking and start fucking, so I continue the conversation.

"The bullying... is that why you never watched Star Wars? Were you afraid kids would make fun of you?"

She sighs, so I wrap my arms around her, just under her breasts. She rests her arms on mine.

"Yes, and no. I didn't watch a lot of movies to begin with. I read books though. When the bullying started, I realized people might think I was a nerd if they found out which types of books I liked and especially if they found out I watched fantasy or science fiction movies. So, I decided to never watch them again.

"My senior year of high school, one of the theaters in Jonesboro—where Lana and Tyler went to college—was having a marathon of all the Star Wars movies. Tyler begged me to come up for the weekend and go with him and Lana. They were his favorite movies, or maybe it was Star Trek he loved so much—"

"How dare you confuse the two?" I say, and thankfully, it makes her laugh.

"I'm pretty sure he liked both."

"So, what happened?"

She twists around and places her palms on my chest.

"He collapsed on the football field the Friday before we were supposed to go."

Shit. I just made a joke during her heartbreaking story. I'm such a dick. I take her hands and bring them up to my lips, kissing her knuckles, then her palms.

"I'm sorry, Rebecca."

"You know what?" She smiles, and I wait for that smile to falter into the grief I've seen cross her face far too many times. "It's okay. I'm okay."

"You are?"

"Yes."

She straddles my lap and folds her hands behind my neck.

"I never told anyone about that. It wasn't in my book either. I mean, Lana knew, of course, because she was going to go to the movies with us. But..." she chews on her lip before continuing. "It was nice sharing it with you. Talking about my grief and sharing Tyler stories outside of what I wrote in the book usually hurts too much."

She leans in and kisses me. It's a soft kiss, gentle. She's thanking me.

When she tilts back, her eyes are glossy with tears. Except, I don't think these are sorrowful tears this time.

"Can I sleep with you tonight?"

I pause before answering. Two nights in a row of cuddling until we fall asleep? I want nothing more than to have this woman in my arms tonight. Though, it'll be hard to resist her. Leaving the bed after I tasted her was already difficult enough. I desperately want to be inside her, but we have to be up early tomorrow for the wedding.

Rebecca must see the battle on my face.

"I'll be a good girl, I promise."

I laugh at her words, mirroring my own from the other night.

"I'm not worried about you."

Chapter 10 - Jensen

4 Years Ago

I'm nervous.

Today is the first day of filming. I'm going to see *her* again. I haven't seen Rebecca in-person since the day we met for script negotiations. Any time we needed to discuss the movie, we did it through email, text message, or a quick—and very professional—phone call.

At least I already ran into Mylan and don't have to deal with the anticipation of that reunion. My former best friend shouldn't be here filming this movie. He's still recovering. It's too soon.

I considered dropping out of the project and risking paying a fine or facing a lawsuit. Though, the other directors stated creative differences and somehow skirted the fines and suits. Plus, my parents are both high-profile entertainment lawyers and would have been able to get me out of both.

But I didn't drop out.

I didn't because of *her*.

Because if I drop out, this movie won't get made, and I won't do that to Rebecca.

Why do I care so much? Why does she make me care? Is it because she needed someone that day in the bathroom? Because she needed me?

No one except Mylan has ever needed me. Growing up, we'd always be there for each other. Even when our friend Rey got too busy and strayed from our friend group, Mylan and I stayed close all those years. Which is why it hurts so much that he refused my help. Which is why I refuse to let myself care for anyone ever again.

I get to set early to finish prep work and go over my story boards. I have every single shot planned out. There's been a few more script changes over the past couple months, all Rebecca approved (and with no fight, I should add), so I'm going over those changes to make sure we don't run into any major issues the first day of filming. We'll only have a few rehearsal takes to get it right. Especially if we want to stay on schedule and within the budget.

By the time I'm done with prep, the cast is arriving to set. I'm standing with Michelle Miller in the high school hallway, where we'll be shooting the first scene. Michelle is playing Lana Young in *Tyler's Team* and she wanted to go over some of her lines with me. Before we start, I glance up.

My heart skips about a million beats a minute the moment I spot Mylan walking in, holding hands with the real-life Lana Young.

The fierce woman narrows her hazel eyes at me and scowls. I deserve that after how I behaved at her bar the other night. I walked in looking to start a fight with Mylan. It was childish and unprofessional of me. I went to Lana's bar, hoping to piss Mylan off enough that he'd punch me and get fired. Then there'd be nothing holding him back from going to longer treatment.

An idiotic move on my part because what if him getting fired triggered him to return to the booze and pills? I would have been responsible for that.

I also hoped I'd piss him off enough that he wouldn't want to revive our friendship. If he hates me, then I can't get hurt again. I can't get hurt if I convince myself I no longer care about him.

But that's the problem. I do still care about him.

I care enough to worry about this new romance. I saw Lana console him after our confrontation at the bar. She brought him down when his temper reached a point where he definitely would have punched me if she hadn't stopped him. It was like a switch. Her touch was all he needed.

Mylan has obsessed over women before. His last girlfriend, Olivia, broke his heart because of it. That relationship sent him back into his addiction. What if this woman does the same?

I'm brought back to reality by the sound of Michelle stumbling over her words.

"Oh, um, yeah, well... I just meant you're all tattooed with red hair now."

What the hell did Michelle just say to Lana?

"Sure, sweetie," Lana responds, and I hold back a smirk.

Lana is a plus-size woman. Being a plus-size man in this toxic industry, I bet Michelle made some fat phobic comment. It's happened to me far too many times from co-stars who make backhanded comments about my body, pinch at my fat rolls, or comment about what I'm eating.

I swallow my anger at the model-turned-actress and acknowledge Lana and Mylan.

"Lana," I say, my eyes dropping to their embraced hands. "So glad you could join us on set today."

My words are hesitant, forced. Not because of displeasure, but of concern.

Mylan glares at the side of my face. I refuse to look at him because I know the hatred I'll see will break me. I *wanted* this. I *want* him to hate me. At least, that's what I *thought* I wanted.

This is why I don't do emotions. It's fucking with my head.

I wave my finger between Mylan and Michelle. "You two should get to hair and makeup and wardrobe. We start filming in an hour."

Mylan's brows pinch together as he looks back and forth between me and Lana. He doesn't want to leave her with me.

"It's fine. I'll be fine," she tells him.

"I'll take good care of her," I say, adding fuel to Mylan's animosity towards me. I don't miss the disapproving glare Lana gives me.

Mylan nods and kisses Lana on the forehead before stalking down the hall with Michelle Miller following.

"I appreciate you helping him," I say the moment they round the corner. "And I'm sorry about my behavior at the bar."

Lana leans back at my words, clearly not expecting me to say that.

"What happened between you two? I've asked Mylan, but he always changes the subject to avoid talking about it."

I swallow hard and scratch the stubble forming along my jaw. I look around the area. With crew members setting up, there are too many prying eyes. Not that they would share what they hear or see on set with the tabloids and risk getting fired. Still, I wave my hand, prompting Lana to walk with me.

I lead us down the hallway away from the holding area, where there are fewer people shuffling around.

"Mylan and I were best friends. Then he let his addiction get between us."

Lana scoffs. "You mean you let his addiction push you away?"

I narrow my eyes at her, mostly because she's right. "It's not that simple. I was there for him. I cleaned up his messes and covered for him far too many times. I offered him help. I *wanted* to help, and yet, he never accepted it. What was I supposed to do?"

"Not give up?"

I shake my head, despite berating myself for this exact thing a million times.

"It was too hard. Have you ever seen someone you love willingly wilt away? Destroy their life with no regard to those around them?"

I know addiction and alcoholism is a disease, but he's been to rehab two other times before this last stay. I can't keep hoping that this time will work because it tears me apart when it doesn't.

"Mylan needed support. He needed friends," Lana says.

We reach the end of the hallway and turn around, leisurely heading back towards the holding area where directors' chairs line the lockers.

"Mylan had support. He had friends: me, Bruno, Eloise. He had people who begged him to get help." *And for longer than one month*, I silently add, because talking about this, about losing the only person I ever cared about, has my voice shaking. I hate feeling this way. "He reached a point where he was so far gone that I no longer recognized him as my best friend."

"Maybe this last stint worked. He's doing better now. He hasn't had one drop of alcohol or any drugs." She winces as if she doesn't necessarily believe her words.

"Yeah, he does this. It's a vicious cycle. He'll stay clean for a while. Sometimes weeks, sometimes months, then something will happen, something will trigger him, and he'll start falling again." Something I should have told myself before walking into Lana's bar Saturday night. *Idiot.* "You should know while booze was an issue, it wasn't the root of his problems. Not until he started adding the drugs—opioids, coke, molly, whatever he could get his hands on."

I stop myself from revealing Mylan's intentional overdose. It's not my place to tell.

And it's not like I'm telling her all this to scare her away. I'm just making sure she knows how bad it was. How bad he could get again. If she plans to be in a relationship with him, she should tread lightly. Because the last woman Mylan dated broke his heart. I can't let her do the same.

"I should also warn you—"

"Lana?" A shrill, familiar voice cuts through the hallway, cutting off my words.

Fuck.

It's her.

Rebecca.

She's here.

"Lana," she repeats in her honey sweet voice. That fucking accent is going to kill me. It coats my skin like icy rain on a hot day. It awakens my cock, begging to be claimed by her.

Rebecca opens her arms as she approaches, swaying those wonderfully wide hips like she's on a runway at New York Fashion Week. She's wearing a purple wrap dress, clinging to her body and showcasing all her curves. Her long brown hair falls in waves.

Damn, she's beautiful.

"Rebecca," Lana says. There's a hint of displeasure in her voice.

The two women hug, and I look away.

"I didn't know you'd be here," Lana adds.

"Of course, silly. I wrote the book *and* the screenplay. This project has been my baby for nearly thirteen years. I plan to be here every day."

I sigh, heavily. Right. She's going to be here every single fucking day. She's been near me for seconds and my dick is already begging for relief. How will I last three months?

Rebecca's blue eyes cut to me. She purses her lips and raises her chin high. "Jensen."

"I need to finish prep," I lie and to Lana say, "We'll talk later?"

I don't give her time to answer before I'm walking away as fast as I can. I round a corner and slam my back against a wall, tearing the white poster board with the school's mascot of a panther drawn in black.

I close my eyes to calm my racing heart and fast breathing. *Get yourself together, dammit.*

I stand there, panicking, for at least five minutes before someone finds me.

"What the hell is wrong with you?" a tiny, angry voice asks. I turn and find a short petite woman wearing jeans and a black fitted blazer with a white blouse underneath. Her braided blonde hair hangs over her shoulder.

"Hey, Eloise."

Mylan's personal assistant gives me a snarl. She's not my biggest fan. We used to be cool. She's been Mylan's assistant for about two years now. It's the longest anyone has held the position—between him going all male diva, him hooking up with them, or them only wanting the job because he's Mylan

Andrews. Eloise is the only one to put Mylan in his place. She doesn't put up with his bullshit.

She once told me she had an uncle who was an alcoholic. She knew how to deal with this disease. Having her with me in the clubs the few times my busy schedule allowed me to hang out with Mylan, helping me watch over him to make sure he stayed in line, was a relief. We became close because of it. We both did our best to keep him away from the drugs and alcohol, but he'd still find his way back to it. All we could do at that point was babysit him.

Then she saved his life when he overdosed. It should have been me. I should have been there. What she experienced that night... I can't even imagine. And yet, she stuck by his side while I was the one to abandon him. She probably resents me for that.

Now, here she is, likely thinking I'm flustered because of Mylan and not the woman who makes me question everything about my entire existence.

Though, working with Mylan these next three months also has me on edge.

"I'm fine," I finally say and step away from the wall. I adjust my black-framed glasses and tug on the bottom of my long-sleeved flannel shirt.

Instead of saying something nasty to me, as I deserve, her face softens. She places her palm on my arm.

"He's doing great this time."

I say nothing. I can't. So, I nod and walk away.

I somehow avoided Rebecca the rest of the day. Well, sort of. She was there, always there, sitting in one of the director's chairs—watching the scenes, watching me work, leaning in to Bri Downley, my first assistant director, to share her thoughts on certain shots and suggesting additional takes. Bri would then relay the message to me.

At first, I wanted to ignore Rebecca, but I changed my mind after observing her during a scene. She didn't see me staring, but I saw everything as she watched her memories come to life. Her palm resting over her heart. Her eyes wide and glazed with tears. The way she sucked her lips into her mouth so they wouldn't tremble.

Goddamn her for chipping away at my cold, dead heart.

So, I accepted all her suggestions to re-evaluate, re-shoot, re-position.

Now, it's late. The crew has packed up; the cast is gone, and it's just hours until we're back for day two.

I'm the last to leave. Walking down the hallway, I pass a security guard making the rounds as he watches over the equipment. He's one of a few guards patrolling at the school, monitoring the set to make sure no fans or crazed paparazzi sneak in.

I round a corner and stop in my tracks.

Rebecca is still here?

She's standing in front of a glass case in the middle of the hall. I walk towards her, my feet near silent on the carpeted floor. She doesn't hear me approaching and when she finally looks over at me, she glances away, wiping at her face.

I stop by her side, turning to the case to see what has her so upset.

In the center is a picture of her brother. He's in his football uniform. Sweaty light brown hair clings to his forehead. He's smiling with his arm around a younger Lana who is wearing a cheerleading uniform.

"This was the night he secured his football scholarship to Arkansas State University," Rebecca says quietly.

She smiles sadly and huffs a laugh.

"He could have gone to any college in the U.S., but he wanted to stay here with Lana and be close to family. He didn't even really want to play football. He wanted to be a social worker. But we weren't rich, so he kept playing football because it paid his way through college."

She pauses and I'm not sure if she's going to keep talking, so I say nothing. Then she clears her throat, glancing at me and frowning.

"Anyway..." She turns to leave.

"Are you okay?" I blurt out.

She stills mid-turn and moves her head back toward me just enough that I can see her profile.

"No. Not at all."

I should say something. Tell her I'm listening; tell her I think about that day in the bathroom almost every single day.

I don't because I'm already distracted by her being here. I have to focus on this film. This is a huge opportunity for me. It's already getting Oscar buzz. I can't fuck it up by getting involved with Rebecca Taylor.

But mostly, she deserves someone who can offer her the type of relationship where she comes first. Right now, I can't be that person for her. I can't offer her the attention she deserves.

My silence speaks volumes.

"I wish you'd stop doing that," she finally says.

"What?"

"Stop acting like you care, then decide you don't. It's frustrating and confusing and I can't stand it."

With that, she leaves me in the hallway.

Chapter 11 – Rebecca
Present Day

After soaking in the jacuzzi, Jensen toweled me off. It was so gentle and intimate that it had me questioning everything I ever thought about this man.

We both put on robes and climbed into his bed, snuggling together. The moment my head hit the pillow; I passed out.

I wake up before him. The rising sun pours into the room because neither of us drew the curtains closed last night. I watch Jensen sleep. His long eyelashes flutter as he dreams, his mouth is open slightly. He's not snoring, but his nose makes a whistling sound when he breathes in and out. It's adorable. He's adorable. So very innocent and at peace right now.

The things he's told me about his past, his experience in Hollywood as a plus-size man, his parents offering him no love, his friendship with Mylan... I can understand now why he's been so cold to me. Why he refuses to open up.

He's scared. His entire life has been back-to-back let downs—a series of people overlooking him, judging him, not appreciating him.

In a way, we are too similar. I let people judge me and changed everything about myself. My parents used to love me, then took it away as if love was a toy. I let myself date men, powerful men, famous men, just because I thought they could offer me status, something I felt would validate me when no one else did. Except those relationships all failed because I was unhappy. Because they weren't with the real me.

My phone vibrating on the table next to me brings me back to the present. I check the time and realize I only have about fifteen minutes before I'm due in the bride's wedding suite for hair and makeup.

I peel myself out of Jensen's arms, and he stirs.

"Come back." He mumbles.

"I have to get ready for the wedding. You should wake up and start getting ready too."

"Mhm."

I graze my lips over his cheek, and his eyes flutter open. He palms the side of my face.

"How did you sleep?"

I smile. "Very well, actually."

He takes my hand and kisses my palm.

"Good. Because we're not sleeping tonight."

He gives me a cocky grin before turning over on his side, his back to me. He's already fast asleep.

We're not sleeping tonight.

Fuck me.

I'm thankful for the bath with Jensen last night because I had no time to shower or even look in the mirror this morning. I dress in a pair of leggings and an oversized button-up shirt. After putting my hair into a messy bun, I slip on some flip-flops and grab the bag containing my bridesmaid's dress and ballet flats. I make it to Ginger's bridal suite at the other side of the resort with one minute to spare.

People are running around taking care of the last-minute wedding details. A woman takes my bag, hands me a robe to change into for hair and makeup and points me to a bathroom. Once I emerge, a different woman collects my discarded clothes and hands me a glass of champagne. Then a third woman clutches my elbow and leads me through one massive room to another massive room (everyone is moving so fast that it's all a blur, and I can't even admire the décor) where the bride, Lana, Gram, and Bruno's mother are sitting.

"Rebecca!" Lana holds up a near-empty glass of champagne, waiting for me to clink my glass with hers, and giggles.

"Are you drinking?"

She nods giddily, looking away from me after I accept her offered toast. She proceeds to clink her glass with Ginger's almost full one and Gram's half empty one. "Champagne to celebrate Ginger's big day!"

"She's clinked our glasses five times already. The booze is going to her head," Gram snorts.

"It is not," Lana gasps, giggles again, then playfully slaps at her grandmother's arm. "I've only had one glass."

"Being that you never drink," Ginger begins, smiling at her best friend, "and the last time you had a drop of alcohol was, what, over twenty years ago in college... I'd say you're feeling pretty good right now."

"And you feel the effects of champagne faster because of the carbon dioxide in the bubbles," I add. I learned that the hard way while briefly dating a politician. He took me to a charity event in Washington, D.C. and I had way too many glasses of champagne. I got wasted fast and tripped over my dress, knocking into a server, who spilled food all over a table of rich donors. Let's just say, I immediately left that event, hailed a cab, and holed up in my hotel room for the rest of the night. The following day, I nursed a killer headache and ignored the politician's calls until he realized I would never show my face around him ever again.

"Okay, fine," Lana concedes. "My head is a little woozy and now my stomach hurts, but it's totally worth it."

Ginger rolls her eyes and snatches Lana's glass, setting it far away from her. When she turns back, her eyes land on me and widen.

I look down to make sure I'm not flashing her.

"What?"

Of course, me saying that has Lana and Gram looking at me closer too. Lana cackles so loud, I swear I saw the walls vibrate.

"Did you have fun last night?" Gram asks, a mischievous grin on her wrinkly face.

"Oh yes. The bachelorette party was a blast."

"What did you do after?" Lana prods.

My heart thuds in my chest. Do they know? How could they know?

"I... went to sleep?"

"Liar!" Ginger and Lana yell at the same time.

A woman standing near a wall of windows with a fantastic view of the ocean looks up from the clipboard to stare at us. Bruno's mother, who doesn't speak a word of English, smiles and darts her eyes between us all. She doesn't speak English, but she sure understands it.

Eloise, who had been sitting in a chair in a corner, messing with her camera, hears the commotion and stands to join us. Her brow raises pointedly at me. "Damn girl, who left that hickey on your neck?"

I suck in a breath, my eyes bugging out, as my palm slaps the side of my neck.

Shit.

I'm going to kill Jensen.

I open my mouth, about to explain... to say anything but the truth.

"Don't you dare try to lie to us." Ginger waves her finger up and down my body. "You have a glow."

"I do not."

"An orgasm glow," Lana adds.

"I see it. You're definitely glowing," Eloise says, sitting next to me on the couch.

"Shut up." I jerk my eyes to Bruno's mother, Sophie, who saw the hickey, and is giggling with the rest of these insufferable women.

Gram is the worst of them all, laughing up a storm, slapping her leg, and wheezing. "All I have to say is finally."

"You too, Gram?" I ask, betrayed.

"Oh, honey, I may be old, but I ain't blind. I saw you two together last year. You clearly have the hots for each other."

I throw both of my hands up in the air. I'm being ambushed. It's annoying.

Yet, I can't stop the grin forming.

"Spill!" Ginger says, giddily.

I roll my eyes and my grin spreads across my face.

"I don't know what's happening between us. I mean, we hate each other. I think. But last night, he came back to the suite with a purpose. He looked at me without an ounce of the disdain I usually see. He was like, a whole different man."

I've only seen glimpses of that man. Jensen keeps him hidden behind a guarded wall. Every once in a while, I'd see shadows of his attraction to me.

Did he ever see mine?

"And?" Ginger and Lana bark at the same time.

"And... We didn't have sex, but... he still made me come twice."

"Ooooooo," Ginger and Lana howl in unison again. I swear they are the same damn person.

Before I can go on, a short and voluptuous Black woman walks over, interrupting our gossiping. A wave of relief washes over me. As fun as this was, I don't want to talk about my sex life with Gram here. Even though she seemed to egg me on the most.

"Ginger, I'm ready for you," the woman says.

Ginger stands and sucks down the rest of her champagne. "Time to get my hair and makeup done."

I'm not the one glowing. Ginger is. She's the bride. It's her day. Why were we making such a big deal about me?

Because that's what friends do.

The thought warms my belly. I do have friends now. Lana, Ginger, Eloise. Friends who gossip, who share happy moments with each other, who hype each other up.

A white woman with pink hair styled in a retro-fifties curls and wearing a vintage dress to match approaches. Rockabilly. That's the style. And it's adorable. I could pull off rockabilly. How cute would Jensen and I look together, him in his hipster lumberjack attire and me dressed like I'm about to shoot a pinup calendar?

Wow. Where did that thought come from?

"Maid of honor?" the woman asks in an Australian accent. Lana waves and stands, following her to a chair next to Ginger.

While those two are getting their hair done, I'm placed into a chair next to them for makeup.

We're all done after about three hours, so we have a late lunch delivered to the bridal suite, then we head down to the beach to pose for an endless number of pictures. Pictures of Ginger and Lana... Ginger, Lana, and me... Lana and me...

Lana, me, and Gram. Someone even took the camera to shoot a few pictures of Eloise with us all. Then the wedding planner shooed us back inside to the bridal suite so they could bring the groom and groomsmen out for their round of pictures. After the ceremony, we'll all return to the beach for group photos before the sun fully sets.

My heart thunders in my chest, anticipating seeing Jensen. It always beats wildly when I think about that man. It aches just a little after our eyes meet and an emotion I can't quite understand crosses his face.

I always thought it was hate.

Now I'm not so sure. Now I wonder if he even hated me at all.

I never hated him. I hated how he'd open up to me, show me he cared, then take it all away. I hated when he pushed me away. All I ever wanted was for him to be that man in the bathroom that day over four and a half years ago.

We've been in this battle of false hatred, and I'm done. Now I want to fight *for* him not with him. Because he needs to know that there are people who see him, who want him, who need him. I just wonder if he'll let me... if he won't shut me out like he typically does.

After thirty minutes, the men are done with their pictures. The wedding planner herds us back downstairs, through the lobby, and outside to the beach where the ceremony is taking place.

The guests are in place, the decorations immaculate yet simple. Bruno stands at a white arch decorated in colorful tiger lilies, blue cornflowers for the national flower of Germany, and rose gold ribbons. I have a feeling those lilies were Lana's idea. It's her favorite flower.

The sun is on its way to setting, making for a magical background as we line up at the back.

I stand ahead of Lana, fidgeting on my feet. My heart jumps when I hear Mylan's voice behind me, praising how sexy his girlfriend looks in her dress.

Because that means...

A wave of amber, honey, and citrus hits me before his voice.

"Fuck," Jensen whispers as he joins me at my side.

"Like what you see?" I tease.

He doesn't answer, so I turn to look at him. His eyes explore my body—down my chest and the chiffon fabric of the long rose quartz dress where it hugs my hips and ass. He reaches out a hand and brushes his fingertips over his mark on my neck—now covered with makeup—then he snags the dress's spaghetti strap, stroking his fingertip back and forth, until I'm blushing and my nipples pucker.

Lana clears her throat behind us, and we straighten, but not before I check out Jensen's plump ass. He's wearing black slacks, a white long-sleeved dress shirt, black suspenders, and a black bow tie. I bite my lip and hide my smile behind the bouquet of flowers I'm holding.

"Like what you see?" Jensen echoes.

Before we can continue our flirting, an instrumental song I don't recognize starts playing. Ginger said it was a traditional song played at German weddings. The wedding planner frantically waves at us to walk.

Jensen holds out his elbow and I weave my hand through. The moment we step onto the sand, Eloise's camera clicks away. We smile and nod at people as Eloise walks backwards, snapping photos of this moment.

Jensen leans in to me.

"I'm already thinking about taking that dress off you later tonight," he says in a voice low enough only I can hear.

"Oh yeah? What if I want to keep the dress on?"

"That's fine. I'll fuck you with it rolled up your hips."

I tighten my grip on his arm, and he chuckles.

"Does that turn you on, Rebecca?"

Rebecca. Damn him for listening to me and ditching the nickname.

We're almost at the end of the aisle now. Before we part, he ducks his head even lower, his lips so damn close to my ear.

"I know you're not wearing underwear underneath that dress."

I raise a brow. "I didn't want any lines to show." I wink before letting go of his arm and take my place on the bride's side.

I swear I hear him growl before he goes to Bruno's side, leaving a space for Mylan.

Lana and Mylan walk down the aisle next. They smile and wave and whisper to each other, likely saying inappropriate things like Jensen did with me. When they reach the front, Mylan kisses Lana on the cheek and they part. She gives me a suffocating hug before joining my side. Lana's eyes are already wet with tears and the ceremony has barely started.

The music changes over to an instrumental version of *At Last* by Etta James and the guests stand. Ginger appears at the end of the aisle with Gram and Pa on each arm. Gasps of admiration fill the air.

"Wunderschöner engel," Bruno says within a breath.

Ginger's dress has a corset top and ballgown skirt with rose gold fabric under white lace and sheer tulle. Her hair is styled in tightly coiled curls with one side pinned up with a light pink lily.

She looks like a queen.

I knew I'd cry the moment I saw the bride. I glance away to wipe the fast-falling tears. When I turn back, Jensen is staring at me with his eyebrow quirked. I roll my eyes and shrug.

The ceremony begins and I'm already distracted by the man standing across from me. Jensen can't stop scanning his bright green eyes up and down my body.

When he notices me staring, he tilts up that brow again. I raise mine to accept his flirty challenge. I lick my lips, then move my hand to sweep my long hair off my shoulder. I graze my fingertips over the makeup-covered mark he left on me. His eyes follow every strategic move I make.

"Cut it out," Lana says out of the corner of her mouth, amused. At the same time, Mylan elbows Jensen in the side.

Busted, I mouth to Jensen.

He bites his lower lip and covers the front of his pants with his clasped hands.

The rest of the ceremony was beyond beautiful, and I cried a lot. It was short enough that it was over before the sun finished setting. Bruno and Ginger wrote their own vows. Bruno said his in English, then repeated in German for his parents. Then Ginger said her vows, first in English, then in German.

Bruno nearly fell to his knees hearing his soon-to-be bride speak his language. Ginger learned for him; told him she'd been learning for the past three years. The big man bawled like a baby.

They exchange rings and then a nearly inappropriate kiss ends the breath-taking ceremony. Bruno takes his new wife's hand, and they raise up their embrace as everyone cheers loud enough to be heard across the ocean.

The newlyweds walk back down the aisle and veer off to the side where we'll all wait for the guests to clear so we can pose for the rest of the wedding photos with the bride and groom. Lana and Mylan leave next. Mylan desperately tries to console Lana, who is a sobbing mess.

When I reach Jensen to follow, he stops me. He lifts his hand and gently wipes the tears streaking down my cheek with the pad of his thumb. Then he winks and holds out his arm for me.

As we leave the beach, my throat aches; it burns, with this overwhelming need for more of this man. The one from the day in the bathroom. The one he keeps showing me glimpses of. He has so much compassion to offer, yet he always second guesses himself.

Maybe this time is different. He hasn't retreated into himself yet. One thing's for sure, I'm not about to let him take it away from me this time.

Chapter 12 - Jensen

I'm desperate to get Rebecca back up to our room. She knew exactly what she was doing wearing no undergarments with that skintight dress. It clings to her body and highlights all her curves. I never thought a woman could look more beautiful with clothes on as Rebecca does in that fucking dress.

Keeping my eyes from ogling her during the ceremony was unavoidable, and I don't regret getting caught by Lana and Mylan.

Now we're at the reception, held in one of the resort's banquet halls. The small room—since only about twenty people were in attendance for the wedding—is decorated in blues and silvers: balloons, ribbons, flowers, and even the tablecloths and chairs. The dimmed lights allow for a spotlight to flash rainbow colors around the dance floor.

Eloise has been on top of it all night, documenting every moment. Dinner was served a while ago, Lana and Mylan gave speeches and the newlyweds cut the five-tiered cake, then adorably smashed it into each other's faces, followed by a slow dance to *Kissing You* by Des'ree. I remember the song from *Romeo + Juliet*. Baz Luhrmann is a brilliant director. His films are chaotic, poetic, and I've watched them all dozens of times, especially any time I need inspiration.

When everyone joined Ginger and Bruno on the dance floor for that first dance, I worked up the courage and offered my hand to Rebecca. She hesitated but took it, giving me a beautiful grin with her ruby red lips. I held her tight against my body, her small hand tucked into mine, my cheek pressed against her hair since she's so much shorter than me, and my fingers splayed hungrily across her lower back.

It should scare me how much I enjoyed slow dancing with her. Instead, my chest tightened with sweet anticipation at the thought of dancing with her like that all night. Or at least, as long as we're obligated to stay at the reception before taking Rebecca back to the suite.

The part of me afraid of caring for someone is being overshadowed by the attraction I have for this woman. I brought it on myself by offering to let her stay in my suite. After having a taste of her last year, there was no way I was going to pass up the opportunity.

I spent the past year not fucking anyone else because I knew they wouldn't compare.

The DJ, who's a bit curvy and has deep tanned skin and tattoos up and down their arms, chats with Eloise who finished her wedding photographer duties for the night. The two laugh and sneak in some sexy dancing to the fast song currently playing, just like the past ten fast songs the DJ played. They even played a few songs that involved choreographed dance moves. I sat out all those songs because I have two left feet and refused to make an ass of myself. At least I have company. Mylan is probably a worse dancer than me. Though that never stops him from trying to make an absolute fool out of himself.

I'm sure he would have been out on the dance floor right now if it weren't for Ginger, Rebecca, and Lana huddled together. They're all shaking their asses, swaying their hips and twerking to the Nicki Minaj song playing, like they're her actual backup dancers.

They're amazing and look sexy as fuck.

Ginger changed out of her wedding dress into a silk, white pajama set that matches the one Bruno is wearing with the words Newlyweds and Mr. and Mrs. Stein inscribed on the back.

Lana is still in her bridesmaid's dress, the same one Rebecca has on. The fabric is soft and breathable, flexible enough so that it twists and turns with every move Rebecca makes.

Every dick-raising jiggle her ass makes. Every bounce her beautiful tits make.

"You're drooling," Mylan says next to me. I wipe the back of my hand along my chin, then scowl at my best friend for lying to me.

"Asshole."

He chuckles and fake punches my arm.

"You're so in love with her."

"I am not," I say too quickly. "I just want to fuck her."

He cracks up again, slapping my back as if I've just told the best fucking joke in the world. He stands, shaking his head.

"We're being summoned," he says, pointing to the dance floor.

His girlfriend pretends she's holding a fishing pole and starts reeling in the line. Mylan plays along and flops around like he's an actual fish.

They're so adorably gross and in love, and I hate how it makes my chest ache with jealousy.

I want that.

When my eyes find Rebecca, she arches an eyebrow and runs her tongue between her lips. My cock jerks at the move and before my brain can talk me out of it, I'm following Mylan out onto the dance floor. The song changes, playing another rap song.

Once Mylan reaches Lana, he grabs her hips from behind. She grinds her ass into his dick and lifts her long hair off her back seductively.

Jesus. That's hot.

Icy fingers clutch my jaw, turning my head away from the near sex scene in front of me.

"Your turn," Rebecca whispers next to my ear over the music.

She smashes her back to my front. Her arm wraps around my neck and her palm latches on at the nape. She presses her ass into my cock and starts swaying her hips back and forth. I close my eyes, attempting to control the erection already forming. It feels so fucking good having her body against mine.

The song's beats are fast and energetic, yet Rebecca's moves are slow and torturous. As if we're the only ones in the room and I'm getting a private dance.

My hands skate down her sides and over her stomach, then back up, stopping before reaching her breasts. I'm doing my best to keep it PG-13. The dance floor is dark, but people can still see us. Anyone in this room with a phone could start snapping pictures or taking videos of us being sexual to sell to the tabloids.

Mylan must have realized that too, because he and Lana have toned down their own not-so-private dance. Lana is attempting to teach Mylan some moves and laughing her head off because he looks like one of those red inflatables you see flailing outside a car dealership. Lana used to be a cheerleader. Of course, she's killing it out here.

I press my lips to the side of Rebecca's neck and she hums, grinding her ass harder. I dig my fingers into her hips.

"If you keep doing that, I'll bend you over right here and fuck you in front of everyone."

She laughs and turns around, draping her arms over my shoulders like we're at a middle school dance. Not that I went to middle school. I was home schooled or taught on film sets. But I've played characters who attended school dances.

The need to keep touching her grows, so I skim my palms up and down her back, and over the slick fabric of her dress.

"What? You don't believe me?"

She sucks in a sharp breath. "I don't, but I sure am picturing it right at this moment."

I place another kiss on her neck before moving my mouth back to her ear. My teeth latch on to her lobe and nibble. She lets out a quiet moan, which doesn't help my boner.

"When can we go?" I ask, refusing to stop caressing her backside, refusing to stop giving her more kisses and nibbles.

"Well," she begins, out of breath, "dinner is over. The cake's been served. The crowd is thinning. It's been just over four hours since the ceremony—"

"Four hours?" I lift my head and meet her eyes.

She nods.

I take her hand and we join Lana and Mylan, who gave up on fast dancing and they're now slowly swaying to an old-school hip-hop song that I recognize but can't remember the name of.

"We're leaving," I say and pull Rebecca up beside me so she can say goodnight to them.

I don't miss the wink from Lana and the blush across Rebecca's cheeks that follows. Mylan gives me a knowing smirk.

Seriously? What's wrong with them? Why are they making such a big deal about this? We're just going to go fuck.

I roll my eyes at these two assholes and drag Rebecca behind me as I search the room. Gram and Pa left a while ago. The only people we need to find are the newlyweds. I spot them standing in a corner with Bruno's parents.

"We're leaving," I say the same time Rebecca says, "the wedding was beautiful."

"Yes, it was. Congratulations," I add, trying not to sound too eager.

Rebecca and Ginger hug. Bruno and I bump fists, then we switch, and Rebecca hugs Bruno and I hug Ginger.

"Don't fuck this up, Boliver," Ginger whispers in my ear before releasing me.

I smile nervously at Ginger's threat. The two women didn't always like each other. I don't know exactly why, only that it had something to do with turning *Tyler's Team* into a movie. Now they're friends, and Ginger will totally kick my ass if I break Rebecca's heart.

I weave my fingers with Rebecca's and lead us out of the banquet hall. It's late, nearing midnight, so the only people around are the ones stumbling around the lobby after hitting up the bar, people taking advantage of a night swim in the pool, or those leaving another wedding reception being held on the property.

We reach the lobby and I press the up button. The elevator in the middle opens seconds later and I hurry us in, smashing the button for our floor, then desperately pressing 'close doors' to make sure no one else joins us. The moment the doors shut, and we're alone, I swing Rebecca around and press her up against the elevator wall.

I cup her face in my hands and my lips descend on hers, rough and appreciative. She whimpers and parts her mouth, letting my tongue in to stroke hers. The wine on her breath is sweet and makes me hunger for more of her taste.

We make out until we're almost to our floor. I end the kiss by sucking on her bottom lip until she whimpers for me once more.

"That's what I wanted to do two nights ago."

"I would have let you," she whispers.

The doors ding open.

I brush my thumb over her cheek, making her eyes flutter. Then I interlace my fingers with hers and we exit the elevator.

Inside the suite, my heart begins racing. I've never been so nervous about fucking. Don't get me wrong, I know what I'm doing. I know my way around a woman's body, but this is the first time I want to be touched, to be looked at, to be *wanted*.

Rebecca stops at the table next to the kitchen area and starts taking off jewelry I didn't even realize she was wearing: a necklace, bracelet, and a ring. Next, she slips her feet out of her sandals.

"Rebecca," I say, my voice deep and full of lust. "Stop stripping. I want to be the one to peel you out of that dress."

She takes a predatory step towards me, and my already frantic heart nearly explodes. I'm not used to women being so dominant with me. I always have control over what I let a woman do to my body. I sleep with women who don't want a commitment, who will fuck me and forget me. Women

I meet who will do anything I say, submit to me in the bedroom, just because of who I am.

I know that sounds bad, but I never... *ever* took advantage of that. I'm transparent in what I want, which is always one night.

"Begging, Jensen?"

"Yes. Do you want me on my knees?"

The way her pupils dilate tells me yes, she does.

"I'll make you a deal," Rebecca says, low and sultry. She places her cold palms on my chest. "I'll let you undress me if you let me suck your cock."

"And what do you get out of this deal?"

"I get to take care of you and taste you and feel the moment you come undone by my mouth, just like you did for me yesterday."

She glances down at the bulge in my slacks.

"You want that, don't you?" she places a sweet kiss on my lips.

"Yes," I whisper. I start removing my suspenders and go to work on the buttons of my dress shirt.

Rebecca bats my hands away.

"If you get to undress me, then I get to undress you."

I gulp, trying to wet my dry throat.

She leans in and says next to my ear, "Bring me to your room."

Hand in hand, we walk out of the kitchen area, past the living room, and into my room.

"Where do you want me?" I ask. My heart has finally calmed, my tense body relaxed now that Rebecca is giving me orders.

"Stand next to the bed," she says, and I obey. I wait for my next instructions, hands on my hips.

"Good boy," she purrs.

My dick jumps at the words, and she saw it. What the hell? Why did I like that?

"Jenny, Jenny, Jenny," she mocks. "Do you have a praise kink?"

I don't even care that she used the nickname. Coming out of her mouth, in this moment, I'd gladly get it tattooed on my ass if it meant she'd keep saying it.

"Not that I know of."

She's in front of me now. She raises an eyebrow and her hand cups my throbbing erection.

"Look at this cock getting hard just for me. I'm so proud of you."

I groan, and my dick grows beneath her touch.

"Okay, maybe I do have one."

This is new. I never knew how much I wanted Rebecca's praise.

She removes her hand so she can unbutton my shirt, untucking it from my pants and whisking it off me. Then she kisses all over my chest while her palms glide over my stomach and my sides.

"Relax," she whispers and sucks on my nipple.

My eyes flutter at the jolt of lust that ripples through me as her tongue and teeth play across my skin.

"That's better," she says before getting to work on my pants.

She's taking her time, torturing me, letting my anticipation build. She undoes the belt, slowly threading it out of the loops. Then she unzips my pants, tugging them down over my wide ass and thick legs.

She hooks her fingertips behind the band of my boxer briefs and brings them down to pool at my feet. She helps me step out of the discarded clothes.

I look down, and she's on her knees staring up at me. My cock is hard as fuck, pointing at her, waiting patiently.

Still, she doesn't take me in her mouth.

Instead, she admires the tattoos on my left leg. *Star Wars* may be my favorite movie, hence why I have an entire tattoo dedicated to it, but horror is my favorite movie genre. After my next project, I want to direct a horror movie.

"Jensen," she muses. "These are terrifying."

She traces the tips of her fingers over Freddy from *Nightmare on Elm Street*, Jason from *Friday the 13th*, and Michael Myers from *Halloween*. There are a few other horror elements mixed in like a bloody knife, skulls, gravestones, and even a zombie hand.

"Not a horror movie fan?"

"Not at all," she laughs and bites her lip. "I'm a wimp, easily scared, but I kinda like these."

She smooths her palms over the ink.

"They're sexy," she adds.

Before I can respond, she wraps her hands around my length, and I gasp at the feel of her soft, cold hands. She starts twisting and squeezing and I nearly topple over.

"Sit on the bed," she says.

"Let me undress you first."

"Not yet. Sit."

I do.

"So obedient, and obedient boys get rewards."

I lean on my palms as she closes her hot mouth over the tip of my dick, licking up the pre-cum.

My head tilts back. "Fuck, that's good."

She slides me all the way down her throat then back out, sucking hard with her tongue wrapped around the shaft. She does this over and over while one of her hands squeezes the base of my cock and the other fondles my balls.

The pressure building in my spine, and in my stomach, means I'm close. I want to grab her head and choke her on my dick. I want tears to stream down her face.

But she's in control right now.

She releases me with a pop.

"Do you want to take over and fuck my mouth?"

As if hearing my thoughts, she drops her hands.

I stand and thrust into her mouth as hard and deep as I can go before she gags. Then I do it again and again until tears—like I had just silently begged for—start falling. She hums and I grunt, pounding into her faster, rougher.

She holds on to my thighs, digging her sharp nails in hard enough that I'm sure I felt the skin break.

The humming, the pain of her nails... it's too much.

With one final thrust, I stay seated in her mouth and come—hard. My release pours down her throat, and she takes it all.

When I remove my dick, she runs her finger around her lips to clean up the excess cum. Then she licks her finger like she just ate the best dessert in the world.

"Fuck, that was good, Rebecca," I say, cupping her cheek.

She smiles up at me, proud of herself.

"Now it's your turn," I add.

Chapter 13 - Rebecca

Sucking dick has never been something I enjoyed. But tonight? It was like some sex goddess took over my body. My pussy aches with need after Jensen came down my throat, and I swallowed it all.

I'm wet. So wet it's beginning to leak down my leg because I didn't wear underwear. Giving Jensen a blow job turned me on so much that I nearly orgasmed.

How is that possible?

Maybe it's because he gave me control. Maybe it's because he praised me for the way I was pleasuring him. Maybe it's because he made me come twice yesterday, expecting nothing of me in return.

No man has ever done that for me. No man has ever taken care of my needs over their own.

Sex shouldn't be one sided, yet that's all I've ever experienced. With Jensen, it's like I've entered some euphoric dreamland. Could our hate for each other be fueling this lust?

He lifts me off the floor where I was kneeling as if I weigh nothing, yanking me against his body and claiming my mouth. I savor the minty taste from the gum he's been chewing all night as he dips his tongue in. He massages my own with such fierceness it's almost like he can't get enough.

Almost like he's thanking me.

He slows his kisses and with one final pull on my bottom lip with his teeth—something he loves doing—he gives me a quick peck.

"Turn around," he whispers against my mouth.

I do and hold my breath with anticipation as the sound of the zipper of my bridesmaid's dress unlatching from top to bottom pierces through the quiet of the room. My skin prickles when Jensen's palms smooth over my spine and up to both my shoulders to shift the fabric off my body. He places soft kisses on the side of my neck as the dress falls to the ground.

"Do you have any idea how cruel it was to wear nothing underneath that dress? Do you have any idea how hard it was not to take you to a dark corner tonight and fuck you? How badly I wanted to slip my fingers between your legs and find your soaking wet cunt?"

He snakes his hands around my front and down until his fingertips brush against my clit. When he presses down and starts massaging, pleasure jolts through my body. I push my ass against his dick. It's not quite hard since I just drained him.

"Where should I fuck you first, Amidala?"

I pause, my brows pinching together. "What the fuck did you just call me?"

"Amidala."

I turn my head so I can look at him and wait for him to explain. Instead, he grins mischievously.

I shove him away and spin around, placing my hands on my hips. "Explain."

He closes the space between us—his intoxicating cologne of sweet citrus enveloping me.

"Your reaction is exactly why I called you that. You are unrelenting and demanding, like a queen. But you don't want me to call you queen, so instead you are my Amidala. Queen Padme Amidala is a character from one of the Star Wars films. Which, as you know, are my favorite movies."

Amidala. I sound it out in my head. Ah-me-doll-uh. "I don't hate it."

He scrapes his teeth over my neck, and my entire body melts into his arms. I sigh as he sucks and kisses and nips my skin.

"I'm glad you don't hate it, my Ami."

Ami. Ah-me. It's so similar to mi amor yet nothing like it. Because it's mine. All mine. Well, and the Star Wars character, but still I groan.

"You like that one better?"

"Anything but Becky."

Not that there's anything wrong with the name, but he uses it as a weapon. He's the one who made me hate it.

He chuckles against my throat, his hot breath fanning my skin and causing goosebumps to prickle.

"So, tell me, my Ami. Where would you like to be fucked first?"

This time when he grinds his heavy cock into my soft stomach, it's harder, almost ready for me.

Damn. That was fast.

Since we're already next to the bed, I step away from him and crawl to the middle. I open my legs and start touching myself.

He narrows his eyes as if angry that I'm touching what's his.

"I don't think you're quite ready yet." I glance down at his dick. "Watch me pleasure myself until that cock is pointing at me and leaking."

He tsks and turns to the dresser and digs around in the top drawer before removing a row of condoms.

"Oh, I'm ready, Rebecca." He holds up the packets like a prize fish he just caught. "We have a long night ahead."

He removes a condom and tears it open with his teeth before rolling it over his dick. He strokes his fist over his length a few times and returns to the bed to descend on me.

The tips of his fingers trace my slit up and down before he plunges one inside.

"You're definitely ready for *me*," he smirks.

I gasp as he pumps into me faster. "Yes."

His thumb teases my clit, and I arch my back off the bed. He removes his fingers, bringing them to his mouth to lick them clean and then he lines the head of his dick between my legs, rubbing up and down through my arousal.

The anticipation of him entering me is almost too much. He's stalling, perhaps to get harder for me. He kisses my stomach, then he moves his kisses up to my breasts and covers a nipple with his mouth. His free hand cups my other breast, the fingertips playing with the hardened nub.

The moment he pinches one nipple while taking the other in his teeth, he thrusts into me... hard.

I scream and see stars.

He waits for me to adjust to his size before he slowly draws out. He lets my arched back descend to the bed, then he slams into me again, anchoring his hands on my hips to piston into me.

"Fuck," he grunts. "You feel so good."

My hand moves down to my clit, and I rub it while he lashes into me viciously. He's big, the biggest I've ever had, and I've never felt so full. He's hitting spots I never thought possible, causing my eyes to roll into the back of my head.

I'm not going to last long.

"I'm close, Jensen," I wheeze.

He slants over my body, somehow fucking me deeper. My walls constrict around him, and he moans. Damn, that was hot. I love it when men are vocal during sex. His reaction to my body, his thrusting, and me massaging my clit puts me over the edge.

Jensen pauses and waits for my pussy to stop spasming. Then he pounds into me again.

"Give me another one, Rebecca."

I'm already highly sensitive down there, but it only feeds into my overwhelming need for him.

"Kiss me," I demand.

He slows his thrusts to find my lips. I sweep my tongue into his mouth, burying my fingers into his hair while my lips move over his. I hum just a little and that prompts him to pick up speed again.

The way he's tilted over me puts his dick at the perfect angle to graze my G-spot. Not fully hitting it, but, fuck, does it get me to my orgasm quicker.

"That's it. Come for me again," Jensen says, clearly feeling me getting close.

He drives into me relentlessly until I'm coming undone. Jensen joins me this time, stilling as his release fills up the condom.

Unmoving inside me, he rests his head in between my breasts. Once he catches his breath, he carefully removes himself. He takes off the condom, tying it closed, and throws it away in the bathroom.

When he returns, I'm on my side, head propped on my palm.

"Tired yet?" he asks, planting his hands on the edge of the bed so he can kiss me like it's the last kiss he'll ever get.

"Not at all."

"Good. Because I promised to fuck you all over this room and we're just getting started."

Jensen's refractory period is impressive. Within ten minutes, he was ready for another round. I mounted his lap and rode him. He especially loved burying his face in my tits while I bounced up and down on his dick.

We'd worked up quite the sweat, so we showered. Me soaping him up got him hard all over again. He promised to fuck me in the shower, but I argued we should finish washing first and that the condoms were in the other room. He ignored me, jumped out with his wet soapy body, and returned with the condom rolled on. Then he fucked me against the shower's wall.

Once done, we got out of the stall and took turns drying each other off. Of course, that only caused both of us to get hot and bothered again.

We barely make it out of the bathroom before he's tearing off another condom and bending me over one of the hotel chairs to enter me from behind.

His hand crashes down hard on my ass cheek. I grunt and arch my back at the pleasant sting. He does that repeatedly, alternating between rough slaps and gentle massages, until my skin burns.

"I know you like that by the way your cunt grips me," he says as he twists my long hair around his wrist, hoisting me until my back is nearly flush with his chest. He continues to pound into me as if his life depends on it.

"Your ass is so beautiful bouncing on my dick," he says quietly next to my ear.

His free hand squeezes my breast and twists my nipple before moving down to pinch my clit.

"Fuck me," I groan. He hears that as a command and thrusts harder.

I come apart, and he fucks me through the orgasm until he's coming too.

We lie there, his soft front on my soft back as we both catch our breaths. Then he removes himself—always ever so carefully—and leaves me bent over the chair while he gets rid of condom number four.

I don't know how I'm going to last all night. I want him to follow through with his promise, but my vagina is already pleasantly sore.

Jensen's hand skims up my spine, and he grinds his dick into my ass.

"Already?"

He chuckles. "Not yet, Ami. Just admiring your body."

I stand up straight and turn around. "I want to admire *your* body."

My palms do just that, sliding across his damp, hairy chest, then back down over his stomach. He tenses, seemingly holding his breath as I move over his sides. I explore his back, from his broad shoulders down to his plump ass.

With my head so close to his chest, I can hear his heart beating frantically.

"You don't like being touched, do you?" I ask, my chin resting between his pecks so I can look at him.

"I like being touched by you." He leans down to give me a kiss.

"Me, but no one else?"

"Correct." His lips form a fine line.

"Not even during sex?"

"Especially during sex."

"I don't understand. You never let women touch you during sex?"

"I..."

He's freezing up on me, so I release him from the hug and grab his hand, bringing him over to the bed. I fold the blankets back and get in. Jensen follows, tucking me to his side.

"It took me a long time to accept my body and weight. I've always been chubby. I got roles *because* I was chubby. Of course, the roles were always so demeaning. My character was often the butt of the joke. Did you know my first ever kiss was on a TV show?"

I caress his chest, his stomach, his arms. His tension seems to fade away with every brush of my fingertips.

"The kiss was embarrassing. First of all, I was only seventeen. I didn't know what I was doing. But mostly, it was embarrassing because the storyline was about a bully paying a girl to kiss my character in front of the entire school and say she was grossed out by it. Can you imagine? Your first ever kiss being one big joke because of how you looked?"

"Jesus Christ, Jensen. That's horrible."

He shrugs underneath me. "I know."

I gently place kisses along the same spots my fingers just caressed, letting him know to keep talking.

"Being a man and fat is more acceptable than being a woman and fat. I understand that. But being famous and fat makes it harder to ignore the criticism. Especially since I grew up with it. My fatness always overshadowed my talent. So, I did everything I could not to open myself up to those criticisms. Like fucking in the dark so women wouldn't see me naked during sex. Not letting them touch me. I took control in the bedroom to protect myself from any judgement they may have had. It got so bad that about a year before we met, I started hiding myself in public with my clothes."

"The long-sleeved flannels," I say, piecing it all together.

"Yeah."

"What about your tattoos? You got them just to hide them?"

"I got the tattoos for me. To remind myself that no matter what the world thought, I still had things I loved like thunderstorms and nature. Things I was passionate about, like watching movies and directing them."

"But you're not dressing like that anymore? You're not covering them up?"

"No."

"Why? What changed?"

"Before this trip, I had a session with my therapist. I told her about Ginger's threat about my wardrobe—"

"Ginger threatened you?" I gape at him.

"Yeah, she told me no flannel or beanie caps allowed."

I bury my head into Jensen's stomach to hide my laughter. I didn't hide it very well because Jensen chucks the blankets off me and spanks my bare ass so hard, I yelp. It's still sore from his insistent spanking a few minutes ago.

"Done laughing?"

I pinch his nipple, and he feigns pain.

"Anyway, I've been working on my body image issues with my therapist for a while now. I don't know, I guess the lumberjack hipster look, as you all like to call it, became a comfort to me. I didn't have to think about what I was wearing. People would see the clothes before my body. It was a relief. That being said, I knew the long-sleeved flannels, jeans, and beanie weren't practical for a tropical island. So, I ditched them for this trip."

"And how does it feel? Not having your comfort outfits?"

"It's been... nice, actually. I've gotten a lot of compliments."

"So, it was Ginger's threat that ultimately forced the change?" I muse.

"Honestly? Lana kinda inspired me. She doesn't give a fuck what the media says about her body. At least, she doesn't let it affect her. So why should I? I've been following her lead for the past four years, and I'm still adjusting, but the idea of silencing the public's view of me has been liberating."

Liberating. I haven't felt liberated since I was a kid. I sit up. "I have an idea."

I crawl out of the bed and stand.

"Let's go skinny dipping."

He laughs. "What?"

"It's 4 a.m. The sun rises in a couple of hours. Let's put on our bathing suits and go swim, then ditch the suits and fuck in the water. Then when we're done, we can watch the sunrise."

"I'm not done fucking you in this room."

"We've got plenty of time for that." I hold out my hand. Jensen takes it and stands. "Come on. I've never been skinny dipping before."

"I have once in Santa Monica with Mylan and Rey when we were teenagers. But I'd rather not get arrested for public indecency. Or get our pictures taken."

"So, let's borrow some of Mylan's bodyguards he hired for this weekend."

"You noticed them? They were supposed to blend in."

"I saw them move in a couple times when someone got too close to Mylan and Lana, then they backed off when Mylan gave them a hand signal."

Jensen laughs and shakes his head. "I think having them out there will draw more attention to us."

"True. But, also, do you seriously think the paparazzi are going to be out there right now? They've got to sleep sometime."

"I mean, technically, they're not allowed on the property unless they're a guest. I'm pretty sure they've either been sneaking in or they're paying people to snap shots of us all." He purses his lips. "You know what? Fuck it. Let's go. If we get caught, then it'll be a fun story to tell."

I squeal. Actually squeal. "It's like we're going on an adventure. We're spies, trying to slip past the enemy that is the paparazzi. Mission: Don't get caught!"

A wave of nostalgia washes over me. For the first time since I stopped letting my imagination run wild, I'm excited.

I'm excited about letting loose and having fun. To feel like a kid again. To *live*.

Chapter 14 – Rebecca
Age 17

It's been three months since Tyler was diagnosed with stage four Acute Lymphoblastic Leukemia. It spread fast. Too fast. None of the treatments are working and the doctors don't know why. They're giving him only a few more months to live.

It's Christmas break and Tyler and Lana moved back to Silo Springs to live out the rest of his days. Lana is taking next semester off college to be with him and to mourn. Since I don't turn eighteen until the summer, I asked my parents if I could also take time off school, but they said no. I don't understand. I'm his sister. I love him just as much as Lana, if not more.

Any time I try to bring up Tyler's diagnosis, they dismiss me like I'm some dumb kid. I want to know what's going on, but they're not including me. They won't let me go to the appointments. Lana has been the only one to tell me anything. She's been there to console me, but she ends up getting sadder and I have to console her instead.

Why is this happening?

Why did it have to be him?

He deserves to live in this world more than anyone. He had dreams of helping others. It should have been me.

I've been praying every night for God to let me switch places with him. I've never been religious. My parents never took us to church, but we sure have been going more these past three months.

Are they praying for the same thing? Do they want it to be me?

Christmas is tomorrow morning, and Mom has been in the kitchen all day preparing the big meal. Everyone will be here. Lana's grandparents, Ginger's parents, my grandparents who I never see because they live all the way on the West Coast in Oregon. They're staying a while. Weeks. Months. Until...

"Why the long face?" Tyler asks, entering the room. "Are you a horse? Neighhhhh."

He's wearing a baseball cap because his hair is starting to fall out from the treatments that aren't working. He's pale. So unlike him. He's always been tan from being out in the sun—either from sports, working in the yard, or out at the cliffs with Lana.

I stick out my tongue, and he laughs... then he coughs. A lot. He has to hold himself up by the table in the dining room where I'm cleaning up for tomorrow.

I drop the stack of papers I've been filing and rush over to him.

He holds up his hand. "I'm fine."

Tears prick my eyes, and I turn before he sees them fall.

When I finally compose myself and face Tyler again, he wags his finger at the mess. "Hurry up with that."

"What? Why?"

"Because I want to show you something."

"What is it? I'll go get it."

"It's not something I can bring you. Just... meet me out back in thirty minutes."

I frown at my brother's back as he slowly retreats from the room.

After thirty minutes, I stop cleaning to go meet Tyler. I still have a few things to pick up in the dining room before I move on to my room. I don't know why Mom insists my room be spotless. It's not like anyone will go in there. My grandparents aren't even staying with us this time because

Lana offered the spare bedroom at her house. The one her parents left her when they died in a car crash when Lana was nine. The one Tyler and Lana had planned to make their home before his diagnosis.

I follow Tyler through the black iron gate of the white picket fence behind our house and walk out to the woods. He has to stop several times to catch his breath and I try to convince him to turn around at least three times, but he refuses. He let me be his crutch at least, leaning on my held-out arm as he leads us down the worn path.

A path I used to walk every day until middle school.

I never come out to these woods anymore. They make me sad. They remind me of how happy I used to be when I didn't care about the wicked rules of the real world. When I didn't let others bully me into changing my entire look and personality.

Tyler squeezes my arm when we get to the massive oak tree we used to climb as kids. I used to hang out on the branches until dark. Tyler hung a tire swing on the lowest elongated branch. I remember catching him out here one day, pushing Lana and stealing kisses from her when she'd swing back to him. I remember pretending to be a spy and hiding behind trees, armed with a Nerf gun and ambushing the love birds because they unsuspectedly moved into my territory.

I start crying because now this oak tree that played a big part in my childhood has a treehouse.

"You built a treehouse?" I sob.

We stop and stare up at the small wooden structure. It reminds me of a cabin in the woods—square with a triangle roof. It's small, big enough to fit three, maybe four people. I count two windows and wonder if the other two sides—which I can't see—have windows too.

Tyler tugs me to his side. "I didn't build it, but I hired someone."

"You can't afford that."

"You're right. They actually did it for free."

"Why would they do that?"

"Because I'm dying." He shrugs and laughs.

"Not funny," I sob again, hiding my face in my hands so he can't see.

"Oh, Becca Bear. I'm so sorry. I didn't mean..." He sighs and wheezes. "Let's go up."

"You can't..."

"I can and I will."

He's already leaving my side and closing the distance to the tree, pausing before ascending the nailed pieces of wood because he's struggling to breathe.

He climbs every sturdy rung, flings open the access door on the treehouse's floor, and shakily crawls inside before falling onto his back. I'm right behind, collapsing beside him. He's breathing as if he just ran a marathon.

"Water," he rasps. I dig in the backpack he handed me before we set out walking and find two bottled waters. He sits up to drink. Once Tyler is done, downing the entire bottle, I stare him down, narrowing my eyes.

"Why did you do this for me?"

He lays back down and takes one deep breath. "Because I know how hard it's going to be these next few months and the months after I'm gone. You'll need somewhere to go. Somewhere to escape to."

The ache in my throat builds.

"Becca, my life is getting cut short and there were so many things I wanted to do, like help people in tough situations. I had hopes and dreams. I wanted to marry Lana and travel the world with her. We wanted to adopt since she can't have kids. Now I won't be able to do any of those things."

He pauses and I say nothing because I know he has more to say.

"Tomorrow is not guaranteed. You should be living every day like it's your last."

I groan.

"I know how cliché that sounds, but Becca, you have to promise me. Promise me you won't waste one second of your life once I'm gone. Promise me you'll follow your dreams, no matter how silly you think they are."

"I promise," I whisper.

He holds out his pinky, and I latch it with mine.

"Pinky swear, because I know you've stopped letting yourself imagine. You've stopped writing. You used to love writing stories. They were wonderful. I loved reading them, but you stopped writing because you let the popular girls at school judge you. I get it. Really, I do. I was the popular guy too. You just want to fit in, but at what cost?"

"What do you mean?"

"You're changing yourself to become someone I no longer recognize. You're becoming someone who's not real. A version meant to please others. I'm worried the real you, the one who dreams, will get lost and you'll never get her back. Promise me you won't let her get lost."

I'm crying and shaking my head because something about making this promise feels final. A goodbye. I'm not ready to say goodbye. I never will be.

"Tyler," I cry. He lets go of my pinky and opens his arms. I fall into them, crushing myself to his chest. He kisses the top of my head and rubs my arm.

"I love you, Becca Bear, and I just want you to be happy. I want you to live your life, not someone else's. You just have to find like-minded people. Friends who want to cosplay in parks or watch sci-fi movies or read fantasy books about hidden kingdoms and magical powers. And don't settle. One day you'll meet someone who will support you and challenge you and bring out your inner child. You'll feel so comfortable around them that you'll drop this mask you're so determined to wear and no one else will matter. Only they will."

"My own Lana Banana?"

"Exactly. And when you find this person. Never let them go."

Chapter 15 – Jensen
Present Day

I've never seen Rebecca Taylor so... animated. She holds my hand and skips down to the beach under the dark of night. There are tiki lamps lit throughout, but they thin out the closer we get to the water.

I scan the beach for any signs of paparazzi or people who might recognize us. Thankfully, only a few people are out: a couple walking along the beach hand in hand, three men stumbling back inside the resort after a night of drinking, and a resort worker cleaning up.

Rebecca slips off her sandals, approaches the water's edge, and sticks her feet in the crashing waves. She has a drawstring bag on her back that she said is to hold our suits when we take them off in the water.

"It's warm." She looks at me, a huge smile plastered on her face.

I can't help myself and tug her against me, kissing her deeply. As deep as the lowest parts of the ocean.

"Ready?" she asks, her grin never faltering.

I squeeze her hand and nod. "Ready."

We enter the water slowly, watching our step since it's pitch dark out. We go in far enough that the water reaches our chests, and we can still touch the ocean floor. Any further out would be too dangerous. Hell, we're probably dumb for going this far at night.

Rebecca removes her bathing suit first and puts it in the bag. I strip my tank and swim shorts and stick them on top. She draws the strings shut and puts the bag on her back.

"We're skinny dipping," she beams.

"We're so fucking naked," I say, beaming back at her.

She wraps her arms around my neck and brings me in for a kiss. Her legs fold around my waist and my hands find her ass, squeezing the cheeks. She gasps, obviously still sore from my earlier lashings. My dick is already getting hard, poking at her entrance. One thrust and I would be inside her.

"Fuck me, Jensen," she murmurs against my mouth as if reading my mind.

Oh shit. I freeze. She continues kissing me but stops when she realizes I'm not kissing her back.

"I forgot to bring a condom."

"I don't care. I'm on birth control, and I'm clean. I get tested twice a year, and I haven't slept with anyone in over a year."

"A year?"

"Hey, no judging. How long has it been for you?"

I bite my lip, and she swipes her thumb over it, pulling it from my teeth. "I'm clean and... it's also been over a year."

"Why that long?"

Because I was waiting for you. "Why a year for you?"

"I'm asking the questions here, buddy."

I chuckle and nuzzle her neck. She slaps at me before I can leave another hickey.

"Hey!" a man's voice interrupts. "Get out of the water. It's not safe at night."

Rebecca immediately hops off me and frantically starts digging into the bag. She shoves my swim trunks and tank at my chest, then puts on the one piece she wore out here.

"Sorry, sir. We're coming out now!"

She giggles and holds my hand as we wade back to the shore. We collapse onto the sand and let the waves wash over our legs. The man who was yelling at us walks over.

"The jellyfish get pretty bad this time of year, especially at night. I'm surprised you didn't get stung."

"Sorry, we didn't know."

He shakes his head at us, amused, and saunters off, picking up trash along the beach. There's not much, so I know this man does his job well. The beach is always spotless.

"Look!" Rebecca sits up and points at the horizon. "I think I see a peek of the sun. It must be close to sunrise."

She leans over me and grabs a handful of sand, letting it cascade over my chest. I squirm a bit because it tickles.

"Let me bury you in the sand," she says.

"Hell no. I don't want to be digging sand out of my ass crack for the next week."

She tosses her head back and laughs. "Fine. Then build a sandcastle with me."

This woman who I've only known to be reserved, who never seems to relax and let loose, has transformed into someone I don't recognize. I've seen her laugh and smile, but neither ever seemed genuine. Tonight, she's a breath of fresh air. As if the weight of the world has melted off her shoulders and replaced with an electrified energy that makes her feel alive.

"Now that I can do. I'll make the biggest and best castle for my Amidala."

She gives me a quick peck on the lips before sitting up. We crawl away from the water to a dry spot on the beach to get to work.

We're silent for the first few minutes as Rebecca concentrates on building the first tower. We need tools. I search the beach, squinting to see through the dark. The flicker of light from nearby tiki torches helps enough that I spot something blue.

"Aha!" I stand and walk over to the closest lounge chair. "Some kid must have left this bucket."

"Perfect," Rebecca grins and takes it from me to start filling it up.

We're almost done when the sun finally starts rising. We make our final touches to the palace just in time to relax and watch the show mother nature is putting on.

The moment we collapse onto the two lounge chairs next to our small five-towered castle, we both let out a breath, then a laugh in unison.

"Do you still hate me?" Rebecca asks when silence falls between us.

"I never hated you, Rebecca."

She scoffs. "You did a good job of pretending you hated me. Makes sense. You're an actor, so pretending can't be hard, right?"

"I still didn't hate you."

"You said I made your job a lot harder."

"You did, but I understood why you were fighting against the changes."

"If you understood, then why were you always such an asshole to me? Why did you push me away at the end of negotiations? You saved me from having a mental breakdown, then you acted like consoling me was the most horrible thing you've ever done."

"I'm sorry. I thought I was doing what was best."

"For whom?"

"For me."

"I don't understand."

I take Rebecca's hand and rub circles in her palm with my thumb.

"Because it's how I grew up. I told you how the word love was never said in my home. It was never shown. My parents never hugged me, never told me how proud they were of my acting career, which began when I was five. I was good, especially for a kid. Even being overweight, I was landing role after role. They never took me out to celebrate. I'm talking no celebration: birthdays, holidays. When I won the Oscar for *Tyler's Team,* I got a text from them. A text. Can you believe it? I had a nanny who was more of a parent than Jack and Julie Boliver ever were.

"For my fifteenth birthday, my cousin came over to hang out with me. He was two years older than me, and I'm pretty sure his parents forced him to show up. Anyway, his father and my father hate each other. My cousin told me he overheard his dad saying that my dad and mom didn't even want to have kids. That I was a mistake."

"Oh, Jensen." She lifts our embraced hands and kisses my knuckles. I close my eyes at the gentle, caring gesture.

"They were forced to become parents, and I paid for it. I honestly believe the reason they never told me they loved me is because they don't. Or maybe they just don't know how. Or maybe they also grew up in a home where the word love didn't exist. So, they show their love through material things like buying me whatever I want. I used to let them, too, thinking it would make me feel better. It never did. Now I accept nothing from them unless absolutely necessary.

"So, when I found you in that bathroom and held you... you hugged me back so strongly, as if you'd never let go. You *needed* me, and I wasn't used to that. But it felt so right. Then my thoughts turned against me, convinced me I could never offer you, or anyone, love because of how I grew up. Stupid thoughts, really, but I didn't want to take the chance. I shut down, shut you out. I always do with women. This is something I'm working on with my therapist. She says I'm making progress.

"Then working with you on the movie... I saw a lost soul. The more I was around you, the more I wanted to fight with you because in those moments, you blazed with life. I'm just as lost as you, but when we're together, I don't know... I don't feel so abandoned."

"Yet you still pushed me away."

"Yes, I did."

"Why?"

"Because I worry I can't give you all of me. I worry I can't care for anyone anymore after Mylan..." I swallow the lump in my throat. "I worry I'll become my parents, and you don't deserve that."

She sits up in the chair and closes the space between us to palm my cheek. I close my eyes, melting into her touch.

"Jensen, you are nothing like your parents. You said they didn't have an ounce of love in their bones. Yet, here you are, on the beach with me, building sandcastles and watching the sunrise. You sought me out that day of negotiations to make sure I was okay. You offered me a ride last year when my driver got a flat tire. And you offered me a room when the hotel lost my reservation. People who lack the capacity to care don't do stuff like that."

She kisses me before I have the chance to argue. Was I going to argue? Honestly, I have no words. She's right. I'm nothing like my parents. Still, the pit of my stomach rumbles with unease. Putting myself out there for someone is terrifying.

Especially someone who, for the first time in my life, I can see myself building a life with.

The thought is unhinged. Who am I?

Rebecca and I are just fucking. She wouldn't want something more, would she? The easiest way to find out would be to ask, but my fear of abandonment settles into my stomach and stops me. I don't want to scare her away. This is new. We may have known each other for over four years, but this part of our relationship has just begun.

After an intense make-out session on the beach that caused us to miss the sunrise, we walk hand-in-hand back to the resort, our bodies covered in sand and suits still wet since we forgot to bring towels. We're in the lobby waiting for an elevator when the middle one dings open. Lana, Mylan, Gram, and Pa walk out.

They freeze the moment they spot us.

"Well, what do we have here?" Mylan says like he's a detective from an old black and white cop movie.

"Who's this fool, Rebecca?" Pa grumbles. "Is he bothering you?"

I don't make a move as Pa, who's met me before, gives me a murderous once-over.

"Norman, calm down. This is Rebecca's boyfriend, Jensen," Lana's grandmother answers. I tense at the word boyfriend, but Rebecca laughs and squeezes my hand.

"He's not bothering me today, Pa, but if he acts up, I'll make sure to send him your way."

"I didn't bring ole Betsy but say the word and I'll find a shotgun somewhere."

My mouth hangs open. Did this old man just say he'd shoot me?

Mylan squeezes my shoulder. "That means he likes you."

"Funny way of showing it."

"It's a southern thing," Lana says, amused. She then scans our bodies from head to toe and wags her brows at us. "You two sure are up early."

I glance at Rebecca, and she winks back and says, "Actually, we haven't gone to sleep yet."

"Hurry on up, Banana. We're hungrier than a hog over here," Pa complains as he and Gram start walking off towards one of the resort's restaurants.

"I'd ask if you two want to come to breakfast with us, but..." Lana taps her lips. "It appears you two need a shower. I'm curious as to how you two got covered in so much sand."

"Sex on the beach?" Mylan asks with an annoyingly smug smile.

"For your information," Rebecca begins. "No, we did not have sex on the beach. But we did in our suite. We fucked a lot. Then we went skinny dipping and got busted by a grounds worker, so we hung out on the beach and built a sandcastle and missed the sun coming up because we couldn't stop kissing. *That* is why we're covered in sand."

I nearly choke on my spit at Rebecca's confession to our entire night.

"And we're not done yet, so if you'll excuse us, we're going back to our suite to fuck some more."

She weaves her fingers with mine and we enter an elevator that just opened to unload hotel guests.

"I have so many questions," Lana says. Her cackling laugh and Mylan's shocked face are the last things we see when the doors close.

"Um..." I mumble.

She shrugs. "What? They were going to find out anyway. If we pretended nothing had happened, they would have forced us to confess. Now they can obsess over it at breakfast without us."

The elevator arrives on the ninth floor. We exit and walk down the long open-air hallway, still holding hands. She

didn't even attempt to let go while talking to Lana and Mylan.

We reach our suite, and the door at the end of the hallway
opens, startling us. A giggling woman stumbles out.

"Eloise?" I ask, amused.

The DJ from the wedding appears by her side, looking
disheveled and well-fucked.

"Oh. Jensen and Rebecca. Hi." Eloise smirks when she
glances down at our embraced hands. "You two have a good
night?"

"We did," Rebecca purrs. "Looks like you had fun as well."

The two steal a look and laugh, blushing wonderfully.

"Yes, last night was amazing." Eloise clears her throat. "But
Kelly—this is Kelly, by the way—has an early flight back to
L.A. and they're leaving me to go pack."

Kelly, who has short dark brown hair with a constellation
of stars designed into the side, wearing a black crop top and
white parachute pants, brings Eloise in for a kiss.

"You have my number. Text me when you're back in L.A."

With that, Kelly leaves and Eloise touches her lips as if not
believing the amazing kiss she just received.

She pops up her head after realizing we're still standing
here. "I'm going to sleep. Goodnight, you two."

She disappears into the room, and I scan the key to our
suite, hauling Rebecca inside.

"Shower?" she asks, leading me to my bathroom.

"Absolutely."

After we shower—surprisingly sex-free—we dry off and put on robes, then we order room service. Thirty minutes later, a cart full of pancakes and sides of scrambled eggs, sausage links, and bacon rolls in. We decided not to order coffee since we're both exhausted and want to go to sleep after eating. I opted for apple juice; Rebecca got water.

Bellies full and eyes barely able to stay open, we crawl into my bed naked and snuggle up to each other.

"When do you leave?" I ask against her neck.

She hums. "Monday evening."

"Same." I place a soft kiss on her skin. "Spend these next few days with me."

"Okay."

"Yeah?"

"Well, you promised to fuck me all over this room and we still have the balcony. Not to mention there's the shared living space and my room."

I growl and grind my cock into her plump ass.

"If I wasn't so tired, I'd fuck you right now. Just like this."

She turns her head and brushes her mouth against mine. "Let's make a deal."

I laugh. "You love making deals."

She kisses me, a long, languid kiss that has my dick aching to be inside her.

"Whoever wakes up first, wakes the other with sex or oral."

I nip my teeth along her jaw, and she exhales.

"Deal."

Chapter 16 - Rebecca

I wake up before Jensen and, as promised, I mount him and start grinding on his dick, which is already sporting a nice erection. I wait until he's fluttering his eyelids open before I take his cock and line it up with my pussy.

"Condom?" he asks, now fully awake and grabbing my hips.

I shake my head. "Not unless you want one."

"Fuck no," he answers, and I sink down to the hilt.

He tilts his head back and digs his fingers into my sides.

"God, your bare cunt feels so good around my cock," he grits out. "I won't last long like this."

Same.

I lean over and rest my palms on his chest for leverage and start moving up and down. One of his hands finds my breast and he rolls my nipple between his fingers, making me moan.

He sits up and wraps his arms around my body to take over, thrusting up into me so hard, his balls slap my ass.

"Yes, Jensen, keep doing that. Harder. Please."

He does, for at least another minute, before twisting us around and fucking me into the mattress.

He takes a nipple in his teeth. I groan, coming undone. The orgasm is long, and stars paint my vision. Jensen gives one last thrust and I feel his warm release pour into me as he grunts with each spurt.

He cradles his head into the crook of my neck and breathes hard after that fast fuck.

I kiss along his shoulder, my hands rubbing up and down his back, then down to his ass, where I give it a big squeeze. I relish in the weight of this man on top of me. For once, he's not trying to hold himself up. He's relaxed and still inside me and I feel so safe at this moment.

But it doesn't last long.

"Shit," he mumbles. "I'm crushing you."

He crawls off and removes his dick. His warm cum leaks out of me. He watches with fascination for a few seconds before using his fingers to lap up his release and put it back into my pussy. I raise a brow at him.

"What? You're the first person I've fucked raw. I want it all in there. Can't let it go to waste."

I cackle.

"What? Why is that funny? I thought you said you're on birth control."

"I am, but you know birth control doesn't always work one hundred percent, right?"

He shrugs and pushes more of his cum back inside.

"Jensen, do you have a breeding kink?"

His eyes shoot up to meet mine. "That's a thing?"

I bite my lip and nod, my cheeks heating at the idea of carrying his baby.

What the hell? That thought was so uncalled for.

He scans my body, pausing on my stomach. His eyes go dark, not with panic as I expected... it's something else. Lust for sure, but maybe hope? A yearning?

He opens his mouth, about to speak, but I hold up my finger.

"Don't. Whatever you were about to say... just... we'll unpack it later."

Because I'm confident he was about to start talking about wanting kids and that's ridiculous, right?

We're just fucking.

He smiles mischievously and picks up his phone off the bedside table, then collapses next to me.

I pick up my phone too and notice it's barely noon. We only got a few hours of sleep, but to be honest, it was some of the best sleep of my life.

I scroll through my notifications, making a mental note to read the email my publicist sent. Probably more pictures of us all here on the island. She asked if I wanted to comment on the photos of Jensen and me at dinner that first night, looking as if I was about to murder him, but I said no. It doesn't matter what excuse I came up with for that photo. People will always make their own assumptions.

There were a few rumors the tabloids printed during the filming of *Tyler's Team* about the tension between us. We barely spoke to each other on set. People must have seen my sneers and his eye rolls and leaked it. I doubt it was any of the crew members. Maybe a background actor.

I open my texts and read through the ones Lana sent.

Lana

Awake yet?

Want to go chasing waterfalls?

Eloise is coming.

> Gram and Pa are too tired to go because we just got done snorkeling with them. Plus, we're taking them to a luau later, so they're going to rest before then. I want you two to go do something fun and adventurey with us before we leave tomorrow night. Come onnnnnn. Gooooooo.

> Okay, waterfall hike and tour booked. If I don't hear from you soon, I'll come knock on the door.

I groan. "Lana is forcing us to go on—"

"A waterfall hike?" he chuckles. "Yeah, I got the same texts from Mylan. He said Ginger and Bruno couldn't go because they're spending the first half of their honeymoon hanging out with his parents. They'll spend a week doing tourist stuff around Kauai, Oahu, and Maui. Then next week, his parents fly back to Germany while Ginger and Bruno head to Italy, Greece, and France."

"I'm so jealous. That's, like, a month-long honeymoon."

I set my phone down and turn on my side. Jensen does the same, reaching out and moving a piece of hair off my face. It's such a caring move from someone who claims they're not capable of it.

"Everyone leaves tomorrow too. So, one more day of friend obligations?"

"And then you're mine," Jensen says and tickles my sides.

I squeal and contort my body away from him.

"No tickling! I will pee my pants, I swear!"

"You're not wearing pants," he laughs, now on his knees so he has better access to tickling me.

"I will piss your bed then."

"We'll just move things to your room."

"Jensen Matthew Boliver, I swear I will kick your ass if you keep tickling me," I say through a fit of giggles.

He stops suddenly. A shit-eating grin filling his face. "I never told you my middle name."

"Yes, you did."

"Nope."

"Then someone told me. Lana, probably."

He wags his eyebrows at me. "No way... you totally Googled me."

I bite my lip, trying not to smile. "So what if I did? I'm sure you looked me up too."

"You think you're something special?"

"I am, and you know it."

"So cocky, my Ami."

I hide my face with my hands at the new nickname. It's super corny, but for him to even connect his favorite movie with me is... sweet.

He pulls my hands down so he can press a kiss to my palm. "Of course I Googled you."

"And what did you find?"

Before he can start listing all the boring articles and Wikipedia details about my life, a loud knock raps on the door.

"It's Lana!"

"And Mylan!"

"Get your horny asses out of bed!"

Lana and Mylan booked a tour of Manawaiopuna Falls, which sits on private land. Only one tour company is permitted to land a helicopter at the fall's base, so Mylan booked through them. But when the family who owns the property found out we were coming, they offered to escort us to a part of the falls near the base no one else gets access to. Apparently, the granddaughter is a huge fan of Mylan's.

Jensen's face lit up the moment Lana and Mylan told us where we were going. He said the waterfall was shown in Jurassic Park.

I vaguely remember that minor detail from when I saw the movie as a kid. What I do remember is watching it with Tyler and how he'd always try to scare me during the suspenseful parts. (Maybe that's where my fear of scary movies comes from.) When the movie was over, he pretended to be a velociraptor by curling his wrists and tucking his arms to his sides and hunting me around the living room.

After he died, I hated the movies and refused to watch them because of that memory.

"You okay?" Jensen asks.

I give him a soft smile. "I'm okay. Just had a Tyler memory is all."

He throws his arm over my shoulders and tugs me to his side, kissing the top of my head. He really needs to stop with the small acts of affection, otherwise I'm going to fall for him.

Maybe I fell a while ago.

I playfully shove at him. "It's too hot for cuddling."

He laughs and lets me go.

We're walking through wet and muddy vegetation to the base of the waterfall, and I'm sweating. We had to put blue coverings over our shoes to preserve the land and prevent bringing contaminants in and out of the area. So walking downhill on a slippery path to this secluded spot near the waterfall's base with no traction because of the booties has been challenging. Jensen hands me a bottled water (that we had to sign a waiver for just to bring it on our small hike promising we won't litter otherwise we'll be fined $50,000).

About fifteen minutes later, we reach our destination. The waterfall is four hundred feet tall, untouched by humans. The water cascades over stone, which has green moss growing at the sides.

We stand at the water basin as the family tells us about the history of the waterfall.

Eloise's camera clicks away as we all relish the beauty surrounding us. I notice Mylan fidgeting on his feet beside me. Once the family's story is over, Mylan leads us all as close to the water as possible. The spray dampens my hair and rainbows pop up as the mist and sunshine collide. I take my phone out of my pocket and start snapping photos of the wonderful sight, then turn it off because my battery is at one percent.

"What the hell are you doing?" I hear Lana say, not angry but... surprised.

I turn to them, and Mylan is on bended knee. He holds an open black box. Lana covers her mouth. Eloise circles around them, taking picture after picture.

"Donut, I know I've asked you a million times before and you kept saying no because I was still healing. I had a long way to go in my recovery, but I think the next step in my healing is being with you for the rest of our lives. You are the best thing to ever happen to me. My saving grace, my will to live, my everything. So, now I'm asking you for the millionth and one time. Please, do me the honor and marry me."

Lana is crying. She wipes away the tears and nods her head like an overly excited child. Mylan stands and wraps his arms around her, picking her up off her feet and swinging her around.

I glance at Jensen and see his phone out recording. I slap him on the chest. "You knew?"

He winks. "Of course, he's my best friend."

I roll my eyes but can't stop smiling. The lovebirds part and Lana reaches up to cup his cheek.

"I can't wait to spend the rest of our forever together."

They kiss, then Mylan slides the ring on her finger. Lana runs over to me and shows it off. It's massive. I couldn't even guess the carats, but I'm betting double digits. Eloise joins us, taking pictures of the blue pear-shaped diamond with a gold band. It's gorgeous, just like Lana.

Excitement surrounds us as we head back to the helicopter. The pit of my stomach hollows as thoughts swirl in my head. I want this. I want love and marriage and kids.

Could Jensen offer this to me? It's clear he's no longer the fearful man in that bathroom over four years ago. Or at least, he's trying not to be. He's changing. I've changed. Still, are we going too fast? This is insane. We went from fighting to fucking to this intense obsession for each other. It oddly already feels like a relationship.

Is that what he wants? A relationship?

By the look in his eyes as he eyed my stomach, surely imagining my pregnant belly...

I rarely give someone my heart and risk them crushing it like so many others have done to me in the past.

But would I risk it for Jensen?

Chapter 17 - Jensen
Age 17

It's the first day of filming for *Metal & Mayhem*. A day I should be looking forward to since I'm one of the leads. This role is going to be great for my career. Except, my character's introduction in the pilot, the thing audiences will know me by, is me getting fucking bullied. Not only that, but I have to kiss someone. I looked up my co-star on the internet, and shit, she's beautiful. She's my age and was in some sitcom before this series. Tiffany Spars always gets cast as the blonde popular girl or the cheerleader. I'm going to get a boner in the middle of filming, I just know it.

I keep my head down as I walk to wardrobe. Even though I sent them my measurements, they never seem to stock clothes that fit me. It's embarrassing and production sometimes gets held up because they're rushing to make alterations or going to the nearest clothing store to find an outfit that works. I've learned to bring my own clothes as backup.

Thankfully, since I'm in a main character role for this show, and it's based in the 80s, the clothes have to be accurate. The costume designers were prepared. They dressed me in a pair of whitewash jeans, a Van Halen black t-shirt, and a pair of Chucks.

After wardrobe, a production assistant directs me towards hair and makeup. I'm growing my hair out for the role, but until I can have my own mullet, I'm stuck wearing a hideous wig.

An hour after arriving on set, I'm officially transported through time to represent an 80s teenager. My character is one third of a metal rock band made up of high school outcasts, started by the new kid at school who had to leave his old band behind when he moved. I've only read the scripts for the first two episodes because the show runners are trying to avoid leaks and spoilers, but the first season focuses on our band gaining popularity and how the three of us deal with the sudden success and the temptations that come with it.

"Yo, Jensen," a scratchy voice behind me says.

I turn to find Mylan Andrews walking up. We met during table reads but didn't really get a chance to talk. He's slightly taller than me with his black hair styled in a pile of curls all around his head. He's dressed in torn jeans, a black graphic t-shirt, and a leather jacket.

Mylan swings his arm over my shoulder. "You ready for this?"

I shrug. While I'm excited about the role, I'm nervous about shooting the scenes when my character gets bullied.

I'll be playing a nerd named Crash—he's called that because he's so big he crashes into everything. I hate it. Fucking Hollywood, I swear.

Mylan is playing Boomer, the new kid with a bad streak who heard Crash playing the drums in the band hall one day and decided they should start a metal band together.

"Crash! Boomer!" a deep British voice calls out to us.

Rey Michaelson walks up, playfully punching Mylan in the arm then me in the chest.

"Your bassist has arrived."

Rey is playing Ryder in the show, a character who's silent and mysterious and barely talks but still makes panties drop with just a look. He's sixteen, Mylan's age, and he told us he just moved to the states with his twenty-year-old sister a couple of months ago. He did some acting in the UK, which helped him get an agent here. This show was his first audition. I wonder if his good looks secured this role.

Like Mylan, Rey is the type of actor you'd see splashed across those magazines for teenagers to swoon over. Aside from his alluring accent, he's handsome with perfect light brown hair, perfect teeth, and in shape. I'm not jealous, but envious. I've always been a big kid. I even loved myself until society told me I shouldn't.

"This show is going to be so much fun," Rey says.

I smile and agree, despite the growing anxiety. Mylan Andrews and Rey Michaelson will have an entirely different experience on this show than I will.

"C ut!"

Making out with Tiffany Spars was a dream. Thankfully, I didn't get a boner. There were too many people on set, too many eyes on us. We did at least ten takes before the director decided the scene was good enough. Tiffany didn't seem affected by our kissing. Me, however, it was my first ever kiss, and I was smiling like a fool.

"Okay, everyone, that's a wrap on day one," the director announces after reviewing the last shot.

"Thank God," Tiffany grumbles.

She walks away from me and joins a couple of other girls cast as her friends on the show.

"If I had to kiss that fat ass one more time, I was going to puke."

I freeze and ball up my fists. I don't think I was supposed to hear that. Though she said it loud enough that me, Mylan, Rey, and two crew members standing next to us heard.

"What the hell did you just say?" Mylan asks, his voice dark and dangerous.

"Mylan," I warn, but he's already walking towards the three girls. Rey stays by my side but sends death glares to our cast mates.

"I... um... nothing," Tiffany stumbles.

Mylan stands in front of her with his arms crossed. He's pissed but surprisingly holding his composure. "What the fuck is wrong with you? Do you hate yourself so much you have to put others down to feel better?"

She sputters over her words, failing to complete a sentence.

"You're pathetic." Mylan points at me. "Jensen is my best friend. Don't you ever say anything about him again. Got it?"

She cowers, wide-eyed, and steps back closer to her friends.

"Got it?"

Mylan stares her down until she agrees then returns to where Rey and I stand.

"You really didn't have to—"

He turns me away from the girls and we start walking. "Jensen, don't ever let anyone put you down like that. You're a human being. You deserve common decency like everyone else."

"That's easy for you to say. I mean, look at you."

"Acceptance of yourself is key. Once you love yourself, the confidence will follow." He glances back at the group of girls who are now consoling Tiffany. She's not crying, but she looks absolutely embarrassed. "Those girls are bullies, but only if you let them be."

He throws one arm over my shoulder and his other one over Rey's and the three of us walk off set towards our trailers. "We are the leads of this show. We are badasses. This is only the beginning for us. In a few years, you won't even remember those girls. You'll be too busy winning awards and making bank."

I smile because I like that sound of that.

"Now, call time isn't until noon tomorrow, so who wants to go get drunk? My friend is throwing a party out in West Hollywood."

"Hell yeah," Rey says.

"I'm down," I add.

I return home wasted and with an older woman's phone number. Well, not much older. She's nineteen and an actress who recently starred in some action movie with Brad Pitt. I'd never met such a bold woman. She flirted with me, kissed my cheek and neck, and tried to kiss me on the lips, but after what happened on set today, I refused. She gave me her number and told me to call when I'm ready to pop my cherry.

I didn't tell her I was a virgin. My refusal to kiss her and the tension radiating off my body as she kept touching me must have tipped her off.

I just don't like being touched.

My parents' Beverly Hills home is dark when I enter, only the light in the foyer is on. The house staff must have already turned in for the night and my parents are probably upstairs in their office, working late. They're entertainment lawyers, so they always have some crisis needing to be taken care of.

I walk up the winding staircase heading to my room, trying not to knock into things because I've never drank so much booze in my life. I got tipsy on my sixteenth birthday with my cousin, but that was on beer. Tonight, I drank the hard stuff. Mylan kept handing me drink after drink like he does this all the time, despite being a year younger than me.

My parents' voices stop me right before I pass the door to my father's office. Most kids would sneak by, quiet and worried they'll get busted. Not me. My parents don't care what I do or how late I stay out.

As if sensing I'm home, my father opens the door and turns the corner, nearly running into me.

"Jen. What are you doing lurking out here in the hallway?"

My father, Jack Boliver, is a big guy like me—tall and bearded, with light brown hair that curls at the ends.

"I just got home," I say and hiccup.

"Are you drunk?"

I shrug and try to hide my smile.

My father sighs and glances at my mother, who's standing in the doorway at his side. Julie Boliver is nearly a foot shorter than my father and petite. She has darker hair that also curls around her face.

"Just... be careful," my father says. "Keep your head up and be on the lookout for paparazzi. And don't get into trouble."

My heart pumps faster. He cares? This is the first time my father has ever shown that he's concerned.

"Your father is right, Jenny. We deal with messes all day. We don't need yours to add on to our work." She pats my arm as if doing so was a chore, then she turns back to my father. "I'm going to bed, sweetheart. Goodnight, son."

My father gives me a curt nod and follows. I stand there, frozen, heartbroken, while they disappear into their bedroom and shut the door.

Today was the first day of my new show. It's a big deal. A network series and I'm the lead. I'm only seventeen and all the entertainment shows and magazines say this will open so many doors for my career. Yet, all my parents could say is don't get in trouble because they don't want to clean up my messes?

Fuck them. Fuck this life. I'm so goddamn alone and no one cares about me.

How can you give birth to a child then pretend they don't exist? And imply that the child is a burden on your life?

I'm never going to have kids. I'm never going to get married. I'm never going to commit my life to another's because what's the point? Love is selfish and if my parents love each other but don't have enough for their own child, then how would I be able to do the same?

I stomp down the hallway and slam my bedroom door shut, falling back and sliding down to the floor.

Would anyone even care if I died? At least I'd no longer be a 'problem' for my parents.

My phone beeps and I dig it out of my jeans pocket. Mylan put me in a group text with Rey.

Mylan

I had so much fun tonight. We gotta do that again

He adds a crazy face emoji and I laugh and wipe my cheeks, not even realizing I'd been crying.

Rey

Fuck yeah, we do

Me

Hell yeah, man. Anytime

Rey

Jensen, tell me you got a number from that absolute fit bird flirting with you all night?

I laugh at Rey's text. The drunker he got tonight, the stronger his accent and British slang became.

Me

Yeah, I got it

Both of them sent a slew of emojis, including the kissy face, the eggplant, and the peach.

Mylan

I know we all just met, but I have a feeling the three of us are going to best friends

Me

I'd like that

Rey

Aye. The best of wankers

I can't help but bark another laugh at that crazy Brit. Best friends. I've never had a best friend. It's hard to meet people when you're home schooled and taught on set. Even my co-stars, some who are my age, never keep in touch after filming is over. Mostly because we're moving on to the next role and don't have time to meet up or hang out. I'm hoping that will be different with Mylan and Rey. We'll be filming five to six days a week, months upon months a year (until the show gets canceled). Maybe that means we can form a better friendship since we'll be around each other all the time.

I lean my head back against the door. Mylan cared enough to stand up for me today. No one's ever done that for me.

Maybe my life is about to get better.

Chapter 18 – Rebecca
Present Day

I'm inspired.

My writer's block is gone, and I'm ready to finish my book. I'm not sure if it was seeing Lana and Mylan's love story reach a milestone. Or maybe it's because of how much time I've been spending with Jensen and how he brings out parts of me I thought I'd hidden deep down inside. But the words are flowing out of me.

I woke up at eight this morning encased in Jensen's arms and peeled myself out of bed to start writing. It's now noon and I've sucked down three cups of coffee, ordered breakfast, and scarfed down the best waffles—topped with fresh strawberries and syrup—I've ever had. I've slammed out fifteen thousand words.

"Ami," Jensen mumbles, stumbling out of his bedroom like a zombie. His hair sticks up all over his head as he rubs the sleep out of his face. He's not wearing a shirt, only flannel pajama bottoms. My eyes sweep across his bare chest, over the intricate ink and bulky arms that feel so right when wrapped around me.

How could this man ever doubt he's beautiful?

He yawns. "How long have you been awake?"

"Since eight."

He grunts and ventures into the kitchen to make himself a cup of coffee. "You should have woken me."

I rest my chin on my palm and smile at him. "You looked so sweet and peaceful, Ani. I couldn't bring myself to disturb you."

He sucks in a sharp breath. "What did you... did you just..."

"I Googled it. You have a nickname for me, and I wanted you to have one. So, I found Padme's nickname for Anakin. That's who she loved, right?"

He laughs and leaves his brewing coffee to join me at the table. He bends over and kisses my neck.

"I love it. Though, if you'd seen the movies, you'd know Anakin becomes Darth Vader. The villain. You don't think I'm an evil villain, do you?"

"Not anymore," I tease. I expect him to argue. Instead, he licks my skin, which makes me shudder. Out of breath and turned on, I add, "Now you're a good boy who gives me orgasms and gets hard for me when I need to be fucked."

He groans and wraps his large hand around my neck, squeezing hard enough to make me whimper. "Do you want this good boy to fuck you on top of the table? Give me the order, my Ami, and I'll do it."

"Yes," I breathe. "Choke me while you fuck me on the table."

Jensen releases my neck and grabs my laptop to move it out of the way. He must have glanced at the screen because he pauses.

"You're writing?"

"Yeah," I say and chew on my cheek.

"That's great, Rebecca. You said you were at a block." He purses his lips. "I don't want to interrupt your flow."

"No. Please. Interrupt. I need you."

He reacts to those three words. I need you. His face drops as if he doesn't believe me. He sets the laptop down and kneels, placing his hands on my bare legs. He rubs his palms up and down my thighs.

"Say it again."

"I need you, Ani."

My phone chimes and I groan.

"Ignore it," Jensen pleads. "It's probably just Lana or Mylan."

"I should answer it. They're leaving this evening and want to meet for lunch."

He grips my hips and drags my ass to the edge of the chair. He undoes the belt of my robe and loosens the fabric, revealing my naked body underneath. A possessive growl escapes his throat as he descends on my pussy. I moan when his mouth covers my clit.

My phone rings this time.

"Jensen," I sigh.

"I changed my mind. You should answer it while I eat you out." He goes back to sucking on those sensitive nerves.

With my legs shaking and my breathing already uneven, I answer. "Hello?"

Jensen plunges his tongue inside me, and I cover the phone to mask my moans.

It's my publicist. She's been sending me article after article of the publicity surrounding Ginger's wedding.

Mostly, she's been wanting to talk to me about the intimate photos of Jensen and me, at the beach that one day we floated in the water, at the wedding ceremony sharing flirty glances, at the reception dancing. I didn't respond because I'm still not sure what's going on between us.

But now she's calling, and she only calls when there's bad news.

And fuck it's... bad.

Jensen lifts his head the moment I tense. He stands and tugs a chair close to me to sit.

"Lexi, let me call you back."

I hang up before she can argue.

"What happened?"

My hands tremble as I set the phone on the table.

"There's an article and a video. It hasn't been picked up yet, but Lexi, my publicist, is worried it could go viral."

"What is it? I can fix it."

"It talks about script negotiations for *Tyler's Team*. About how difficult I was. About how the film almost didn't get made. The video is from set of us disagreeing over a shot. It gets pretty heated. This is on top of the picture from dinner that first night here in Kauai, when I was glaring at you. The article doesn't even mention all the other pictures and videos of us flirting with each other. It's one sided and only meant to make me into the villain."

"I sent a statement to my publicist explaining all the pictures of us. Didn't you?"

I shake my head, ashamed.

"Rebecca."

"I know. I just didn't want to deal with it."

He stands. "Even so, they published the article without asking for our side." He stands and walks off into his room, returning with his phone and charger in his hand. "My phone must have died last night when we got back from the waterfall tour."

After plugging it in the outlet next to the table where I'm sitting, he reaches his hand out and rubs my forearm.

"My phone died too. I charged it this morning, but I always have it on silent." I scroll through my notifications. Lana texted at some point. She tried calling a few times this morning too. I'd been so in the zone writing; I didn't notice the screen lighting up with notifications. "My lawyer and publicist have been trying to get a hold of me since last night. So, they did try to get our side before publishing."

I lower my head into my hands and start crying. Jensen stands to console me, rubbing my back with his warm hand.

"They make me out to be such a bitch. I wasn't doing it to be a bitch. This was Tyler's life... I... I just wanted it told in its truest form."

"I know, Rebecca."

"Did you know when the movie was announced, people emailed me? They threatened me."

"What?"

"They told me I better not let Hollywood change a single thing. People connected with the book. It helped them grieve and move on. There was this obsession with it. Dedicated fans found Lana and forced her to move. She changed her number and disappeared from social media. I fought not only because of Tyler's legacy, but because I was scared. I just didn't want to let anyone down." I pause to catch a breath because this is the first time I've told someone other than my lawyers about this. "Then it came out with the changes, and I worried for nothing. Everyone loved it. Aside from a handful of death threats, which were handled by the police, not a single person was disappointed in me. Not even my parents. It was the first time they even acknowledged something good in my life since he died."

Jensen stands in front of me and I wrap my arms around him. I bury my face into his stomach.

"We'll fix this," he says into my hair and kisses the top of my head.

"How?" I ask, my voice muffled.

"I'll call my parents."

I pull back, tilting my head up to see his face. "What?"

"They're entertainment lawyers. Powerful ones. Big name ones. They'll get the article and video taken down. They'll find out who leaked it and make sure they never work in this industry again."

"You'd do that for me?"

"Of course."

"But your parents... they were horrible to you."

"Shh." He kisses my forehead, my cheek, my mouth. "My parents are only good for one thing. They love legal shit like this. Especially if it's getting traction. Anything to get their name out there more. They'll do this for me. For you."

"I can't accept their help. Not after everything they've put you through."

He releases me, holding me out by the arms. "You said you needed me earlier?"

I nod.

He briefly closes his eyes before saying, "Not many people need me. Let me help. Please."

I scan his face, looking for any sign that he's bothered by doing this for me. All I see is concern.

I cup his jaw and scratch his beard. He closes his eyes and groans. Okay, he loves getting his beard scratched. Noted.

"You're a good man."

He smiles. "Finally. Lana has been trying to tell you I'm nice. Gram even said it that one time."

I laugh, and his face lights up at the sound. I'd tell a million jokes if it meant I could see him smile beautifully like that again.

After charging his phone for thirty minutes, Jensen got to work making calls. Mylan and Lana showed up after I responded to her texts. She said the tabloid also contacted them for their side of the story, but they didn't get the emails until this morning.

Now they're here in our suite while we deal with this scandal.

Lana sits at the table with me while Mylan and Jensen pace the living room floor. I've been making calls myself for the past couple of hours. I had my publicist release a statement saying everything I'd mentioned to Jensen. I never told anyone about the death threats, but now it'll be reported by every single entertainment publication and TV show.

I also told my publicist to contact my lawyers about Jensen's parents taking over. She gasped in my ear when I told her *the* Jack and Julie Boliver were on the case. I didn't realize they'd represented dozens of A-listers.

We ordered room service: greasy comfort food from the resort's restaurant.

I'm picking at my fries, separating the crispy ones from the soggy ones, when Lana reaches out and rubs my forearm. "It's going to be okay."

I pop the crunchiest of fries into my mouth and smile. "I know. It's just... I was thinking maybe the article is right. Maybe I'm a difficult and horrible person. The things I said to you when you didn't want to be a part of the movie anymore..."

"Rebecca," Lana warns. "You apologized."

"I should have never said them in the first place. That makes me a bitch."

"I'll kick your ass if you keep calling my friend that."

I roll my eyes. "I told you that you never loved my brother. That was a bitch thing to say."

Lana frowns. "Fine. It was. But I know you didn't mean it."

"I didn't believe it either. Writing the book and having it turned into a movie helped me grieve, but I never considered that it'd be the opposite for you. I was holding you back from moving on. Then I convinced myself you abandoned me all because I couldn't deal with my grief. You were all I had when Tyler died. My parents weren't there for me. I'm pretty sure they wished I had died—"

"What?" Lana nearly screams.

"Yeah. Anytime I wanted to talk about Tyler, they'd make up an excuse. Most of the time, they'd say they were too sad to talk to me."

"I didn't know, Becca. I'm so sorry."

"It got to a point where they just didn't seem interested in anything I said. It was almost as if me being around reminded them Tyler was no longer here."

Lana scrunches up her nose, a look of disappointment at what she's hearing crossing her face. "Grief is brutal, and everyone handles it differently. I am not excusing their behavior. What they did to you is wrong, but it had nothing to do with you. I hope you realize that."

I nod, not entirely sure I believe that. My parents are not the same ones from the time Tyler was alive. I've accepted that. I no longer let their lost love affect me. Or at least, I'm working on trying to not let it affect me.

"You were always there for me. I think you were the reason I was able to function. You let me help with the Tyler's Team organization and that kept me connected to him. So while I've apologized for the words I said to you, I don't think I ever thanked you. Thank you for being the sister I never had."

Lana hugs me and I melt into the understanding and acceptance she's offering me. I sit back and sag my shoulders, relieved to get all that off my chest. My guilt over the things I said to Lana never faded, but the more she brings me into her life, the more that guilt chips away.

"Did you know your brother kept all the stories you wrote?"

My eyes lift to find Lana's hazel gaze. "He did?"

She smiles. "Every single one until you stopped writing them in middle school. He kept them in a pile on his desk in college and any time he was sad or homesick, he'd pick one up and read it. I actually think I have them in my Tyler trunk, in my garage in Malibu. You should come by and get them before you fly back to New York."

My heart skips and tears well in my eyes.

"He never gave up hope that you'd start writing again." She points at my laptop. "And here you are, writing again."

I glance at Jensen. He's still pacing, one hand running through his hair, the other holding his phone to his ear.

"Tyler told me I'd one day find someone who supports and challenges me. He told me I'd find the person who I can truly be myself around."

Lana follows my stare.

"If you think that's Jensen, you should tell him that."

"Don't you think it's too soon?"

"I think it's about damn time."

Chapter 19 - Jensen

After nearly three hours, the original article was taken down. My parents' firm also sent out cease and desist notifications to the few organizations that picked up the story. It'll take longer to go through all the social media posts that people made, but eventually, those will be taken down as well. My parents are now working on finding out who leaked the video in the article.

The good thing is it's no longer being circulated by big media. The bad news is we're getting tons of requests for interviews to try to confirm the details of that article so it can be rewritten and posted. Which means the paparazzi will be even worse these next few weeks.

It's nothing new when it comes to this project. The movie took so long to get made; articles were written speculating the cause of the delay. The production company would only say it was due to creative differences. Sometimes the directors who bowed out would hint about Rebecca being difficult when questioned about it. This time, the issue is the video taken on set.

Mylan and Lana rescheduled their return to L.A. by a day, sending Gram and Pa back without them. Eloise stopped in before her flight. She gushed about her date tomorrow with DJ Kels aka Kelly. I've never seen the small woman so happy. She's always quiet and reserved. I know Mylan cares about Eloise like a sister, and the prospect of her finding a partner has both him and Lana thrilled.

Everyone around me seems to be finding a partner.

I've never imagined a life where I'd settle down with anyone. I never thought I was good enough. But *she* makes me *want* to be good enough.

Rebecca has been avoiding my stares all afternoon. When Lana mentioned hitting up a farmer's market, Rebecca jumped at the chance. But with the article about us, there was no way we'd be able to do that without being seen. Of course, Lana and Mylan brought disguises. They started wearing them while traveling a year into their new relationship in an attempt to hide from paparazzi.

Lana chose to wear mom jeans—rolled thickly at the bottom—a white t-shirt reading Hawaii in rainbow colors on the front that she bought in the resort's gift shop, oversized glasses, and an oversized straw hat over a curly blonde wig.

Mylan's blond wig is a mullet. He's wearing a mustache, white-wash jeans, and a white tank top that says Metallica.

They are so ridiculous; I swear.

Rebecca chose a baggy blue dress covered in a colorful floral design and a bobbed black wig with bangs. She topped the look with a big floppy hat and sunglasses. Mylan had another mullet wig, black instead of blond, so I wore that paired with a pair of khakis and a plain gray t-shirt that had the sleeves cut off.

We are so ridiculous.

But it worked because no one has paid us any attention in the past hour we've been here. Well, I wouldn't say that. The paparazzi didn't give us a second glance when we walked by them out of the hotel, but now, as we stroll through the market, people are giggling and whispering and staring at the rednecks in Hawaii.

It's something old me would have been embarrassed about but now I feel alive with the adrenaline pouring through my body. Rebecca is having a blast as well, walking arm in arm with Lana ahead of Mylan and me. They've been talking up a storm, laughing like they're trying to tell the most jokes in a row.

She's happy.

Then why won't she look at me?

"What's wrong?" Mylan finally asks. He must have sensed I was questioning everything. Or maybe he noticed my hands balled up at my sides.

"Nothing," I lie.

"You've been looking at Rebecca, longing for her attention, since getting off the phone with your parents."

"She's avoiding me."

"Why do you think that?"

"She won't look at me."

"Maybe she's still embarrassed about the article and having your parents help."

I shrug. "Maybe."

Though that doesn't sound like Rebecca. Still, I can understand if that was true.

"You're worried. Why?"

I forget how observant Mylan can be. We've been best friends for over thirteen years now and despite both of us always being busy and barely seeing each other anymore, he still knows me better than I know myself. He knows my mannerisms. He never forgot them.

"What if she won't look at me because she realizes she deserves better?"

Mylan laughs. He fucking laughs.

"Are you serious? You just spent hours on the phone helping her with a crisis... with your shitty parents I might add."

"I thought you liked my parents."

"Hell no. Jensen, I saw how they treated you. That's why Rey and I came over all the time. They needed to see you had friends who loved and cared for you."

"Wait. If you knew how shitty my parents were, then why did you always call me Jenny? You knew I hated it. It's because of them."

"Yes, I knew it was because of them. I was hoping you'd redirect the memories behind the nickname to me instead of them."

I huff and look away, pretending to be interested in the row of tents with hand-crafted merchandise underneath. Mylan's plan worked. Eventually, Jenny became Mylan's name, not my parents'.

"What else is bothering you?" Mylan asks after a while.

My therapist told me I need to talk to my best friend more about my feelings, especially if they involve him. I'm nervous. What if he hates what I have to say and never wants to talk to me again?

"I gave up on you."

"What?"

"When you went to rehab that third time. I gave up on you. I was selfish. Then I pushed you away again when I found out you started drinking during the filming of *Tyler's Team*. You crashed into the sign at Lana's bar. You could have died and the only thing I could think of was myself. I was letting you back in my life, then as soon as something bad happened, I shut you out."

"You were protecting yourself. I told you I understood that in the letter. But what does that have to do with Rebecca?"

Fine. I'm just going to let it all out.

"What if I run away from her too when things get bad? What if I abandon her like I did you?"

He opens his mouth to say something, but I cut him off.

"Mylan, you stood up for me more times than I can count. You cared for me more than I deserved, and I turned around and left you when you needed me most. I'm a horrible person and she deserves better."

"And what about me?"

My head snaps up to him.

"Do you think I'm a horrible person for putting you through that?"

"No, but—"

"You were my best friend who tried to help me countless times, and I refused. I was the selfish one. You are my family. You've been my family since that first day on set for *Metal & Mayhem.*"

He's repeating everything he wrote in the letter to me.

"Look. We're not horrible people. We're human and humans make mistakes. All that matters is we're here for each other now. We have the rest of our lives to apologize and repent. We're good."

We're good. It's what we always say to each other after a disagreement or a fight. It's what I said to him in response to the letter he wrote me in recovery. No harm, no foul. We're good.

We stop walking while Lana and Rebecca enter a blue tent with a bunch of cute sun dresses. Mylan and I stand outside.

"I get it. Believe me. Your trust in others has been tarnished. By me, your parents, all those assholes who bullied you, the public who feels they need to comment on your body. Something good is finally happening to you and you're letting the behavior of others convince you that you don't deserve it."

"What if I can't offer her everything *she* deserves? What if I'm not enough?"

"You are." He puts his hand on my shoulder and squeezes. "You can't see what Lana and I have seen this entire trip."

"What's that?"

"Two people who are constantly aware of each other. Who are lonely and lost and have been in denial of their feelings for the past four years. Who finally *see* each other as an escape. You see a future with her, and I think she feels the same."

I rub my palms over my face. "That's cheesy as fuck, My-lan."

He throws his head back with a guttural laugh. "What can I say? I've lived through it. I *am* living through it. And it's the most beautiful experience of my life."

"What is?"

"Love."

I don't respond for the longest time before I turn to him. "I haven't told her about my next job."

Mylan's eyes go wide for a brief second and I wince. "I know."

"Maybe she'll go with you."

"I can't ask her to just give up her life for a year."

"Then you'll have to decide what's important. What do you want to prioritize right now? A relationship with her or your job."

"That's impossible."

He sighs. "Jensen, you'll always be a movie director. There will always be jobs lined up for you. How often will you come across a woman who looks at you like that?"

He points his chin to the tent and Rebecca glances up from the rack she's perusing. She gives me a small, shy wave. I wink at her, and she glances down, blushing.

Mylan leans in. "*That* is a woman in love."

We return to the resort an hour later after stopping at a local bakery for dessert. We ate homemade Hawaiian sweets and bought extra to snack on tomorrow. Mylan and I carried bags upon bags of clothes, jewelry, artwork, and more that the women bought from local artists and businesses. Then we said goodbye to Lana and Mylan, who have an early flight tomorrow and we won't see them until the next time Lana forces us all to have a get-together. Ones that I pretend to hate being forced to attend, but I always leave feeling fulfilled.

There are things I need to talk to Rebecca about. Why was she acting weird this morning and refusing to look at me? I want to ask her what we're doing. Does she want to be in a relationship with me? I want, no… I need her in my life. But I'm leaving in a month for a job that will last a year. How can I ask her to be with me when I won't be around? As much as I want her to come with me, there's no way she'd go. She has her own life and her own career.

I'm too scared to bring any of this up and ruin what we've had the past few days. Because I have plans for her tonight.

Rebecca stands near the door to her room. A room that she hasn't slept in once this entire trip. She wrings her hands.

"What are you nervous about, Ami?"

"I'm not nervous," she whispers.

I stalk to her, and she sucks in a breath.

"Let me help." I kiss the curve of her neck. "Let me fuck the worry out of you."

"I'm not worried. I just—"

A moan cuts off her words when I tweak her nipple.

"No talking. I want to worship your body for the rest of tonight and tomorrow. We'll talk Monday morning before we leave."

"We should—"

I kiss her, desperate to distract her. Thankfully, it works, and her tense body melts into my arms.

I walk us away from the bedroom and to the balcony, which stretches from her bedroom, past the living area, to the end of my bedroom. While still attached to her lips, I open the door and we stumble out.

Finally, I release her mouth.

"Turn around and hold on to the railing."

Her brow shoots up. "I thought I was the one who got to order you around?"

"Then order me to fuck you on this balcony."

She bites her lip and smooths her palms up and down my chest. "What if someone sees us? Paparazzi are still lurking around. They might sneak in and take pictures and..."

Her face falls, obviously thinking about this morning and the article. I take my phone out of my pocket and I type out a message.

Me

> Can you do me a favor and call in a sighting to divert the paparazzi away from the resort?

The three little dots pop up almost immediately.

Mylan

> Done

He follows up by sending me a ton of emojis, including a smirking face, the kissy face, an eggplant, the peach, and the one that looks like jizz. I reply with a middle finger emoji.

"It's taken care of. The paparazzi won't catch us."

She watches me set my phone on the small table between two lounge chairs. "What did you just do?"

"Mylan is going to call in a sighting. All the Rats will scurry away from the resort, hoping to get a shot of him."

"Fake sighting? Rats?"

"The paparazzi are scum. Rats. Mylan will tip them off that he and Lana are out and about. Maybe he'll say they're at a club. They'll go nuts, especially since he never goes out anymore."

"Smart."

"Yeah, and it's going to piss them off. But that means they won't be lurking around here trying to get pictures. And even if they are paying guests to get shots of us, no one knows which room we're in. We're on the top floor. If anyone looks up here, it'll be too dark to recognize us. We'll just be two strangers fucking on a balcony. If you still want to, that is."

"Oh, I want to."

"Good. Now, give me my orders."

"So demanding."

I get on my knees before her and bow my head. "Please, Rebecca, tell me what you want."

Her fingers comb through my hair and I close my eyes, mewling at the sensation of her fingernails scraping over my scalp. With one hand, she grips the strands in a fist and tugs my head back. With the other hand, she runs her fingertips over my beard, across my lips, and down my neck.

My dick is already straining in my shorts.

"I want to touch you," she says and releases her hold on me to step back. "Stand."

I contain a whimper and stand.

"Undress."

I do, a little too fast, though.

"Slow down."

My fingers shake eagerly as I lift the shirt over my head and toss it to the floor. Rebecca leans against the railing of the balcony and watches. My eyes dart down to her breasts, and I ache to squeeze them, to put my mouth over her hard nipples.

She snaps at me, bringing my attention back to removing my clothes.

I start working on the shorts. Rebecca bites her lip as she ogles my chest and stomach. It's something that would have made me uncomfortable if it were anyone else. But having Rebecca's heated gaze scour over every inch of my skin only makes my dick harder.

"Like what you see?" I tease.

"No talking," she barks, and I laugh. She smiles, clearly having fun taking on this regal role.

My shorts join my shirt on the ground, and I hook my fingers in the band of my briefs.

"Wait," Rebecca says and steps to me.

Her palms smooth over my chest, through the fine hair, and along my tattoos. She moves her hands down over my stomach, at my sides, then around to my back, up and down. She touches every inch of me, jiggly parts and all.

She loves touching me and the more she does it, the more I crave it.

Her fingertips return to trace over the stretch marks around my belly button and on my love handles.

"I have these too," she whispers.

"I know, and they're beautiful."

She kisses the middle of my chest. Her soft lips move on, dropping more gentle kisses and leaving a trail of goose-bumps. A jolt of pleasure shoots down to my cock when she gingerly bites down on my nipple.

My head tilts back.

"You like that?"

"Yes."

She does it again, biting down on my other nipple at the same time she squeezes both my ass cheeks. My dick leaks, desperate to be free of my briefs.

I groan and gently push her away.

"Please, let me fuck you. I'm not going to last if you keep touching me like this."

"Now you like touching?"

"Only your touch."

She steps away. "Don't take your eyes off me, okay?"

I swallow hard. "Okay."

She grasps the fabric of the over-sized dress she's wearing—the disguise from our trip to the market—and gracefully drags it over her head. She's not wearing a bra. She slips her underwear off next and steps out of the fabric.

She swats at my hand, and I realize I reached for her. She moves to me and hooks her fingers in my boxer briefs to strip them off.

My dick bounces out, still leaking pre-cum. She strokes me in her palm, and I grunt at how cold her hands are despite the warm night. Her hot mouth covers the tip, and she sucks so hard, I nearly topple over. She releases my cock with a loud 'pop' then she fists me, up and down the length, squeezing with just the right pressure. She's slow at first, then she picks up speed.

"Rebecca," I wheeze. My balls tighten and I'm so fucking close to losing it.

She releases me with a smirk.

"Are you edging me?"

She tsks. "That would be cruel." Naked and glorious, she turns her back on me and takes hold of the metal railing of the balcony. "Now fuck me, Jensen."

I'm on her before she can finish the command. I line the head of my dick to her wet center and thrust into her, hard and to the hilt.

"Fuck," she screams, and I cover her mouth with my palms.

"Quiet, my Ami," I say while pumping into her. "The Rats may be gone, but we still don't want to put on a show."

She groans into my hand as I relentlessly pound her from behind. My free hand reaches around to her clit.

"Play with a nipple for me. Pinch and pull it nice and hard," I whisper against her ear.

She has no problem with me taking over control now. She lifts one of her hands to her tit while keeping her hold on the railing. Her body jolts the moment I press the pad of my middle finger against her clit and start massaging while she tweaks her nipple.

The waves crashing on the beach and music playing from an outdoor bar at the resort barely mask the sound of our slapping bodies. I slide in and out of her, picking up speed the closer she gets to orgasm.

"Choke me, Jensen," she mumbles against my palm.

I remove my hand from her mouth to wrap my fingers around her throat. I squeeze. Not too hard at first, but enough that her walls tighten around my cock.

I keep my hold firm on her throat, squeezing harder with every brutal thrust. She whimpers, letting me know how much she loves wearing my hand as a necklace.

I pinch her clit again, and Rebecca's orgasm explodes. She shudders and I keep thrusting until jets of my cum spurt inside her.

I rest my forehead on her back while we both catch our breaths, then I remove myself. I poured a lot of cum into her this time and it's starting to come out. I fight the urge to put it back inside her pussy where it belongs like I did the other day. I think it freaked her out. To be honest, it freaked me out.

Do you have a breeding kink?

I grew up adamant about not wanting kids. I worried if I ever had kids, I wouldn't care about them the same way my parents didn't care about me. But Rebecca has shown me a side of myself I didn't believe existed.

Maybe I do want kids. A family. I'm thirty years old. Maybe I should start thinking about settling down.

Would that mean breaking my contract on this new directing job to stay close to Rebecca?

Fuck. We really should talk.

I kiss her spine and stand up straight. "Come on. Let's get you cleaned up."

Chapter 20 - Rebecca

Unease wrecks my stomach. Jensen is quiet in the shower as he washes my body. He doesn't say a word while shampooing and conditioning my hair. Instead, he offers me light kisses on my forehead, my lips, my neck, my shoulders.

No words.

It's almost as if he's savoring this moment like it's the last one he'll get.

When it's my turn to wash him, he tries to refuse me. We stare at each other for nearly a minute before he relents. He closes his eyes as I soap his body and clean his hair, sighing with every brush of my hand. With every touch.

Still, neither of us speaks.

It's not until we're out of the shower and he's drying me off that I finally ask, "What's wrong?"

"Nothing," he says almost immediately.

I consider trying to force him to talk, but I worry he's mentally preparing himself to end things.

No. He wouldn't do that. Would he?

The real reason I don't push him is because of the progress he's making with his fear of putting himself out there. He no longer retreats to a shell of a man when faced with an onslaught of emotions, and we have been drowning in emotions for the past couple of days.

We both care for each other and it's not something either of us is used to experiencing.

So, while he may be quiet and refuse to talk about what's bothering him, I let him work it all out in his head. If I force him, he may never feel comfortable talking to me.

Once clean and dry, he leads me out of the massive bathroom into his room.

"I want to make love to you," he whispers against my lips and sinks me down onto the bed.

We've had a lot of sex over the past few days, and this, by far, is the best he's given me. It's raw, sensual, patient.

He doesn't give me control. He doesn't take control either. It's just the two of us, surrendering ourselves to one another.

After seeing stars and experiencing the most mind-blowing orgasm of my life, we cuddle. He wraps his burly arms around me, and my cheek rests against his chest. He rubs his thumb back and forth over one of the scars underneath my breast. Scars he's yet to ask me about.

I can feel his heartbeat thudding frantically, and I'm not sure if it's from the sex we just had or his nerves.

"Are you okay?"

He kisses my neck, then inhales deeply. "Yes."

"Jensen, we should talk about what happens when we leave here."

He tucks his finger underneath my chin and turns my head to look at him. "I know." He slants his mouth over mine and kisses me with such desperation. "Tomorrow, okay? I just want to hold you tonight."

Before I can argue, his lips return to mine and suddenly I'm okay with waiting until tomorrow.

I wake to an empty bed, cozy beneath soft blankets tucked to my neck, which I'm guessing Jensen did when he left. My stomach dips with worry that he's gone. That he didn't just leave the bed but left the resort. *Left me.* But I spot his suitcase and belongings still strung across the floor at the foot of the bed.

I get up and use the restroom, then put on a robe. I find Jensen at the table in the dining nook next to the kitchen, wearing a black t-shirt and black boxer briefs. He must have woken up in the middle of the night to take out his contacts, because he has his black-rimmed glasses on.

He looks like a sexy professor sitting in front of his laptop, a cup of coffee in his hand.

"Hey," I say, my voice hoarse from sleep and sex.

"Good morning, Ami. How'd you sleep?"

"Amazing." I glance at the clock on the TV in the living room. 9 a.m. "Why are you up so early?"

"I got thirsty and came out here to get water. Then I saw your laptop, and it was open to your manuscript."

Wait. That's not *his* laptop, it's *mine*.

"Oh." I perk up, my back straight and shoulders back. He's reading my book? No other person has set eyes on that book yet. Not even my agent.

My stomach twists with nerves, tangling with anger that he helped himself to my personal laptop.

"I see you're getting pissed, but I swear I was going to just close it because you didn't have it plugged in and it was about to die. Actually, did you turn off the screen saver and sleep mode? You should really turn all that back on, so it'll save power when you're not actively using it—"

"Jensen," I interrupt because he's rambling.

"Sorry. Um, so my eye caught what was on the screen. I started reading and was immediately hooked. I found your charger, plugged it in, and kept reading and reading and it's been two hours and I'm probably halfway done now."

"Really?" My anger fades, replaced with shock. "Is it... What did you... How is it?"

He smiles, and it's a confusing smile. He looks proud of me, happy for me, but his eyes are so sad and that has my chest in knots.

"It's amazing, Rebecca."

"You really think so?"

"I really think so."

I sit down next to him at the table. "I'm a little behind on my deadline. My first draft was due last week. I didn't think I'd ever finish, but I only have a few chapters left now."

"This is going to sell millions of copies."

I laugh. "Yeah right."

"I'm serious. It'll be the next Game of Thrones."

I snort at his over-exaggerated enthusiasm. "I hardly do enough character killing to be on George R. R. Martin's level."

His face lights up and he takes my hands in his. "I want to make this into a movie. Or a TV show."

"What? Jensen, that's crazy. You haven't even finished reading it. What if you don't like it?"

"I will love it. I know I will. You're extremely talented, Rebecca. Do you know how many times I read *Tyler's Team*?"

I suck in a sharp breath. "How many?"

"At least five times."

My bottom lip trembles and I'm going to cry. I hate fucking crying. I've cried too damn much in my lifetime. Yet, these tears are different. They're happy tears. Because no one has ever believed in me as much as this man. No one since Tyler.

He scoots his chair over so he can hug me. Rubbing my back, he says, "Don't cry. You deserve this. You deserve the world."

"What about you? What do you deserve, Jensen?"

I want him to say he deserves me. That he wants to be *with* me.

Instead of answering right away, he releases me and stands. I accept his offered hand and follow him into the living room to sit on the couch.

"My next directing job is in Hungary. It's an apocalyptic movie."

"That sounds awesome, Jensen," I say quietly, cautiously, waiting for the bomb to drop.

He searches my face, stalling, as if dreading his next words.

"It's going to take a year to film."

"Oh." There it is. The bomb dropping.

"I know I should have told you sooner—"

"Why didn't you?"

He locks his jaw and his nostrils flare as he carefully words his answer. "Because I didn't know... I didn't expect..."

"Didn't expect what?"

His head pops up, a crazed yet hopeful look taking over. "Come to Hungary with me."

"What?" I repeat because I can't think right now.

"You can write there, and we can keep doing this."

"This, what? What are we doing, Jensen?"

He stands and starts pacing. He doesn't answer my question.

"Is it just sex? Because if you think I'm going to drop everything and follow you to Hungary for just sex, then you've gone mad."

He stops and stares at me, his hands running over his hair and making it stand on all ends.

"Of course it's not just sex, Rebecca."

My heart gallops inside my chest. "You want more?"

"I do but..."

But he's going to be gone for a year.

I stand and cross my arms. "You're asking me to come with you, but you haven't thought this through, have you?"

He shakes his head.

"What happens if I go, and this doesn't work out and we break up? I'll have sacrificed my own life, my career, and for what?"

"For me. For us."

"Jensen, we don't even know who we are outside of that bedroom." I point to his room to solidify my point. "We don't know what our relationship looks like back in the real world. Up until a few days ago, we hated each other—"

"I told you. I never hated you. Did you hate me?"

I bury my head in my hands, buying myself time to form my answer. Because he won't like what I have to say.

"I hated the way you made me feel. I hated when you offered me a glimpse of a man who cared, then took it away when he got scared. How do I know that won't happen again?"

"I..."

"A year is a long time. As much as I want to go with you and start a relationship with you... I can't. I can't put my life on pause. I'm almost done with this book. They're streamlining the release. It's out in six months. They'll want me to go on tour and I still have book signings scheduled for *Tyler's Team*."

My heart sinks. I wanted so badly to have a life with Jensen, to show him he deserves to be cared for and loved.

"Our lives and our schedules would make it too difficult to be together. We're too busy. We're always traveling. We'd never see each other. Even if I move to L.A.—"

"You would move to L.A.?" He steps toward me but stops, as if expecting that I won't allow him near.

"I was already planning to leave New York. I don't have anyone there. At least in L.A., I'd have Lana and Ginger."

My voice cracks and I turn away from him. He comes close enough that I can feel his heat against my back.

I have to get away before I change my mind. I walk back to the kitchen area.

"Where are you going?"

I grab my laptop and head to my room. "I need to finish writing the last few chapters then I'm going to pack. I think it's best that I change my flight for tomorrow."

"Rebecca."

"Jensen, please. These past few days have been wonderful, and I don't regret any moment I spent with you... but the timing just isn't right." Defeat washes over him, and it hurts my heart. "You know our paths will cross again. We always find each other. Let's make a deal."

His head jerks up, his eyes hopeful.

"A year from now, when you're back, we'll reconnect. I don't know where I'll be, if I'll have book tours, but we'll find each other. We always do. Maybe next time will be the right time, the right place."

I'll wait for you. I'll wait because I love you.

How do I say that out loud? What if I say those words and he decides he no longer wants to go to Hungary? I can't let him miss this great opportunity for his career.

I turn away before his face can convince me to stay. His beautiful face that I just know is full of pain and disappointment right now.

My flight is at 6 a.m. I was originally scheduled to leave on the same flight as Jensen. But after he told me about Hungary, I called my assistant the moment I got to my room, the room I haven't slept in this entire damn trip and had her rebook it for first thing this morning.

There was no way I could sit next to him on that plane after what I said last night.

Sleeping without Jensen's strong arms around me last night felt wrong. I tossed and turned and got maybe two hours of sleep.

After gathering my nerves to emerge from my room, I find him on the couch. His arm is tossed over his eyes, leg propped on the back and mouth hanging open. He makes a light whistling noise every time he breathes in and out.

Is he out here to catch me before I leave? Would he stop me or tell me goodbye?

I wish I could take everything I said back. I wish I could go with him. I want us to be together. But how do we begin a relationship when he'll be on set all day? I'd be so bored and lonely and frustrated and end up hating him. It would never work out.

I sneak around, trying not to wake Jensen as I gather my belongings. He stirs when I open the door, then he turns to cuddle up to the couch cushions.

I force my feet to walk out, and I cry all the way down the hallway, in the elevator, and in the car to the airport.

Chapter 21 – Jensen
4 years ago

That's a wrap. Filming for *Tyler's Team* is officially over.
Well, almost over. We still have to do two more weeks
on a sound stage and a green screen for the hospital scenes.
Mylan can't lose enough weight to appear sick, so we'll do it
with special effects.

Mylan.

I can't believe how great he's doing with his recovery this
time. I was worried when I learned Lana wasn't coming to
Jonesboro with him for the two months we've been filming
at the college. She seems to be an anchor for him. But the
two months flew by, and Mylan came to set on time. He was
alert and performed amazingly.

I get back to my hotel room when the sun is rising, and I
crash on top of the plush bed. The moment my head hits the
pillow, I fall asleep.

The next day, I order some room service, scarfing down a burger and fries before packing up my luggage and heading down to the lobby to check out.

Instead of flying back to L.A., I hop in a hired car to drive me three hours back to Silo Springs, where the town is hosting a wrap party for us. I don't think about how I'll likely see Rebecca again. It might be the last time we see each other until press for the movie. Though, I'm sure she'll request we don't get paired together during the day-long junkets.

I pass the time by sending a few emails and making some calls on my next project: a science fiction movie that I'm so fucking hyped to direct. Before I know it, the driver is slowing down to pass through the town's downtown area.

The wrap party is being held at a small convention hall owned by the city. Cars already pack the parking lot, so the driver drops me off at the front. He'll find a parking spot and wait. I only plan to stay a couple of hours before I head to Memphis to fly out.

Music hits me when I open the glass double doors. People are crowded around the stage dancing as the band plays a cover of an Aerosmith song.

I search for familiar faces: Mylan, Lana, Bruno, Ginger, Eloise, but can't find them anywhere. That's weird. Are they not here yet?

My eyes stop on a gorgeous brown-haired woman, flirting with Shane, one of the camera guys from the film. She's breathtaking tonight, wearing black stilettos and a strapless black dress that falls mid-thigh. Thighs that are covered in patterned tights.

My body fills with jealousy when she places her hand on Shane's arm. I stomp over there to break them apart. Then I realize that's insane because she's not mine and I'm not hers, so I swallow my jealousy and compose myself by the time I reach them.

"Hey, Jensen," Shane says.

Rebecca's back is to me, but I notice her stiffen at my name.

"Hey." I scan the crowd one more time, then look back at Shane. "Have you seen Mylan? Or Lana?"

"No," he says, sounding somewhat angry that I've interrupted his flirty conversation with Rebecca. "Though someone said Mylan was here earlier. Then he left suddenly. Ginger and Bruno too."

"Hmm."

Rebecca finally turns to look at me. "Have you tried calling them?"

I narrow my eyes at her snark. "Not yet."

I step away from them and do just that, but my call to Mylan goes directly to voice mail. I scroll to find Lana's number and her phone rings, but no answer.

Bruno, Eloise... nothing, and I don't have Ginger's number to call.

"Is everything okay?" Rebecca asks, leaving Shane to join me where I stand along the wall.

"I don't know... I... I have a bad feeling."

Rebecca sets aside whatever animosity she holds against me. "Come on, let's go find them."

I follow her out the door, and we walk to her rental car. She starts it up and some country song blares over the speakers. She scrambles to turn it down.

She laughs, nervously. "Sorry. A Carrie Underwood song came on right before I got here. I love her, so I had to blast it."

The image of Rebecca singing at the top of her lungs while driving makes me relax. I even almost smile.

Rebecca pulls out of the parking lot and heads back through the downtown area. We filmed in this town for a month, so I'm familiar with it enough to know she's going to Lana's apartment, which is over the bar she owns.

As soon as we approach, there's a tow truck loading up a black SUV.

"What the fuck?" I grit through my clenched jaw.

"Jensen," Rebecca whispers, her palm covering my balled-up fist.

I rip my hand away and before she's barely put the car in park, I'm flying out of the door.

"What the fuck happened?"

The man operating the tow truck shrugs. "Car crash."

"Obviously," I snarl.

"Jensen." Lana's voice grounds me, stopping me from losing my fucking mind.

Her arms are wrapped around her stomach as she approaches, and my anger fades quickly. Her eyes are bloodshot. Ginger stands near the door to Lilies with the same solemn expression.

Rebecca walks past me and brings Lana into a hug.

"What happened?" she asks, smoothing strands of hair off Lana's face.

Lana sniffs and wipes her nose with the back of her hand.

"Mylan crashed his driver's car into my sign. He'd been drinking."

"What?" I choke out.

She stares at me for the longest time as if choosing her words carefully. "He lost control again, Jensen. He's sick."

"I knew it. I fucking knew it."

I turn to walk back to Rebecca's car.

"He said he'd go to rehab longer this time. A year-long recovery program," Lana yells after me.

I spin back around.

"How did this happen?" My voice wavers and I suck in my devastation.

"He was drinking on days I couldn't be there." Lana starts sobbing.

"This isn't your fault, Lana," Rebecca quickly adds.

"I know... I..." She turns back to me. "What are you going to do? With filming? You still have two weeks left, right?"

I lift my arms with no purpose, then drop them to my sides. "I don't know. I have to speak with the producers and the studio head. But if it were up to me, I'd fire his ass."

This time when I turn around, I keep walking, ignoring the protests from Lana, Rebecca, and even Ginger. I drop into the passenger seat of Rebecca's car and stew.

This is so fucked up. What the hell was he thinking?

If it were up to me, I'd fire his ass.

Who am I kidding? We're too far into filming for it to even be possible. The production company is going to do whatever it takes to finish the movie, even if that means stopping Mylan from entering rehab right away.

Rebecca returns to the car about ten minutes later. I'm laying back in the seat, covering my eyes with my arm.

Without saying a word, Rebecca starts the car and drives away from Lana's. Five minutes later, we're back in the convention hall's parking lot.

Neither of us gets out.

"Are you really going to fire him?"

I lift my arm just enough to see her. She's gripping the wheel hard enough her knuckles turn white.

"It's not up to me."

"But you would if you could?"

"Yes."

"Why?"

I sit up and put the seat back in its upright position. The move was so fast, Rebecca jumps.

"Because, Rebecca, I'm an inconsiderate asshole."

I get out of the car and weave through the parking lot to find my driver.

Rebecca gets out too, stomping after me.

"He's your best friend, and he's in trouble."

"You heard Lana. He's going into a longer treatment program."

"Jensen, you're clearly upset."

I spin around. "Upset? Upset? Fuck yes, I'm upset. Did you know I asked the producers not to hire him? I told them this would happen. I told them he would relapse because that's what he does."

"You can be there for him—"

"I'm always there for him, but he refuses my help every time. I can't keep loving him while he continues to break my heart. Fuck! He drove a car while drunk this time. He could have killed someone. He could have killed himself."

That did it. Those words broke me. That flashback to him being carried out on a stretcher the night he tried to take his life has me crumbling to the ground on my hands and knees, crying like a big fucking baby.

Rebecca rushes over to me, but I cower away from her.

"Don't touch me. Please. I... I can't do this right now."

"Do what?"

"Let you care about me."

"Jensen, you're–"

"Please, just leave me alone."

It's quiet for so long that I wonder if she actually left.

"You know," she begins, her voice quiet and calculating, "one of these days, you're going to push every last person in your life away and they won't come back. Everyone deserves compassion. Even inconsiderate assholes like you."

This time, she leaves and I'm alone once again.

I take a red-eye back to L.A. and go straight to bed when arriving at my Silver Lake condo. I wake up a few hours later at 9 a.m. to do damage control.

Shyon and the head of the production company called a meeting to discuss the situation with Mylan. The crash stayed out of the media after Lana and the driver chose not to press charges. They didn't even call the police. Mylan wrote a check to the driver, triple what his car was worth. He also paid for Lana's sign to get repaired.

I barge in, demanding Mylan be fired. Mylan sits at the table next to his manager, saying nothing. He doesn't even react. Guilt gnaws at my stomach. I convinced myself I wanted him fired but really, I'm just hurt and grieving our friendship once again.

"Calm the fuck down, Boliver," Shyon says and sighs. "It'll be too expensive to fire him and reshoot the role."

I knew this would be the case. They hired him right out of rehab. Did I really think they'd fire him with two weeks left?

Shyon is taking control of this meeting. The head of the production company is sitting next to her with his fingers woven together. His face reveals nothing. He's an older man with graying hair and wrinkles all over his face, just like his hands.

Shyon turns her svelte body to face Mylan. "Let it be known, Mister Andrews, if this would have happened a week or even a month into filming, you *would* have been fired."

Her head moves slightly to Tony. The man is in his sixties and balding. He looks like he could be on the Sopranos with his designer suit and ring-covered hands.

"Well, Tony? You're the one who put your career on the line and made promises that clearly couldn't be kept. Will we be delaying production for a year while your client gets help?"

Shyon never calls anyone by their first name. The two definitely know each other. It makes sense since Tony was the one to call in favors and land Mylan this role.

"Mylan will film the final two weeks, then he'll check in for treatment."

Shyon crosses her arms and narrows her eyes. She's just as suspicious as I am.

"He'll be sober," Tony adds.

Haven't we heard that before?

I t's been a week since that meeting. Today is the first day of filming on the sound stage. Mylan shows up sober, as promised, and with a smile. A smile I've seen too many times from my best friend. He's putting on his best show. Behind the calm mask he's wearing, he's actually terrified.

He could be worried about many things: Lana not taking him back after being separated for a year, him not being able to last the year in treatment, me not forgiving him this time.

Because I'd been trying to mend our friendship these past couple of months.

"Jensen," Mylan says, approaching me.

"Alright, everyone. Let's get started," I say immediately. I can't hear any more excuses from him.

"Come on, Jenny."

"Don't." It's all I say. It's enough to shut him up. "Every time I give you my trust, you rip it away."

"I know. I'm sorry."

"I can't keep doing it, Mylan."

"I know."

The look of pure regret on his face almost breaks me. "Please go find your mark."

He nods and drops his shoulders, defeated.

He turns away and I add, "I'm glad you're finally going to the year-long treatment."

I can't say anything else because Rebecca is right. I want to push him away so badly. I don't, because I'm hanging on to a thin string of hope that this year-long treatment is exactly what he needs.

Chapter 22 – Jensen
Present Day

She left.

She said she was leaving.

Still, a part of me hoped she stayed.

I didn't beg her like my heart wanted me to do. I couldn't risk her changing her mind, because this book she's writing is coming from a part of herself that she's kept hidden. *Tyler's Team* was a tribute to her brother. It was her way of grieving for him. This new book is her way of finally moving on and finding herself. She's letting her imagination run free again.

If I would have told her I loved her, because I do so fucking much, then would she have said it back? Would her love have been enough for her to come with me? Even if it was, I would have never let her put her life on pause to choose me.

I could always break my contract. But then what? Would I follow her around the country on her book tour?

She's right. We'll cross paths again. We can wait.

I can wait for her.

I returned to L.A. late and pass out. My back and neck are killing me from sleeping on the hotel's couch. I thought I'd wake up before she left, that I'd hear her getting ready. Then I would have... what?

Maybe I would have begged her to let me fuck her one last time. Maybe I would have been angry and pushed her away further because that's what I do. I let myself fall in love when my gut told me I didn't deserve it.

When I wake this morning, I grab my phone off the bedside table. My stomach drops because I don't have any missed calls or unread texts from her. Of course, I don't.

Instead, I have some from my best friend.

Mylan

Hey. I heard

You good? Need to talk?

Lana and my joint charity event is tomorrow night. I know you RSVP'd but if you don't want to come, then I can come by today

Let me know

They already found out? That was fast. Did Rebecca text Lana to tell her? Is she okay? I should call her.

Setting my phone down and rubbing my palms over my face, I realize that the only time I've ever called or texted Rebecca Taylor was over four years ago to discuss changes to the *Tyler's Team* script. She may not even have the same number. We were together 24/7 this past week and I didn't even think to ask her if it was still the same.

I could easily get it from Lana or Mylan, but I'm scared. What if she doesn't want to hear from me?

What if she does? What if you're breaking her heart by not calling her?

I need my best friend. He'll help me work this out.

Picking my phone up, I text him back.

Me

I'll be there

The collar of the red dress shirt digs into my neck as I secure my black tie. I tug at it, trying to breathe as my anxiety chokes me. Tonight's fundraiser is a black-tie affair, so I'm wearing my favorite black tux.

It looks good on me. It's always looked good on me, but now my brain believes it. For so long, I refused to love myself because I let the world tell me I wasn't worthy. That being fat meant I didn't deserve to be treated like a human.

Then I met Lana four years ago, and she gave the world and their unrealistic beauty standard the middle finger. She stopped giving any fucks, and she was *happy*. She *is* happy.

Lana inspired me to start this body acceptance journey. I've been doing it for four years now. It opened my eyes to other aspects of my life. I diverted my focus from my body to my work. I made damn good films, networked my ass off, and landed on lists of the most desirable movie directors to work with.

Tabloids would still report on my weight, posting pictures of me out at lunch or at bad angles that made me appear fatter.

Jensen Boliver Gaining Weight?

But there'd also be more articles about my work and my success.

As my confidence grew, so did the way I approached others. I'm a quiet guy. An introvert, if you will. But I found myself starting conversations instead of being forced to join them. Women had always shown an interest in me, but I'd no longer be the leftover, paired with the friend who didn't score with the sexy, built guy at the party.

The hardest part for me to give up were my comfort clothes. While I'd started testing out new clothes a month ago, this past week not wearing my long-sleeved flannels, the beanie hat, and jeans was the first time I'd finally felt like myself. I was still vulnerable, sure, but it was freeing. I even emailed my stylist, who was ecstatic—mostly shocked—to go shopping for an entirely new wardrobe for me.

It was a relief to have the weight of my toxic self-esteem lifted.

Forgoing contacts tonight, I adjust my glasses, choosing a semi, black-rimmed pair, hoping to appear studious and sexy-smart tonight.

Not that I have anyone to impress.

The clicks of my Dior dress shoes echo in the stillness of my Silver Lake home, reminding me of how lonely I am. How lonely I have been.

Spending time with Rebecca, waking up to her scent and her body against mine, makes this two-story home feel incomplete. I suppose it's always felt that way. I filled the place with expensive furniture. The two spare bedrooms have never been used, and no one has ever seen the pricy artwork decorating the walls of my bedroom.

Because I've never wanted to bring a woman here. We'd always hook up at her place, or at the hotel I was staying at during a job, or in a bedroom at the home of whatever celebrity was hosting a party.

My home has never felt like my home because it was missing something.

It was missing her.

Fuck. I'm an idiot. I let her go.

My phone vibrates with the notification from the driver saying he's arrived. I give myself one last look in the mirror next to the front door, pocket my house keys and cell phone, then head out.

The Gala, which is booze free tonight, is a joint-venture for Beyond the Bright Lights and the Tyler's Team Foundation. Mylan and Lana's charities. Both organizations help people during their worst days. Tyler's Team assists families whose loved ones are undergoing cancer treatment or have recently passed, providing resources and support. Mylan's foundation helps those recovering from alcoholism and addiction.

They'd invited me to this event a while ago and I said I'd come. I already donated a million dollars, half to each foundation. A part of me wanted to cancel, but tonight, Lana and Mylan are being honored with Governors awards for their work in the foundations.

They're good people. Inspiring. It makes me want to start a non-profit. It's actually something I've considered for a few years. I want to help men like me who have struggled with body dysmorphia. Something I didn't realize fat people could have. I only thought it was for skinny people who viewed themself as overweight. My therapist told me anyone who feels uncomfortable in their body can have body dysmorphia.

'It's a mental health condition,' she said. 'You spend too much time worried about your appearance and how others view you, over-exaggerating your flaws when others likely don't see what you see.'

Except, I'm a celebrity and my flaws are splashed all over the internet. All my life, even as a child, tabloids published articles about those flaws. I'm guessing that's what caused my body dysmorphia.

But my therapist was right. I obsessed over my appearance, my body, for far too long.

My driver rolls to a stop at a red carpet that leads to the guest entrance. I step out to flashing lights. Reporters stick out their microphones and yell my name, attempting to lure me over for interviews.

They'll only want to question me over the article about Rebecca, or about our relationship in Hawaii. They'll ask why she's not here tonight and I'm not ready to talk about any of that.

Also, tonight isn't about me, so I only offer smiles and waves as I quickly pass by the horde.

I'm stopped by the public relation teams for Mylan and Lana's foundations and pose for pictures in front of a massive backdrop with both charity logos plastered all over it.

"Jensen Boliver?" a voice calls from my right side.

I turn and see a beautiful woman with dark blonde hair styled in loose curls down her back, wearing a red mermaid-style dress.

Holy shit. Tiffany Spars.

My co-star from *Metal & Mayhem.*

I hadn't seen her since the show was canceled after three seasons nearly ten years ago. Her career has gone downhill lately, not getting roles like she used to. I wonder why that is. She's aged gracefully, even more beautiful than I remember.

As she moves to me, I tense. She may be beautiful, but that's all she has going for her. I remember the hateful words she said about me, behind my back and to my face. Despite Mylan threatening her that first day, she'd still snarl at me every chance she'd get. She'd hide my food and make snide remarks under her breath, far out of Mylan's hearing.

She's a horrible, hateful person.

Her tiny hand lands on my arm, and her red lips spread to the fakest of smiles.

"It's so good to see you." She scans my body from head to toe. "Wow, you look phenomenal."

She squeezes my arm and raises a brow, waiting for me to fawn all over her.

"I do look phenomenal, thank you."

When I don't feed into her compliment baiting, she purses her lips. "Let's take a picture together."

The cameras are going wild, lights strobing with how fast they're clicking to document our reunion. One I'm sure they'll hype up to be flirty and happy.

When Tiffany attempts to turn us for a pose, I jerk my arm away. I step close to her, tilting down so only she can hear.

"You think I want to take a picture with the vilest human being I've ever met? Who made my life miserable all because I'm fat? Fuck you."

Standing tall, I adjust my jacket and smile to show her I can be just as fake. I turn and walk away, stopping at the door next to a worker holding a clipboard.

"Is that woman on the list?"

I give her Tiffany's name and she scans the pages. She stops and frowns.

"She's listed under invitees for the Tyler's Team foundation."

Right. Mylan would never invite her. Somehow, she snuck her way onto the guest list for Lana's non-profit because Lana wouldn't know who she was.

"Un-invite her."

The woman holds the clipboard against her chest. "Um. I'm not sure I have the authority..."

"I have the authority," Lana says, appearing next to me. "And if he says that woman shouldn't be allowed inside, then I trust his judgment."

The young girl smiles nervously and nods, touching her earpiece to speak into the microphone on the headset she's wearing. Seconds later, two big security guys walk over to Tiffany, who is still posing for pictures. One leans in and says something next to her ear. Her eyes widen and she places a palm over her chest. Then her sights find me and those eyes narrow. She starts for me but is immediately stopped by one of the security guards who wraps his hand around her upper arm.

The paparazzi go crazy snapping pictures of the drama. I cannot wait to see the headlines tomorrow and make a mental note to email my publicist to write a statement about my past with Tiffany. I could let it go and keep the past in the past. But people should be called out for their horrible behavior to remind others it's not right and won't be tolerated.

Inside the Beverly Hilton where the gala is being held, and out of sight of the media, Lana turns to me.

"What was that all about?"

I smile at her tone. It's not concerned or angry but amused. "She co-starred on *Metal & Mayhem* with Mylan and me. She was horrible and bullied me a lot."

"Seriously?"

"Yeah. Mylan actually stepped in the first day when he heard her say something about my weight. He threatened her, but I never told him she kept doing it behind his back."

"What a fucking bitch," Lana says the same time Mylan says from behind me, "she did what?"

I turn around and Mylan's standing with his hands on his hips, jacket unbuttoned. A few escaped curls fall from his slicked back hair and onto his forehead—hair that's always been curlier than mine.

"Sorry, I never told you. You had your own shit to deal with while filming the first season. Your mom..."

I let my words trail because this isn't the place to talk about mine or Mylan's troubled past. He was only sixteen when he became emancipated. His father was an abusive alcoholic who died when Mylan was ten. His death sent his mother into a deep depression and for six years, she neglected him. He finally got control over his own estate and finances, then placed his mother in a psychiatric facility where she stayed for nearly nine years before he re-connected with her during his year-long recovery after filming *Tyler's Team*.

Mylan and Lana are being ushered away by event organizers needing them to meet with potential donors. He locks eyes with me before walking off, silently telling me we're not done discussing this.

The rest of the night was uneventful. Mylan and Lana schmoozed, getting millions of dollars in donations for both their foundations tonight. They were honored with their service awards, gave emotional speeches that had my throat burning with tears. I didn't cry, but there were plenty of people around me who did. After their moving speeches, we all sat for a steak dinner followed by a sweet, donut-inspired dessert, of course.

Lana, Mylan, and I talked about our trip to Hawaii and Ginger's wedding with the rest of the guests at our table. People I didn't recognize but were probably insanely rich.

I wonder what Rebecca is doing.

Eloise isn't here either. She had a late shoot tonight for some fashion magazine.

Several people stopped by to congratulate Lana and Mylan on their engagement. While the women gushed over Lana's ring, Mylan turned to me to tell me about how they had to deal with the aftermath of faking a sighting for me.

Mylan posted a picture on Instagram of Lana holding up her engagement ring and it went super viral. Then paparazzi and fans packed the club they said they were celebrating at.

Things got out of control at that club and the police had to be called in. Mylan had to issue an apology, basically saying they never made it out the door because they decided to celebrate privately.

It wasn't until the gala was nearing the end, and the crowd was thinning, when Mylan turned to me. "Ready to talk about it?"

"About Tiffany?"

He rolls his eyes. "I don't give a fuck about her. Besides, after tonight, I doubt she'll work in this industry again. I had my lawyers do some digging and there have been other complaints from actors and crew members. It's why she can't get jobs anymore. Tomorrow's article—and you know there will be an article—officially puts her on the blacklist."

I shake my head at my best friend. "You did all that while making the rounds asking for donations and getting a freaking award?"

He smiles like it's no big deal.

"Have I ever told you that you're awesome?"

Mylan barks a laugh. "No. But say it again."

Lana returns to the table after saying goodbye to someone and sits down next to Mylan, kissing his shoulder and rubbing his arm.

"Is he ready to talk about it yet?"

Okay, clearly, they mean talking about Rebecca. They're teaming up on me. Despite their insistence, I'm relieved to finally share my thoughts with someone.

"Yeah, yeah. I'm ready." I sigh and swallow a huge gulp of my iced water. I rub my sweaty palms on my pants and inhale deeply to ease the tension plaguing my body. "I'm in love with her."

I expect a reaction from them. Anything, really. A gasp of shock, wide-eyed doubt. Instead, I get a blinking stare.

"Right. You both know that."

"Does Rebecca know you love her?" Lana asks.

I grimace and tell them everything that happened from waking up and seeing her laptop to when she holed up inside her bedroom. I told them how I didn't want to say 'I love you' because I was scared she'd say it back.

"How can we start a relationship when we're on opposite sides of the world? Or worse, what if she pauses her career to come with me?"

"Why would that be so bad?" Mylan asks.

"What?"

"Why would her pausing her career to be with you be so bad?" Lana clarifies.

I open my mouth, expecting an answer to come out, but I've got nothing and clamp my mouth shut.

"If she's in love with you," Lana adds, "and you love her, if you both want a future together, then maybe she wants to prioritize that over her career."

I grind my teeth, trying to form a response to that.

"Why would she... I mean it's... me."

"Would you fucking stop with that?" Mylan's hands form fists on the tabletop. "Stop thinking you're worthless or don't deserve to be happy."

Lana squeezes Mylan's upper arm and he relaxes slightly.

"How many times do I need to explain this before you get it in your thick skull?"

Oh, shit. Mylan is pissed. It takes a lot for this man to get pissed.

"You're my best friend, and I wouldn't be here today if it weren't for you." His voice cracks, and he clenches his jaw. "I'm talking about when we were teens. When I was dealing with emancipation and getting my mom help while filming *Mayhem*, I was a mess. You kept me grounded. Too many times I thought how easy it would have been to give up. Too many fucking times. Then you'd text me and tell me something funny that happened on set. Or you'd send me pictures of you and Rey with paint all over your faces because you idiots fell for another of my many pranks. Or you'd call and ask me to hang out and play video games just because. Or when you and Rey would show up at my place at three in the morning after I had a really bad day on set, and we'd go fuck around and shoot one of your many short film projects."

I sniffle and wipe my cheeks because I'm crying, and I never cry.

"So, yeah, you're worthy and someone would totally prioritize a life with you."

I bring my best friend in for a hug. The man who actually saved me more times than I can count. Who forgave me after I abandoned him and still loves me as much as I love him.

"Okay," I say when we part.

I stand.

"Okay? That's it?" Mylan muses. "That's all you're going to say?"

"You got it through my thick skull."

My best friend smiles and shakes his head.

I walk away from the table, then stop and turn on my heel, holding up a finger.

"She's back in New York," Lana answers my unspoken question. "She leaves for her book tour in a couple of weeks. I'll text you her address."

I return to the table, kiss Lana on the head, then run out of the venue.

Chapter 23- Rebecca

I flew into LAX from Kauai to pick up the stories I wrote that Lana had kept in her box of Tyler memories. When I landed, the paparazzi were waiting. They crowded me, bombarding me with questions about that damn article and why it was taken down, about Jensen and our time together in Hawaii, and about other things that all merged into one loud ringing in my ears.

Thankfully, airport security came to my rescue and Mylan let me use his jet to fly back to New York to avoid more of the media rats.

Now it's Friday. Jet lag killed me, so I slept fourteen hours the first day back, then the next day I moped around my apartment, binging Netflix and stuffing my face with ice cream and fried foods.

If it weren't for needing to go to my publisher's office to talk about my manuscript after I emailed the first draft on Monday, I'd spend another day lounging and self-hating.

After the chaos at LAX, my publisher wasn't taking chances. They sent a car and a bodyguard to pick me up from my Upper West Side loft. I'd never been famous enough to have a bodyguard. Maybe it's time to consider hiring one. The protection my publisher sent is only temporary until this mess dies down.

My meeting wasn't as bad as I expected. Their critiques were helpful, and it shouldn't take me long to fix all the issues they found. I step out of the Midtown building with a smile, slipping on my sunglasses to block the bright sun with no clouds to hide behind on this warm August day. It's almost September. Almost fall, which is my favorite season. I love walking through Central Park at the end of October to see the foliage.

With my new bodyguard, Jeremy, by my side, we head toward the car parked up the street ahead of other black cars waiting in a line to pick up people more important than me. Jeremy is a bulky white man who's at least six foot three with a bald head and stone-cold face. He works for Bruno's security detail company and Bruno personally selected him for me.

I feel safe with this man and I'm thankful my publisher reached out to Bruno's company to hire him.

We pass by a newsstand—a silver box with a man in-side, selling cigarettes, magazines, lottery tickets, drinks, and snacks—and against my better judgement, I peek at the gossip rags.

I stop in my tracks.

A picture of Jensen beside a gorgeous blonde woman graces the cover of at least two magazines. My heart drops reading the headlines.

Flirty Reunion

Boliver Moving On?

Jensen is leaning down as if he's about to kiss this woman and she's smiling up at him, her hand resting on his upper arm.

What the fuck?

I snatch the two magazines and hold them up.

"How much?"

I pay the man ten dollars and tuck the magazine under my arm, following Jeremy to the car.

Inside, I take a deep breath. I'm letting myself get all worked up even though the media always over-exaggerates the true story.

Once we're moving through traffic, heading back to my apartment, I take out the magazines.

Boliver Moving On?

Written by Angela Borrows, Entertainment Now

> After a whirlwind romance with Rebecca Taylor in Hawaii, Jensen Boliver seems to be moving on. The film director was reunited with Tiffany Spars on the red carpet of the joint Gala for the Beyond the Bright Lights and Tyler's Team foundations. The two co-starred on *Metal & Mayhem* for 3 seasons before the show was canceled 10 years ago. 30-year-old Spars went on to star in hit movies like *Carry Me Home* and *Falling From Nowhere*. 30-year-old Boliver transitioned to work behind the camera, winning an Oscar for *Tyler's Team*. Sources tell Entertainment Now that this is the first time the two had seen each other since leaving the show. They were spotted smiling and flirting...

I stop reading. I don't even pick up the other magazine. How could he do this? How could he move on so quickly? I've been miserable, and he's been out partying?

This happened two nights ago. How have I not seen anything about this already? I mean, sure, I've been holed up in my apartment, refusing to go online, telling my publicist to say 'no comment' to whatever request comes through as long as it's trivial and wouldn't threaten my reputation or career, but certainly Lana would have called or texted me.

You know what? I'm going to call her. I fish my phone out of my purse. She answers after the first ring.

"Did you know?"

"So, you saw."

"Did you know?" I ask an octave higher.

"It's not what it seems." She sighs through the phone. "Did you read the article?"

"I... I started to."

"Keep reading and call me back."

She hangs up on me, and I want to throw the phone at something. I pick the magazine back up and finish reading the damn article.

> ... but looks might just be deceiving, because minutes after the alleged flirty reunion, security escorted Spars out of the charity event. Photos show Boliver and Lana Young watching from the venue's entrance. Boliver released a statement the next day claiming Spars bullied him on the set of *Metal & Mayhem*. We asked if he was the reason she was kicked out of the event but have not yet heard from Boliver or any of the event organizer's team.
>
> It's also come to light that this bullying behavior wasn't a one-time thing from Spars. Other co-stars and crew members from various projects over the years have contacted us with their claims that we are still looking into. Those claims could explain why Spars hasn't booked a role in over three years. Sources tell us she approached Boliver with the intent to ask him for a job.

> We've reached out to Spars for comment, to which she denies all allegations against her.

She bullied him?

What a bitch.

I look at the pictures more closely. Jensen's smile is forced, his eyes full of disdain. Real hatred. Not the looks he ever gave me. He's not comfortable at all. And she's *touching* him.

She's touching *my* Ani.

Lana was right. I overreacted. These magazines are the worst, luring you in with a headline that promises one story, then dishes out another.

It's pathetic.

Instead of calling Lana back, I text her.

Me

Sorry. You're right. It's not what it seems

Lana

Apparently that woman is desperate for work and tried to get in Jensen's good graces so he'd hire her on one of his next films.

Me

That's sad, but I definitely don't feel bad for her

Lana

How are you holding up?

Me

I'm okay. Better today

Lana

What are you up to?

Me

Nothing. Heading home now after meeting with my publisher

Lana

Oh, good. I was wondering where you were.

I raise my brow.

Me

Huh? What do you mean? Are you in NYC?

The three little dots pop up, then disappear, then pop up again. I'm about to call her back, but we're pulling onto my street. As we approach my building, I spot someone sitting on the steps.

"Do you know this man?" Jeremy asks.

My heart hammers against my chest.

It's him.

"Yes. I know him."

The driver barely stops the car before I'm climbing out. Jensen stands to meet me.

"Jensen?" I walk toward him, arms crossed as if that will protect me from the reason he's here.

"Hi," he whispers.

"What are you doing here?"

"I didn't want to wait for our paths to cross again."

I open my mouth to say something, but he moves close enough for me to touch him, and I forget how to form words. His musk of amber, honey, and oranges wraps around me. It's only been a few days and lord I've missed his smell.

He nervously adjusts his black-rimmed glasses and runs his fingers through the loose curls piled on top of his head, then down to the shaved sides. He scratches at his beard and tugs at the fabric of his shirt. He's wearing a white short-sleeved button up with tiny black roses on it and black jeans with the bottoms rolled up to show off his black Chucks.

Why is he so freaking adorable?

Adorable and hot and I want to hold him in my arms.

But I don't because he's about to go into an entire monologue. He's anxious about it too. He fidgets a lot when he's nervous.

"You've been in my life for over four years now."

He takes my hands in his.

"We spent nearly every day together on set for three months. Then I didn't see you again until a year later at the premiere. Do you know how bad I wanted to walk over to you that night, to hold you, to *kiss* you?"

I swallow hard and shake my head.

"Then months pass without seeing you again until the Oscars. Both of us had dates, but neither of us paid them attention because we couldn't keep our eyes off each other."

One of his hands trails up my arm, making the hair stand on end and goosebumps to form. He leans in slightly. His voice low and breathy.

"I let you go for another year before we were together again in that car and I finally got to kiss you, *taste* you. It ruined me. I didn't want anyone else after that. I didn't *have* anyone else after that—"

"That's why you didn't have sex this past year?"

"Yes. I knew no one else would be good enough. So, I waited." He searches my eyes. "Is that... is that why you..."

"Yes."

He smiles and continues. "It was better this way because a year ago, you weren't ready. I wasn't ready. We both had to overcome our insecurities. We both had to convince ourselves that we deserve love. And I love you, Rebecca—"

"You do?"

He smiles as big as his face will allow, his green eyes sparkling. "I think I started falling for you the day I found you crying in the bathroom. It broke my heart that you were hurting. I wanted to hold you and tell you everything was going to be okay. I wanted to take care of you. You were a stranger, but it was as if you were meant to come into my life. Because I was lost and no longer cared about things that used to bring me joy. But that day I cared. I'm sorry it took me so long to stop fearing that feeling."

Jensen reaches up and wipes my wet cheeks. I started crying the moment he said he loved me.

I hiccup through my tears and melt into his touch. "I love you too, Jensen."

He lets out a wavering breath.

"Good. Because there's no fucking way I'm letting you go for another year. I don't want to wait for our paths to cross again."

"I don't understand."

"I quit. I broke my contract, and I won't be going to Hungary to direct that movie."

"What? Jensen, no. You can't."

"I already did it."

He laughs at my reaction. I can't imagine how shocked I must look.

"I've been pushing myself past my limits both physically and mentally by overworking myself. I've been taking jobs back-to-back to cope with my feelings about Mylan and now that I've finally worked through that, I'm ready for a break. Remember what you said to me the night of the wrap party? How one day I'll keep pushing people away?"

I nod.

"Well, this is me no longer pushing. No more pushing people away. No more pushing away my feelings. No more pushing my body past its limits. I want to focus on smaller projects now. Indie movies. Cult horror films. Films that won't take up a lot of my time because from here on out, you will always come before my job. You will never be my second choice."

I suck in a breath. "What did you just say?"

"You will never be my second choice. I will always choose you first."

I cry harder and fall into Jensen's offered hug, letting me sob into his chest. He has no idea what those words mean to me. One day, I'll tell him it's what my brother once said.

But right now, there's one more problem. I step back and he wipes the pads of his thumbs over my cheeks to dry the tears.

"What about my book tour? I'll be gone..."

He shrugs. "I'll come with you."

"Jensen." I shake my head, trying to make sense of how casual he's being after dropping all this on me. As if he didn't just pour his heart out to me. "You'd be so bored. I could never ask you—"

"You didn't ask. I offered. And I want to. I actually emailed your publisher."

"For what?"

"They're going to let me document your book tour. If you'll let me, that is. I'll use footage from the tour, and the behind-the-scenes interviews you did for *Tyler's Team* that weren't used in the extra features release, and I'll make the documentary of your life. Not Tyler's life, yours."

"I thought you wanted a break?"

"Believe me, this will be a break. It'll just be me and my smartphone, recording the woman I love doing what she loves."

"No big crews?"

"Nope. I'm actually excited to see how creative I can get using just my phone."

I wrap my hand around the nape of his neck and yank him down for a kiss. It's a soul-crushing kiss that has me putting the pieces back together just so I can shatter underneath his touch once again. His massive arms snake around me, bringing my body flush with his. He's so big and warm and I never want to let him go.

Except, we're on a sidewalk in the middle of the afternoon. If this kiss gets any steamier, then the people walking around will see a lot more than a passionate kiss between two people who just confessed their love to each other.

I end our kiss and Jensen lets out a soft whimper. I take his hand and lead him toward the steps of my building.

We're barely inside and closing the door to my loft before we're on each other. We strip our clothes off blindly because we refuse to stop kissing.

"Upstairs," I breathe. The living room curtains are open and it's too bright in here to fuck on the couch. Someone walking by would definitely see if they glanced through the window.

We stumble up the wooden stairs nearly naked except for our undergarments. When we reach my room, I move to stand near my bed.

"Tell me I'm yours, Ani." Jensen's eyes widen because he'd said those exact words to me in Hawaii.

"You're mine, Rebecca."

Before I can respond, Jensen is on his knees.

"You're mine and I'm yours. Tell me what you need."

My nipples harden at his words, my pussy pulsing with want. I reach behind me with one hand and squeeze the clasps of my bra, slipping it off and dangling it beside me. Jensen watches as it drops to the floor.

I tilt my chin at him. "Take off my panties."

He's close enough to me to reach out his long arms and tuck his fingertips behind the band. My skin prickles. He grips the fabric and draws me closer to put his mouth on my stomach and pepper it with kisses. He licks my stretch marks there and the ones down at my hips. I thread my fingers in his hair.

"God, you're beautiful," he mumbles into my skin.

"Jensen, please. I need you."

He gives me one more kiss before ripping my panties down. I step out of them, and he tells me to fall onto the bed.

He's in between my legs before I can order him to put his mouth on me. His lips cover my clit, and he sucks and flicks his tongue over the swollen nerves.

I tighten my hold on his hair to bring him closer to me. He chuckles, the vibration and his hot breath make me moan.

As he works my clit, his fingertips tease my opening—up and down—then he slides one in. My back arches and he uses his free hand to skim up my stomach to my breast. He squeezes, then rolls my nipple between his fingers. Hard.

He adds a second finger and starts pumping, slowly at first as he lets my arousal thicken. Then he speeds up while that tongue dances over my clit, and his fingers pinch my nipple again.

"Fuck, Jensen. Go harder."

He does, thrusting into me now with three fingers. His teeth graze over my clit but just before I'm sent over the edge, he removes his fingers.

"No!" I whine.

He climbs onto the bed to kneel between my legs and drags the tip of his cock up and down my slit for lubrication then he thrusts into me.

I scream out my pleasure, and he doesn't stop. He pounds into me, rough and relentless.

"Harder, Jensen."

He uses my hips to anchor himself and picks up speed. He reaches parts of me I never thought possible. The slaps of our bodies, the headboard thumping against the wall, and his grunts mixed with my moans have me working up to my orgasm.

Then he stops and removes his cock from me.

"What the fuck, Jensen," I growl.

He flips me over and adjusts me, so my ass is in the air. The moment he crashes his hand down on my left cheek, he drives into me. He spanks me again, this time on the right. I wasn't expecting it and I buck against him at the pleasant pain. He doesn't stop smacking my ass over and over, not giving me a break.

I don't want him to stop.

I can feel my cunt tightening around him. I'm close again.

He gives me one more hard thrust, then stops. Still seated inside me, he rubs my burning ass cheeks and I groan at how good it feels.

"Stop edging me, you asshole."

He chuckles and I reach back and try to swat at him.

Grabbing my wrist, he maneuvers us so he's sitting, his back against the headboard and I'm straddling his lap.

"I want to see your face while you ride my cock."

I smirk and take hold of his dick. He sucks in a sharp breath as I fist him up and down. It's already well lubricated with my pleasure.

I line the tip with my entrance and sink down.

He grunts, taking hold of my sides as I move. I'm not patient. I'm too worked up to go slow. He's been teasing me, holding me back from coming, and I need an orgasm now.

I hold on to his shoulders as I ride him. He leans in and kisses me, sucking on my tongue, my bottom lip, before moving his mouth down my chin, my neck, and to my breast.

My nails dig into his skin and when his teeth graze my sensitive nipple, I come undone. My pussy pulses around his cock, massaging him until he comes too.

I bury my head in his neck, breathing hard. "Fuck. I missed this."

"Does that mean you're going to let me come with you on the book tour?"

I realize I never agreed to his documentary idea. It actually sounds amazing. I lift my head and place a gentle kiss on his lips.

"I'd love that."

We make out for a few minutes, his dick still inside me, before we finally part.

He cleans me up in my bathroom and then we dress and go downstairs to make something to eat.

We're sitting at the bar that overlooks my living room, finishing our last bites of the sandwiches I made when Jensen clears his throat.

"Do you have plans tomorrow?"

"Tomorrow is Saturday. I have no plans. I'm all yours."

"Good. I have a surprise for you."

Chapter 24- Jensen

I wake Rebecca up at nine the next morning, forcing her out of bed and helping her put on a robe. She curses me out, whining about needing more sleep. We'd stayed up late to watch *Star Wars: A New Hope*. She loved it. I knew she would.

I'd glance at her before an important or exciting scene was about to happen and she reacted accordingly. Though I'm convinced she did that because she caught on that I was watching her. Still, she truly seemed to enjoy it and even said she can't wait to watch the rest of the movies.

I slip on my boxer briefs and a t-shirt from the overnight bag I brought with me, then we head downstairs so I can cook her bacon and pancakes and drown them both in maple syrup.

She hums after sipping her coffee and hums again after each bite of food. It's something she does a lot when eating or drinking or kissing. She hums when enjoying the little things like that first night in Hawaii when she ate dinner and dessert.

I realize there are a lot of little things that we still don't know about each other.

"What's your favorite color?" I ask when I finish my last bite of pancake. I take the plate to the sink and rinse it off, then place it in her dishwasher.

"Purple."

I snort. "For royalty."

"Maybe." She shrugs. "What about you?"

"Red."

She laughs at that. "Because you're always angry?"

"I'm not always angry."

"Fine, but you're at least grumpy."

"You like my grumpy ass."

"I do like your ass."

I wink at her and start cleaning up the rest of the dishes I dirtied for breakfast. "Red because I just like the damn color. Not for any specific reason."

"Favorite type of music?" she asks, picking up on the get-to-know-you game.

"Indie rock."

"Shocking." She pops her last piece of bacon in her mouth and brings me her plate and fork. "I love country."

"Shocking," I say mockingly, and she bumps her hip with mine.

"Favorite food?" she continues, sitting back down.

"Sushi."

She scrunches up her nose.

"It's so good. I could eat sushi every day."

"I'm not a fish fan."

I scoff.

"Sorry, not sorry. I *am*, however, a mac and cheese fan. I'd say that's my favorite food. It reminds me of Tyler."

She smiles, not at all sounding sad about this memory that popped into her head.

"Our parents used to work a lot when we were younger. We didn't have a lot of money, so our meals were usually from a box or a can. Tyler's favorite thing to cook—and probably the easiest thing to make—was macaroni and cheese. He'd always add too much milk, so it'd be more like soup. It was actually terrible, but he'd let me help and we'd dance around in the kitchen to music while cooking. He'd tell me stupid jokes, or we'd pretend we were cooks working in the kitchen of a castle, preparing to serve the king and queen. We'd have accents and everything."

"Oh, I have to hear this accent."

"Absolutely not." She rolls her eyes at me. "Anyway, when Tyler got old enough to work at the Country Mart—that's a grocery store—he'd bring home cheese and meat set to expire that night and our macaroni and cheese would be extra good because he'd add the meat and drown it in more cheese. He was so creative when it came to our boring boxed meals. He could have totally been a chef. He could have been anything and everything. A football player, a social worker, the freaking president."

She giggles to herself. That's another thing she does; she'll let out a little giggle when talking about something she loves, or when she's nervous. Sometimes the giggle comes out of nowhere, as if she thought of something funny but kept it to herself instead of saying it out loud.

Because Rebecca Taylor's mind is an expansive landscape of ideas and stories just busting to be released.

"Why haven't you asked me about the scars underneath my breasts?"

I'm wiping down the counter and pause. The question seemed to come out of nowhere. It's obviously something she's been thinking about for a while.

"I know you've seen them. You've definitely felt them. You always trace your thumbs over the lines when we're cuddling."

She's right. I like the feel of the raised skin. "I figured it wasn't my business unless you made it my business." I wanted to ask her so badly, but it was never the right time to bring it up.

I start washing the pans I used for breakfast, and she joins me.

"I got implants with my first big check from the book. I've always had curves, but my breasts weren't that big. In college, my body filled out more, but my boobs stayed the same. When the book came out and its success grew every day, I convinced myself I needed implants because I was about to be in the public eye a lot more. I've always lived a life based on how society perceived me. For some reason, I believed it would make me more desirable. Instead, it was just another fake thing about me.

"I went from a B-cup to a D-cup. Then, as I got older, I put on more weight. I finally started loving my body with how it filled out. Except my tits grew too big. My D-cup became double D's then triple D's.

"My back hated me, the pain became unbearable, so after *Tyler's Team* finished filming, I took time off to get the implants out on top of a breast reduction. Now I'm at D-cups again."

Now that she's told me this, I had noticed something different about Rebecca when I saw her at the premiere for *Tyler's Team*. She seemed to stand taller, more confidently. The fact that her breasts were smaller never crossed my mind.

I just thought they looked fantastic in the strapless purple cocktail dress she wore.

"Well," I begin, handing her a pan. She puts it in the drainer on the counter, "I thought you had perfect tits when we first met, and I think they're just as beautiful now."

She snorts. "You're a man. You like all breasts."

"Not true. Yours are far superior."

We finish washing the dishes and cleaning the kitchen, sharing more of our favorite things. She knew my favorite movie, and hers is an old Rom-Com starring Drew Barrymore that I'd never seen called *Never Been Kissed*.

We talked about places we've traveled and places we want to go. Rebecca did a book signing tour across Canada and Europe but said she didn't really have time to explore places like London, Dublin, Edinburgh, Paris, and Rome. I'd been to all those cities more than once, plus Switzerland, Tokyo, Singapore, and Dubai. The list goes on.

Some of those places were for film shoots, either acting or directing. Others were trips I took with Mylan. Of course, my favorite vacation was in Tokyo, learning how to make sushi from the world's best sushi chef.

I'd love to take her to these places, if she'll let me.

There are a lot of things we have to learn about each other and I'm hoping today is the start of many years that we'll spend exploring these parts of ourselves—the parts that make us sad, happy, nervous, hopeful, scared, content.

Once the kitchen is cleaned up after breakfast (and we get a quickie in, in the shower) I tell Rebecca to dress in something simple, like a t-shirt and jeans.

She's not going to be wearing today's outfit for long.

Of course, she chose a dress, but it's a flowy one, with short, puffy sleeves. It's white and has colorful flowers on it. The neckline forms to her breasts magnificently.

We leave Rebecca's Upper West Side loft and jump into the car I hired during my stay here in NYC. The driver heads west across Broadway and Riverside Drive and merges onto the Henry Hudson Parkway, driving toward Upper Manhattan.

Traffic is light, so it takes about fifteen minutes before we're passing the George Washington Bridge on the left and entering Fort Tryon Park in Inwood on the right.

She gasps the moment we arrive at The Met Cloisters.

"I love the Met Cloisters," she says. "I come here a lot to write."

I knew that because I stalked her Instagram feed way too many times over the past year. Okay, fine. The past four years.

With Rebecca's hand in mine, we walk up the stairs to the museum, which specializes in European medieval art and architecture. The building resembles a French Abbey, sitting on a steep hill with two levels. There are medieval gardens, gothic windows, and several chapels. There's even a walkway where you can stand and view the Hudson River.

"Wait, isn't it closed?"

"Not for us."

We enter the double doors at the front and a man who I haven't seen in years is standing there talking to a woman who I assume to be the museum's curator.

"Rey Michaelson."

I greet my long-time friend with the secret handshake we created with Mylan. Rey is shorter than me and built like a machine. He hasn't been in any movies in years, yet he must still be hitting up the gym to keep up his physique.

"Rey," Rebecca says with a start. "I remember you. You were supposed to play my brother in *Tyler's Team*."

He lowers his head for a moment, then lifts it with a soft smile. "I was. Sorry I had to drop out last minute because of a family emergency."

She waves him off. "Please. Do not apologize. Family comes first. My brother meant the world to me and now my friends are more my family, and I would do anything for them. I completely understand."

"I appreciate that," he says in his British accent that seems to have lessened over the years living in the states.

"Thank you for doing this," I say to Rey.

"I owed you for dealing with that producer after I had to leave the project. She was going to put up a fight if you hadn't stepped in."

"How are things?"

"They're getting better. I'm going to stay here in New York for a while. I just bought a place across from Central Park on the Upper East Side. Everyone is pestering me about making a return: my agent, manager, publicist, my fans. I might start auditioning for roles again here soon."

Rey moved to L.A. with his sister when he was sixteen and she was twenty. She'd been the one to raise him when their parents died two years before that. Once Rey's career took off after *Mayhem* was canceled, his sister moved to New Jersey with a guy she met, but Rey stayed on the West Coast. I remember Rey telling me he didn't like the guy, but his sister seemed happy, and he didn't want to ruin that.

Then she got pregnant, and the asshole left her. Rey was there for his sister during her pregnancy, and he was there when she died a month after giving birth. He flew back to L.A. a week after burying her to sell his condo and meet with Shyon and me to tell us he had to drop out of the movie and take a break from acting.

He's been raising his sister's daughter as his own ever since.

"A lot of movies and TV shows film here on the East Coast. You'll have no problem finding a project," I say.

He smiles. The same one he gave Rebecca earlier, which doesn't reach his eyes.

"I just have to get some things worked out first, but yes, it'll be nice to get back on sets. I'm glad you reached out to me. I've been needing my friends back in my life. Mylan recently texted me too."

I'm about to ask if he wants to meet up while I'm here to talk, but he glances at the woman next to him. She has light gray hair styled into a tight bun at the nape.

"I have to go get ready, but this is Willa Henderson. She'll take you to the room where you'll be changing." He turns to Rebecca. "It was nice to officially meet you."

Rebecca waves goodbye and the moment he leaves, she slaps the back of her hand on my chest. I pretend it hurt.

"What are you up to?"

"Mister Boliver, Miss Taylor. Please follow me."

The woman walks further into the museum, and I keep having to tug Rebecca along. She's wanting to stop and admire all the old artifacts, which I know she's seen dozens of times before. Willa veers off through a door that takes us down a hallway not meant for the public.

We make one turn before coming to a white door. She waves her hand at it. "Everything for today is in here. I'll be in the office next door if you need me."

She offers a pleasant smile, nothing but professionalism, but her cheeks redden as I thank her and shake her hand.

"She's clearly a fan of yours," Rebecca mumbles when the woman disappears.

"Jealous?"

"Not one bit."

"Liar."

We enter the room, and it's as if we're transported to an old Victorian home. There's a chaise that matches the red velvet curtains, two chairs, floor-to-ceiling bookcases, and a desk in the corner. Sitting in the middle of the room are two racks of clothes.

Rebecca rushes over to the one with dresses.

"Are these... for me?" She runs her fingers over the fabric. She moves to the rack next to it, her hands skimming over the clothes. "And you?"

There's a knock at the door and a tiny blonde pops her head in.

"Lovebirds?"

"Oh my God!" Rebecca squeals and immediately rushes to Eloise, who opens her arms. "What are you doing here?"

The two do a dance hug combo, then part and Eloise holds up her camera. "I'm here on business."

"Business for what?"

Eloise raises an eyebrow and turns to me. "You still haven't told her?"

I shake my head with a smirk.

Eloise rolls her eyes in amusement and points her thumb at me. "He hired me."

"Thank you for flying in to do this," I say.

"I mean, you paid for everything so..." She bites her lip, and her cheeks turn red. "I brought Kelly."

"Sounds like this is more than a whirlwind romance," Rebecca muses.

"Yeah," Eloise sighs, dreamily. "It's been crazy but wonderful and it's happening fast, but we're both taking it one day at a time to see where it goes."

Rebecca reaches out and squeezes Eloise's forearm. "I'm so happy for you."

Eloise shrugs, then glances at the door. "I need to go get ready. I'll see you two out there."

Once Eloise is gone, Rebecca turns her attention back to the racks of clothes.

"Are we going to be wearing these?"

"We are. We're doing a photoshoot. You'll be the queen. I'll be the king. Rey and three of his friends will be your knights. And Eloise, of course, will take the pictures."

Her bottom lip shakes and her blue eyes glaze with tears. "Really?"

"For the queen who was never fit to be a princess."

She thanks me with a hug and a kiss that I never want to end, but she does, too excited to pick out her outfit.

She chooses a breathtaking purple gown with a full skirt and gold-laced trim. The neckline is V-shaped, and the built-in corset pushes her breasts up into perfect round globes. I fight the urge to step forward and bury my face in her cleavage.

My outfit isn't as extravagant. It's a black tunic with purple trim, puffy sleeves, black pants, and boots. I've got a black cape too, which is pretty freaking awesome.

Our crowns match. Rebecca's is decked out with light purple gems rimmed with gold spikes. Mine has a dark purple velvet top inside a gold circle of spikes with light purple gems.

We stand in front of a tall mirror. Rebecca's back straightens, and she stands with a regality about her.

"I feel..." Rebecca begins.

"Silly?" I tease.

She turns to me, reaching out to grab my cape and pull me close.

"Like myself again."

When she kisses me this time, it's slow and soft and thankful.

"My Ami," I whisper against her lips. "Come on. Let's go be models."

Her eyes light up with anticipation.

We find Willa and she escorts us to the Cuxa Cloisters, though Rebecca clearly knew the way since she's been here many times.

The gardens are immaculate, full of rare medieval plants, flowers, herbs, and trees. I don't know a thing about plants, flowers, herbs, or trees, but I spot some lilies and roses in the mix. A covered passageway with connected arches overlooking the courtyard surrounds the gardens. There's a fountain in the middle and stone pathways throughout.

Rey waits, standing next to a black stallion. He's wielding a sword and a lance, dressed in a black warrior tunic with black pants and black laced-up boots. A silver belt to sheath his sword wraps around his waist. Matching silver armor rests on his shoulders. He looks badass, as if he's about to enter battle.

"Holy shit," Rebecca whispers as we approach. She immediately goes to the horse and starts petting it.

Rebecca scans the area. "I can't believe you did all this."

"Believe me, I had a lot of help. I called Rey, and he called his actor friends here in New York. Many of whom take part in the annual Renaissance festival, so they already had the costumes. All I needed was permission from the museum."

She bites her lip. "I've never been to the Renaissance faire they have up here. I'm always either out of town or have no one to come with me."

I take her hand and squeeze it. "I'll go to every single one with you if you want."

Rebecca stands on her tiptoes to give me a kiss, which is interrupted by the shutter of Eloise's camera taking a candid of us.

"Alright everyone, I think we're ready," Eloise says.

She starts positioning us. Rey jumps onto the horse with such grace, as if he does that every day of his life. He's at the end, holding his shield to his body and the lance up straight towards the sky. The female knight, in her warrior faux leathers, stands beside Rebecca. On the opposite end are the two other knights. One holds a flag with a crest on it. A lion and a snake face to face, about to battle. The other man stands at attention with his sword and shield close to his body.

I stand next to Rebecca in the middle.

Eloise has us pose with serious, regal expressions. Then she has Rebecca and me embrace.

"Act like you're in love."

Which isn't hard to do since we are in love.

I'm in love with someone. I never thought I could love like this. It's overwhelming and exciting.

And terrifying.

Trusting others isn't easy, but I've been living in this lonely world where I didn't let *anyone* close. Now with Rebecca, Mylan, Lana, Ginger, Bruno, Eloise, and even Rey, who I hope to have in my life more... This dark world of mine is just a little brighter now.

Eloise takes dozens of photos, then she separates Rebecca and me from the group. We walk around the Cloisters and pose next to all the plants, flowers, and trees. I hand Rebecca a rose and Eloise clicks away. Then we sit next to the fountain, Rebecca running her fingertips over the water while I watch her with adoration.

After at least an hour, we're done.

Rey says he can't stay to hang out. He turns the horse over to the handler then says goodbye to everyone. I told him I'd call him before Rebecca and I leave on her book tour.

Eloise shows us a few of the pictures, and Rebecca glows with excitement. In this moment, she appears so young and innocent. This is the woman she was always meant to be. Who doesn't hold back. Who doesn't care what others think of her.

As we're walking out of the museum, parting ways with Eloise, who hops into the car I hired for her, we pause before getting in our own car.

"I thought you were going to propose to me," Rebecca says with a smile. She grips my shirt in her hands, using it for leverage to stand on her toes.

"You sound disappointed," I say, hover my mouth over hers.

"I'm not."

"Don't lie to me, Becky."

She narrows her eyes and her anger at me using the nickname makes my dick twitch.

"I know how much you love weddings. You cried like a baby at Ginger and Bruno's wedding. And I read *Tyler's Team*—the stuffed animal husbands and ceremonies in your bedroom you made your brother officiate. So, let's make a deal."

She quirks a brow.

"Your book tour lasts three months. We'll be together every day. Every night. You might get sick of me. You might decide you don't want to be in a relationship with me after all."

"You *are* kinda annoying."

"So are you."

"But you love it."

"I do." I narrow my eyes at her. "Stop distracting me." I pause to see if she behaves, then continue. "What I'm trying to say is let's be in a relationship, then I promise I'll propose to you. I'll do it while we're on vacation. Maybe we can visit another island."

"Deal. And I promise to say yes."

I try to kiss her, but she jerks back.

"Do you want kids?"

I choke on a response to the random question that caught me off guard.

"I need to know because I'm old—"

"You're not old."

"I'm almost forty and that's old for having kids, so if you think you don't want kids, because I do then—"

"I do want kids. With you. Only you."

Epilogue - Rebecca
Nine months later

I break down the last box from the move and toss it into a pile that I'll have Jensen take out to recycling later. The place is finally looking like a home.

I moved in with Jensen last month. His Silver Lake house was so bare. Such a bachelor's pad. He had a few paintings in his bedroom that were too expensive to get rid of. It's abstract art with streaks of black and white lines across a white canvas. I'm not the biggest fan of this style, but Jensen loves it and I want our home to portray us both. So, I decorated the rest of the walls with bright paintings and added bookcases with colorful books. I bought rugs to accentuate his beautiful hardwood floors and blankets to drape over his plain white couch and chair.

Even his kitchen was bland with silver appliances, which I replaced with colorful vintage looking ones.

Only a month into my book tour, I knew I wanted to spend the rest of my life with this man. Jensen documented every stop, every behind-the-scenes moment. Now he's editing it. He already sold the rights to Netflix.

My new book came out three months ago. *Cursed Reign* has been on the bestseller list since release day. I had a mini-tour coinciding with the release, then I took a month off to move and unpack. In a couple of weeks, I'll be heading out again for three more months promoting my new book.

It's been nine months since the photoshoot at the Met Cloisters. We posted the photos on our social media pages, officially announcing our relationship. Then Jensen announced his departure from directing the apocalyptic movie. Which worked out because there was another director—one with a few more Oscars than Jensen—who wanted the job. Jensen still had to pay a fine for breaking his contract, but he said his parents got the cost down significantly.

His parents also found the person who sold the video of Jensen and me arguing on set was the actress who portrayed me in *Tyler's Team*. A woman in her twenties who was struggling to find work and, after seeing articles about Jensen and me in Hawaii, she remembered she had the video. She needed money, so she sold it. Now she won't be able to get any job in Hollywood. At least, not any big production jobs.

Jensen's parents really came through for us. They actually want to be in his life more. He'd brought me over to their home in Beverly Hills—a literal mansion—and we had dinner with them. They loved me and it's as if they'd seen Jensen in a new light. It's as if the thought of him dating someone and potentially marrying and having a family of his own activated grandparent mode for them.

Jensen is still hesitant. He sat down with them for hours, talking about how they treated him growing up. They apologized profusely. Jensen said he truly believes they feel remorseful for what they did. Apparently, he was right about both of his parents growing up in a household where love and emotions were never expressed.

I'm also rebuilding my relationship with my parents. They'd finished their cross-country trip, ending in Los Angeles last month. I brought them to one of my therapy sessions. We talked about everything, from how they treated me after Tyler's death to spending less and less time with me over the past several years.

They were shocked and resistant to the idea that they were being horrible parents, but they said they'd be open to talking more about this. They're going to be staying on the West Coast for a while, parking their RV at a camp near Venice Beach.

Next week we have a family dinner planned with my parents and Jensen's and we're both super stressed about it.

We've been relieving that stress with lots of sex.

"Oh, I know that look," Jensen says, leaning on the doorframe between the living area and the dining room. He pushes himself off and reaches me within a few long steps. He slides his arms around my waist and kisses my neck. "You're turned on. You want to get in a quickie before we go?"

I playfully slap his shoulder, and he winces in faux pain. He loves doing that. He's such a nerd. "You said you wanted to do it on the plane."

His mouth moves up my neck to my chin and hovers over my lips. "Why not both?"

We kiss and kiss until those kisses become messy and hungry and we struggle to stop.

"We're late," I say, breathless.

I turn away, and he smacks my ass, making me yelp. He bursts out laughing as I grab my cheek, both hating and loving the sting.

That fucker knows how rough I like it.

We leave the house in a car he hired, taking us to the Santa Barbara Airport where Mylan stores his private jet. We board and select two seats near the back. A few minutes later, we're joined by two familiar faces.

"Eloise, Kelly." I say, standing to give them hugs.

Eloise walks up the aisle, giving Jensen a fist bump. Kelly offers him a nod and the two sit near the front to give us all some privacy.

"If you think them being here will stop me from fucking you during this flight, you're wrong," Jensen whispers the moment I sit back down and buckle up.

"Who said I was thinking that?"

After the crew makes final preps, the plane takes off. The flight is a couple hours long and with the time difference, we'll be landing in Arkansas early evening.

Jensen and I sneak into the bathroom about an hour into the air. The bathroom is bigger than the ones on passenger planes. We had plenty of room to have sex, and it was a sexy fuck. He took me from behind and covered my mouth to muffle my screams. Though I doubt it was much help because our bodies slapping together were plenty loud.

When we finally emerged about thirty minutes later, Eloise and Kelly were scrambling at the front with messed up hair while tucking in their shirts.

I raise a knowing brow at them, which makes Eloise blush.

Once landing in Arkansas, we load up in another hired car to Silo Springs: the town Ginger, Lana, Tyler, and I all grew up in.

It's where the movie was filmed. It's where Lana and My-lan met.

And it's where they'll be getting married.

Well, sort of. We're driving thirty minutes to the next town where the cliffs on Bluffs Lake are located.

It's where Lana met my brother on the worst day of her life when her parents died. She'd packed her clothes and some toys, ran away from her Gram and Pa's home, and went to the cliffs.

We'd just moved to Silo, and my dad wanted to explore the area. We'd driven all around Silo until venturing out further and finding a park by the lake. The park had trails and Tyler wandered off down one of those trails, searching for snakes.

Tyler found the ten-foot-tall cliffs and was standing near the edge when Lana emerged from the woods. She was not happy to see him. She told him to leave. He didn't. Instead, he shoved her off the cliff. He immediately jumped in to save her. I never included that part in the book because it felt like a special moment that I wanted it to be Lana's memory and not the world's.

Despite pushing her off the cliff, Lana and Tyler—and by proxy Ginger—became friends. Then eighteen years after Tyler died and Mylan was cast to play him, Lana, Ginger, Eloise, Bruno, and Mylan all came out here to jump and swim.

I didn't know that Lana had been afraid to jump off that cliff. But it was Mylan who convinced her to take the leap again.

It's strange how life comes full circle sometimes. How important this cliff was to my brother and Lana, and now to Mylan and Lana.

And me because this cliff had always been a sad memory for me. Because I used to come here all the time with Lana, Tyler, and Ginger. I hadn't been back since before he died. Now, this cliff can be a happy memory once again.

We check into the hotel first—the same one I stayed in while in town during the filming for *Tyler's Team* because I didn't want to stay with my parents who would have ignored me the entire time. It's the same hotel Jensen stayed in, down the hall from me. Who I'd see almost every morning before we left for set. Who I avoided as much as he avoided me.

I never let myself think about what it could have been like to be with him all those years ago. Life doesn't work like that. Regrets are useless because you can't do anything about it once it's done and over with. It's all about redemption and how you live your life going forward.

This time, we book a room together. We barely have time to freshen up and change before we're back in the car heading to the cliffs for the ceremony.

It's a simple wedding. No decorations. No chairs. No unnecessary guests.

Gram, Pa, Mylan's mother Marie, Ginger, Bruno, Jensen, me, Eloise, and Kelly.

Rey Michaelson is here too. Rey, Jensen, and Mylan have been rekindling their friendship over the past nine months. Rey and Mylan also just booked a movie together. Not only Rey's first movie in nearly five years, but Mylan's too.

We stop in front of Rey who's holding hands with a little girl.

"Hey man," Jensen says, approaching him. They do the silly handshake greeting like they did at the photoshoot. "Good to see you again."

Jensen leans down with his hands on his knees.

"This must be Addy."

"My name is Adeline. Only my dad can call me Addy," she says, mean mugging him.

Jensen holds up his hands in defense, and I laugh. The little girl's bright blue eyes move to me and widen.

"Are you a fairy princess?"

I look down at my dress. It's light purple with short puff sleeves and a shirred waist. I'm also wearing a crown of lilies, like all the ladies here—Lana's idea since it's her favorite flower—and my hair is styled in big curls around my face.

Jensen stands up from where he was crouched in front of the little girl and takes my hand, bringing it up to his lips to kiss my knuckles.

"She's not a princess. She's a queen."

The little girl giggles. "You're pretty."

"Well, since I'm a queen, that means you can be my princess," I say. She smiles bigger than her tiny face can allow and smashes her tiny face into Rey's leg, wrapping her equally tiny arms around his thigh.

Rey places his big palm on top of her curly red hair. Adeline has Rey's big blue eyes, but that's where the similarities end. Rey's light brown hair is straight. His skin tone is tanner compared to Adeline's porcelain pale shade.

Rey has been Adeline's guardian for a little over five years now. He's the only parent she's ever known.

The media reported that he took over custody of his niece, but he rarely goes out in public with her. The paparazzi are vultures about this part of his life and go feral anytime she's with him. Which is why seeing her here now is surprising.

"Come on, Addy," Rey says and starts walking with her still attached to his leg.

They stop next to Eloise and Kelly. Rey hands over Adeline and she grabs both of their hands. Eloise has been getting a lot of photography jobs in New York lately, bringing Kelly with her, and the two stay at Rey's penthouse. They've all become good friends. They even babysat for him a few times while he tries to find a new nanny.

I greet Bruno and Ginger. Ginger is already crying, and Bruno has his big arm around her shoulder. It's the hormones. Ginger and Bruno are having a baby. Turns out, the reason she wasn't drinking a lot at their wedding was because they were trying to get pregnant and with Ginger being in her forties and also having PCOS, their chances of conceiving were slim.

But they did it and Ginger is six months along.

We split into two sides and Rey takes his place at the front near the cliff's edge to officiate.

Today marks exactly five years since Lana and Mylan met. It only makes sense that they'd get married on their anniversary of the day that changed both their lives.

It's a hot May evening. The sun sets, casting a gorgeous array of colors across the sky. The water is calm since few people are on the lake. Tourist season doesn't technically begin until Memorial Day in a few weeks.

A violin player Lana and Mylan hired starts playing an instrumental version of *We Belong* by Pat Benatar.

Mylan emerges from the woods, dressed in a white, short-sleeved dress shirt tucked into black slacks. His mother is on his arm, dressed in a flowing light pink sundress. She glows as she glances up at her son proudly.

They pass through the middle of where we stand on the bluff. Mylan kisses his mom on the cheek and leaves her next to Bruno and Ginger. Ginger takes her hand and squeezes it.

Lana appears out of the woods next. She's wearing a simple white sun dress laced with pink and purple flower designs. She carries a bouquet of lilies, and on her arm is her grandfather. They walk slowly for Pa, and when they reach the front, the song ends.

Lana gives Pa a big hug and a kiss on the cheek then leaves him next to Gram, who sniffles and wipes her eyes with a tissue.

The ceremony is short and sweet. Lana and Mylan wrote their own vows, and they both gave tributes to Tyler.

Seeing Lana share her life with someone other than my brother should have been weird. But it's not. I'm happy for her. My parents are happy for her too, but they decided not to come today. They said it would have been too hard because this wedding was supposed to be Lana and Tyler's.

'I dos' were said, and the kiss was beautiful.

After the short ceremony, we all crowd together chatting, laughing, and crying for several minutes before Lana and Mylan get our attention.

"The reception is at Lilies," Lana announced. "Being it's Saturday night and an hour until seven... you know what that means?"

"Rock Star Karaoke!" Everyone except Rey and Mylan's mother yells.

I hadn't been to a Rock Star Karaoke night in years. It's where a band, Silo's Symphony, plays instead of a track for people to sing along to. It's become somewhat of a tourist attraction after videos and pictures of Mylan singing to Lana were posted online. He's such a horrible singer, but he performed on that stage without a care in the world.

We all start heading back through the woods to where we parked our cars. Rey says he won't be joining us since he and Adeline have to drive to Memphis early tomorrow morning to fly back to New York.

Gram and Pa head home too, but everyone else joins, including Mylan's mother.

"Are you going to sing?" Jensen asks next to my ear once we enter Silo Springs city limits.

I shrug. "I might."

"We should get drunk and sing a song together."

I bite my lip and turn my head. It's dark in the car, only the lights along the street and from cars allow me to see his face. "I'd be down for a duet."

"Not a drunken duet?"

"No."

"Why not?"

"Because I can't."

"Can't what? Drink?"

I nod.

"Why?"

I say nothing and wait for him to figure it out. After a few more seconds, his entire face lights up. He takes my head in his hands and he crushes his lips against mine.

"What just happened?" Eloise asks. She's sitting next to me while Kelly sits up front.

We hadn't planned to get pregnant before getting married. He hasn't even proposed to me yet. We keep talking about it, but I think he wanted to do something special. We've just been too busy to plan a romantic vacation.

We have, however, been having a lot of sex and there might have been a day, or two, I forgot to take my birth control.

I found out this morning.

I haven't even told Lana yet and I want to keep it to ourselves for as long as possible to make sure the baby is healthy.

Jensen releases me from the most passionate kiss he's ever given me. "I'm going to marry you, Rebecca Taylor."

"Oh my God," Eloise whispers. "You two are engaged?"

He rests his forehead on mine.

"Hell yeah we are."

The End

Thank you

Did you enjoy Rebecca & Jensen's story? Please consider leaving a review for Beyond the Fame!

Amazon

Goodreads

What's Next?

What's Next?

Beyond the Spotlight
Releasing September 15, 2023

Preorder Nowon Amazon (ebook only)
<u>Rey</u>
When my sister died, I put my life on hold to raise her newborn daughter as my own. Now, five years later, I'm ready to get that life back.
But I need help. I need a nanny.

The moment I met Savannah, I knew she was perfect for the job. Not only is she beautiful and funny, but she instantly connected with my daughter in a way no one else has. So, I asked her to interview for the job and she agreed.

There's just one problem... she didn't recognize me. She doesn't know I'm a celebrity and I didn't tell her.

Savannah

I never expected to be on a plane, leaving my life behind after my scum of an ex cheated on me. I need a fresh start and, for some reason, New York City is calling me.

Then I met a hot single dad and his adorable daughter on my flight.

We talked the entire trip and I couldn't stop laughing and smiling. So, once we land, he hands me his card and asks if I want to interview to be his daughter's nanny. I jumped on the opportunity.

But after searching his name online, I find out he's a famous actor. He didn't tell me and I'm not looking to be in the spotlight.

So, I ghost him, thinking I'll never see him again.

Except... two weeks later I run into him at my job.

Acknowledgments

Wow. I can't believe I've written another book. I'm so grateful I was able to feature a new love story between different body types: a plus-size man & a mid-size woman. I will keep writing stories like this where people of all sizes get to be the main character.

I'd like to thank my amazing alpha readers who offered their time amid their busy schedules to read this story in its roughest form. Xan Garcia, Stephanie Patton, and Maranda Perdue. Thank you for always being real with me and not holding back with your critiques.

To my beta readers—Kristyn Habick and Maggie Linton—you were my final eyes before this story was sent to the editor. Thank you for pointing out any final inconsistencies.

To my editor Jenny at Owl Eyes Proofs & Edits—I'm so sorry about all the commas you had to add!

To Kate at Y'all That Graphic, thank you for making this gorgeous discreet cover!

And finally, to my readers and TikTok followers. You are the reason I keep writing. Thank you for all your support. To the ones who've been with me from the very beginning, I see you. I appreciate you.

This book is a reminder that all body types deserve their love story.

Also By Settle Myer

The Off Script Series

Need to catch up on Lana & Mylan's story? Beyond the Bright Lights is the first book in the Off Script series of standalone romances. Available on Amazon, KU, Audible & iTunes. You can also get the paperback online at Barnes & Noble.

The Trinity Trilogy

If you love action & adventure, badass women with superpowers, diverse characters, found family, and fated mates—check out my sci-fi romance trilogy. Book 1 is a clean romance with some cursing and violence, but books 2 & 3 have a sprinkle of spice in them. Trinity Found, Trinity Returns, Trinity Rises. Find them on Amazon.

Social Media

Check out my website and sign up for my newsletter for updates on new books, discounts, and sneak peeks!

https://www.settlemyerauthor.com/

Follow me on social media:

TikTok: tiktok.com/@settlemyerauthor

Instagram: https://www.instagram.com/settlemyerauthor/

Facebook: Settle Myer Author

Join Settle's readers group on Facebook. Search Settle Myer's Stars and be a part of the discussion with other fans. Settle also posts fun facts about her books, characters, and more!

Twitter: https://twitter.com/Settle_Myer

About the Author

Settle Myer lives in New York City with her two cats, Zombie, Michonne & Birdie. She's currently a TV News Producer who hopes to one day leave a world of death, disaster, and politics to write about worlds with plenty of forbidden romance, badass women with superpowers fighting violent villains. She loves all things zombies, cats, karaoke, and tattoos... but not necessarily in that order.

Made in the USA
Monee, IL
10 January 2024